# YVONNE ANTROBUS

# *True to form*

VISTA

First published in Great Britain 1998
as a Vista paperback original.

Vista is an imprint of the Cassell Group
Wellington House, 125 Strand, London WC2R 0BB

© Yvonne Antrobus 1998

The right of Yvonne Antrobus to be identified as author of
this work has been asserted by her in accordance with
the Copyright, Designs and Patents Act, 1988.

A catalogue record for this book is
available from the British Library.

ISBN 0 575 60369 0

Typeset by SetSystems Ltd, Saffron Walden
Printed in Great Britain by
Cox & Wyman Ltd, Reading, Berkshire

98 99 5 4 3 2 1

*To Leo and Chloe*

Thanks to Superintendent Ian Hutchison and
Dr Geoff Parrott for answering questions on
police procedure and medical matters.

# Chapter One

The last three occasions Sukie Buckley had seen Jerry Wearing, he had been holding a knife.

The first occasion.

Sun skimming down a polished table, leaving all the faces in shade. Flash of blade against steel. Plates are passed. Jerry licking blood from his wrist.

The second occasion.

A brick wall. Jerry leaning against it, propping himself with one arm, almost obscuring ... but not quite ... Narrow polished boots, short mackintosh, a face without expression, waiting. Jerry steps back. Blade flash against steel sky. Two hands raised against it. The knife drops to the ground.

The third occasion ...

Think back.

The first occasion. Sunday lunch.

Amanda picking at her cutlery. Amanda Wearing: black hair, eyes like gentians, only the most, explicitly the most expensive clothes. Amanda smiling down the mahogany table at her guests: George and Nicola, Rosamund, Bob and Sukie. Two chairs empty. (Jerry is twisting a corkscrew into a bottle of Chablis. Simon, their son, is late.)

George, check jacket with the gleam of silk, his brogues under the table insist that they are hand-made. Nicola, fifteen years younger than her husband, has the gleam of a salon suntan. Her white trousers, navy blazer and Geiger loafers come from a drawer higher than she does.

Rosamund, gingerbread curls, goitre eyes, laugh like a panting dog: her response to being seated at a promising table on a sunny spring day. A tumbler of neat Scotch is by her right hand.

Bob is quiet. It is the first time he has been to this house. But he appears relaxed in muted tweed jacket and cord trousers.

Sukie wonders if anyone would guess her Armani trousers come from a dress agency. She pushes back her flop of pale hair, perfectly cut to her shoulders, for which she paid the full price.

Plates circle the table. Simon is in his place. Jerry flashes the steel. A heavy, ivory-handled, carving knife against it. Blood on the plates.

The second occasion. At the races.

Sukie holding a folded newspaper at arm's length, to work out form. She has not put on spectacles. Walking and reading with two levels of focus could trip her up. She is frowning, relieved to be alone for a little. And then she sees someone she knows. Over the edge of the paper.

She could pretend she hasn't seen him. And yet . . .

There seems to be no choice. She wants to hide. Hide him from the crowd which hasn't noticed. But she is too small. Smaller than the jockey over whom he bloats. The jockey's face, narrow and sallow, long straight nose, fair hair groomed back. Jerry's shoulders block him out. Shoulders cast in respectability by his well-worn military coat. It carries weight. Then Jerry steps back, hand to his pocket, knife in the sky. Fingers grasp his wrist.

A drowning hand is all that is left of the gesture. But there is an extra blade in the grass, bright, and very sharp, with an ivory handle. And Bob is shaking his head. Bob Teichgraeber, in grey flannel. He sees Sukie. A lightening of recognition. Then everyone is there. Amanda takes Jerry's arm. The jockey turns and is walking away.

The third occasion ... the third occasion ...

Think back.

The first occasion. Tancred House. Jerry and Amanda's place in Suffolk. A blackbird is singing in the garden.

'And why is Simon going to be late?'

Jerry leant on the back of his chair under the low ceiling.

'Oh, some business matter. He won't be long.'

Amanda straightened her cutlery; smiled at her guests down the sunny table. Jerry and Amanda Wearing with George and Nicola Graham-Jones, Rosamund Officer, Bob Teichgraeber, and Sukie, all seated except Jerry who had begun to open the wine.

'Are you seriously asking me to believe that?' The cork burst from the bottle.

Amanda shrugged and turned to help herself from the old Derby plate that Maria was proffering.

'What unusual asparagus.' Nicola craned across at it, honey hair falling forward, catching light from windows at either end of the room. A woman for whom it must always be summer.

'Not asparagus at all. Seakale.' Amanda replaced the silver servers. 'I thought it would be more amusing.'

'I mean, what the hell's he playing at?' Jerry eyed the approaching seakale as though that were the cause of his annoyance.

'Squash. Business squash.'

'Who the hell with?'

'Oh, you know, just Froggy.'

'And what possible business can he have with him?'

9

'I haven't a clue. But the stable keeps Froggy too stretched to make it at any other time, apparently.'

'What utter crap.' The seakale was presented to him. It looked somewhat picked over. Jerry waved it away. 'Froggy's frayed string couldn't keep him stretched during the week, let alone on a Sunday.'

'They could be discussing some sort of partnership?' Nicola patted melted butter from her lips. 'Simon really does so terribly want to train. He told me at your New Year's party.'

Amanda's smile slid round to her. 'Oh?'

Sukie picked up her glass. She knew that smile of Amanda's. The Chablis had a greenish tinge which spread to the faces round the table. She took a large sip, and another; felt ready for anything. Almost. She held on to the stem of her glass. Sweet peas in carnival vase beyond the rim.

'Simon!'

Sukie's glass skidded, spilling wine into the reflection of petals, whey to deepest prune.

Nobody noticed. They were all looking with Amanda towards the narrow window that gave on to the back garden, where a face peered in, indistinct, frowning to see into the shadowed room. Then he seemed to recognize his mother, raised a hand and moved on. They heard him coming in through a side door, wiping his feet on the mat.

'Sorry I'm late. Sorry, Father. Sorry, everyone.' His face was still indistinct. Simon went to his place between Nicola and Rosamund. A boy's face. But dust coloured, the hair, the skin, the eyes.

Rosamund pulled out his chair for him and gave it a little pat. She seemed the most comfortable at the table, in spite of being encased in what appeared to be a brocade bolster cover.

Maria was collecting the plates, everyone trying to look busy, watching their own from table to pile, then all round the table.

Simon leant across to Sukie. 'How are you? You look terrific. It must be the freedom.'

'What?'

'With them both off your hands.'

'Oh, I see.' A quick smile. 'Well, they've only just gone back after Easter, and Alex comes home at weekends. He's only a weekly boarder.'

'Your son is at boarding school?' Bob turned to her with a frown, a little shake of the head.

'Yes. Only weekly. In London. He comes home on Saturdays. But he's gone off on an expedition this weekend. Rock climbing. They do sometimes.'

'Oh, God, we used to do that. Absolute hell.' Simon glanced at his father. 'But we didn't come home at weekends.'

'In London? So, what makes you think boarding education is a good idea?'

Sukie suppressed a sigh, thinking to speak, not knowing what she was going to say. She had found Bob's horn-rimmed spectacles rather stunning. Until now. But he was an American.

'It's the only way.' Jerry was looking around for the meat.

'Absolutely.' George Graham-Jones was sitting well back after Maria had taken his plate. He looked like a baby in a high-chair. 'We were sent away at the age of seven, weren't we, Jerry? Best thing my father ever did for me. Toughens you up.'

'Bring it in, then. Bring it in.' Jerry had caught sight of Maria in the doorway. 'I'm not going to bother with "ladies first". When you see a plate you like, hang on to it.' The blade flashed. 'There'll be some bloody ones coming up in a moment.'

'Toughens you up?' Bob had turned to George.

'Too right. Teaches you to fit in. If not—' he made a throat slitting gesture. 'Remember Portland's Press Gang?' he called down the table to Jerry. 'If any little fink got out of line, they'd get him in the bath and all pile on top of him. And what about Paxo?'

11

'What?' Jerry was trying to get rid of a plate. 'For Christ's sake, Simon, either put it down or pass it on. Otherwise the whole system gets screwed.' He licked blood from his wrist. 'Paxo, yes. Bertie Fowler. We used to stick our compasses in him to see if the fat would run.'

'And Weasel Winterson. His teeth stuck out. We used to tie them to the door and—'

'Yes, well, quite so.' Bob turned to the vegetables: spinach, parsnips and tiny glazed onions.

'All from the garden.' Maria's Spanish accent had a trace of cockney. She glanced shyly at Amanda who nodded, as she arranged the dishes about the table for people to help themselves. Then she left the room, a strong, pale woman with hair in a dark clump.

'So, here's to Triumvirate.' Rosamund Officer raised her claret.

'What?' Jerry flipped some Yorkshire pudding down the table.

'And to *the* Triumvirate.' George had joined her.

'Oh, I see.' Jerry took a slug of wine. 'Yes, well, get stuck in, everyone.'

'Triumvirate is a horse?' Bob was holding his knife and fork like a couple of pencils.

'That's right. Our horse. Jerry's, George's and mine. He's only a baby, but we expect great things.'

'And *yours*?' Bob still had not started on his food. 'Well, I suppose that makes sense nowadays. But without doubt it's a misnomer.'

'We've only signed up Rosamund because we couldn't get a man. Well, not a suitable man, anyway, only oiks.' Jerry folded a slice of beef into his mouth. 'An Officer, Rosamund, if not a gentleman.'

Rosamund chewed vigorously. 'Ha. You bet.'

Think back.

*

The second occasion. Newmarket. Mid-week. The first spring meeting: the Craven. Wind ruffling dark turf. Sky, hoisted to catch the light, mirrors the swish of tails.

In the paddock, Jerry, Amanda, George and Nicola, Rosamund and Sukie. Nicola overdressed in fuchsia silk, Rosamund with brass buttons up to her chin stumping gamely on swollen ankles.

Triumvirate, deep liver chestnut, a little burly, full of himself. 'He's not as fit as we'd like him.' Marcus Irvine, his trainer, lets go the words over his shoulder. Sylvia, his wife, bends to pick up the rug where it has been left on the ground.

'He looks gorgeous to me.' Amanda, arms folded, hip thrusting a provocative crease in her tight skirt. 'So do you, Sukie, by the way. I like the jacket. You should wear yellow more often.'

'Thanks. That emerald green's just the ticket. But you always look good, Amanda.'

'Boring, isn't it?'

There was a movement, a coming together, as though everyone in the paddock was blown in the same direction by the wind. The jockeys had appeared, exchanging the odd remark before peeling off to greet their owners.

Henry Whippet walked alone and, as he approached, half-raised his whip before stopping a little way off, silent and self-possessed. His eyes, clear brown, a little slanted so there appears to be no white. He is watching the horse.

Marcus gave him a leg-up and Triumvirate's quarters swung round, splitting rainbows from the chessboard pattern carefully combed into them. Then the sun went in and, against the moody sky, the jockey's colours became luminous as flowers at dusk.

On the way to the stands, the men striding ahead, the women keeping pace with Rosamund.

'And you've got Henry Whippet up.' Sukie smiled all round.

Amanda halted and sniffed. 'We wouldn't if Jerry had his way.'

13

'But he's the best. I've seen him lift races no one else could have won.'

'Yes, and I've seen him lift even more place money. First, or forget it, that's him. Decidedly ungenuine is Henry Whippet.'

'Yeah, but, come on, Marcus isn't going to put up with that.'

'Ha! Henry Whippet runs circles round him.'

The eleven runners all went very sweetly into the stalls and they were off, the vermilion colours of Triumvirate showing clearly in the middle. Two furlongs out he began to move up on the outside of the leading group; he was cruising. At the furlong marker he was at the girth of the leader; and there he stayed until the final few strides. The jockey hit him once with the whip, urged him on with hands and heels. Triumvirate surged forward. He lost by a neck.

General excitement and congratulations from which Amanda seems a little detached. She is watching Jerry. He and George are still staring out at the finishing line.

'Well, that's done for the odds next time.' Jerry stuffed his binoculars into the pocket of his military coat and hunched off to the second's enclosure.

Triumvirate, restless as horses are after a race, kept butting his lad who stood in front of him holding either side of the bridle. Marcus, smiling vaguely. 'I told him not to give the horse a hard race.' Henry Whippet had already taken his saddle and gone.

'Then why didn't he drop him out when he knew he couldn't win? That's his usual trick.'

'He was doing his best.'

'If that's his best . . . ?' Jerry turned away. 'Well, I suppose you girls think a second still warrants champagne?' He shepherded them out of the enclosure.

Amanda squeezed his arm. 'You're such a Christian, darling. Are you very disappointed?'

'It's only the worst possible result.'

'Till next time. He'll win then.'

14

Jerry settled the women at a corner table and went with George to the bar.

'You watch, he'll get champagne for us, and a pint of bitter for himself,' Amanda whispered to Sukie. 'He only does it for me. Cigarette?'

Sukie hesitated.

'Oh, go on, do have one with me. He's given up.'

'Really?' Sukie's eyes widened over the flame from Amanda's gold Zippo.

'Absolutely. Very strong-minded of him, don't you think?'

'Oh, yes.'

They both looked to where Jerry was leaning on the counter, as though in homage to his strong-mindedness. A joke passed between him and the bar-man, at which George laughed the loudest. Jerry slapped money down and turned with bottles in his hands.

The room was misted with fumes, so that he approached them featureless, bulky, packed into his coat. As he bent to put the drinks on the table, a rogue haze from a light-bulb furred the outline of his head, where the grey wings were clipped short.

'Thank you.' Sukie smiled up at him, thinking that this was the first time she had ever seen his eyes, which were grey and without sparkle set in a square face.

He opened the champagne, so that none of it spilled, then put it down on the table, sat back and slowly poured his beer. 'You'd better get a move on if you want to catch the next one.' He was watching the last drops of foam fall from the bottle.

'Oh, I don't think we'll bother, do you . . .' Amanda looked at Rosamund, at Nicola. 'Sukie?'

'Well, I might just try and catch it.'

'Yes, but you've got a quarter of an hour.' Amanda handed out filled glasses.

'Right, then.' And Jerry was standing, wiping foam from his mouth with a large handkerchief. 'I'm off.'

15

Ten minutes later, Sukie walked towards the grandstand, *Sporting Life* folded for far-vision, studying form as she went. Henry Whippet's mount, that she had fancied over breakfast, had since been withdrawn. She was frowning, trying to read the particularly small print, when something at the top of her paper made her pull focus. Somebody.

It was Jerry. He was leaning against a wall. And he was shaking.

He must be ill, Sukie thought, propped as he was with one arm, until she saw that under that arm, a short mackintosh over his colours, was Henry Whippet.

No one seemed to have noticed. Intent on seeing the next race, they hurried past, animated, purposeful.

Then Jerry appeared to calm down. He stepped back and dropped the arm. Dropped the arm, but not to turn away. Dropped the arm, instantly to raise it. Raise it higher now, with the extension of a small blade.

In that flash Henry Whippet ducked but in that instant, two hands closed on Jerry's wrist, unlocking the fingers, forcing his arm to his side.

'Hey,' Bob said. 'Hey, Jerry, this is not good. Hey, come on.'

Jerry had turned, not in rage but irritation. As he looked at Bob Teichgraeber, all expression left his face. He stared, mouth slack, eyes seeming not to see who was before him. Then he shook his head, clenched and unclenched his knuckles, observing them with curiosity. 'Just a paper knife, for God's sake. Use it to open my letters.' He bent down and pulled the ivory stake from the grass.

Bob was watching Sukie. She attempted a smile but, not sure it was suitable, turned it into a grimace which perhaps was worse.

Jerry was just about to speak again when another hand was placed upon his arm, a hand with shiny pink nails.

'Jerry, darling, we decided to watch it after all.'

'What?' It took him a moment to recognize her.

16

'What on earth's the matter? Have you been overdoing it?' Amanda frowned at Bob. 'Hullo.'

Bob gave a slight bow.

'Not in the least,' Jerry laughed easily. 'Just giving that little shit a piece of my mind.'

Henry Whippet had remained, a step away from the wall. He gave a sideways nod and turned to go.

'So I've got a quick temper. Nothing serious. What the hell,' Jerry called at him.

Henry Whippet paused, one boot flexed, showing a pale new sole smeared with mud, then continued on his way.

The third occasion . . .

Think back.

The third occasion . . . ?

London. Sukie Buckley's flat in Kensington. Triumvirate was beaten today.

Sukie was in the bath, chill of Newmarket dusk seeping from her bones into stinging water. Through the steam was the gloomy vista of the lavatory base lapped by ridged carpet, as though the tide had been over it too many times: there was a distinct smell.

'You can get nice little mats that fit right round the pedestal,' Mrs Tribe had told her, kneeling before it one morning.

A new carpet was a matter of urgency.

But not as urgent as a curry. Sukie threw on jeans, gym shoes and comfortable sweater with a hole in it to set off for their usual place near the Brompton Road.

She had parked her car and was walking towards it when she saw that it was not as she remembered. The ungainly plants, once pressed against the window, had gone. The faded paintwork was now a royal purple with the original name, Star of India, in illuminated pink.

Inside, the tablecloths were also pink, with a carnation in a glass tube in the middle of each. Conversation was discreet. A waiter came towards her, very handsome, very young.

'Can I help you, please?'

She did not recognize him. 'Yes, I've come for some takeaway.'

'Oh. I see. Please come this way.' He led her to a table at the back and handed her a menu of beautifully described dishes and impressive wines.

Sukie chose a buttered chicken and a bhindi bhaji, rice and a poppadom.

He bowed as he took the menu from her. When he returned with the food, he smiled, 'You were thinking of the old place, I think. The one that did takeaway.'

'Yes. I'm sorry. It's been a while . . .'

'It is completely new management,' he said proudly.

'Yes. I can see.' She wanted to ask after the old management, the family who had seemed like friends to Jemima and Alex and herself, but it would have been ungracious.

As she drove home Sukie felt that it was her fault they had gone, that she had failed them. Alex had started to board a year ago, and with Jemima now at university in Bristol, they had perhaps not been there for six months. Then she began to feel cross with the family, as though it were they who had let her down, had not trusted her, waited for her, told her they were going. It was the way she had felt about Peter after he had died.

When Sukie arrived back at the flat, the phone was ringing. She put the bag of curry down on the kitchen table and ran into her bedroom. It was Amanda.

'Oh. I thought you weren't going to answer.'

'I've just come in the front door.'

'Lord. Anyone with you?'

18

'Only a curry. Why?'

'Nothing. Just felt a bit low. Jerry's gone up to the flat tonight. Look, I'll see you next week. We'll have lunch.'

'Fine.'

'Do you want to make a date now or . . . ?'

'Not particularly.'

'You've got someone waiting?'

'No. The curry. It's getting cold.'

'Oh, of course. All right. Speak to you soon. 'Bye.'

In her yellow painted kitchen, Sukie put the curry in the oven to warm up, and opened a bottle of Muscadet. Then she went through to the sitting-room and, without switching on the lights, stood at the window with her glass, looking out at the lime tree in the centre of the square.

The wind had been increasing all day, and now a section of foliage, in the intense light of a street lamp, bubbled and seethed. Sometimes a fanned hole would appear, as when a gust disturbs the fur of a cat. And then it was still: everywhere was silent.

Sukie held her breath, aware of all the lives out there. And somewhere in her mind was Jerry whom, she now knew, Peter had not liked. And the realization shocked her because, of course, she had always known it.

It was nothing that Peter had ever said; it was perhaps that he had refrained from meeting her enthusiasm. He would eye her in a twinkling way, but would never agree. He would smile, but his smile was for Sukie, because her loyalty, her naivety, appealed to him and he did not wish to disillusion her. Then he had had a heart attack and died.

She turned into the room to pour herself another glass of wine, to switch on the standard lamp and wall lights. The room began to swirl. A draught had forced its way over the top of the sash, under the pelmet. Did she really like Amanda? They had been at school together. The huge silk shade of the standard lamp rocked. And Henry Whippet – that couldn't, of course, be his real name

– how, without wishing to notice it, she had seen that in dealing with Jerry, in his forbearance, there had been . . . a certain grace? Or was it something else entirely?

She remembered the curry and hurried out to open the oven door. But it looked quite peaceful in there. She contemplated it, sipping her wine. Then she closed the oven and turned it off, leaning her back against the warm surface. There had been playing classical Indian music in the new Star of India, she now recalled – quite beautiful.

Sukie took the bottle of wine to bed. Sometimes in the night she was aware of the window rattling, people laughing in the street, the crack of a branch. Once, the telephone rang. Just once, as it can in the wind. And then all there was was the storm against the pane, that and the swirling darkness. And the sound of the phone.

The sound of the phone. And still it wasn't morning.

And still it wouldn't stop. Beside the bed. Getting louder. Vibrating. Filling her with shock.

She reached out a hand to stop it, lifted it, and was about to put it back . . .

'Sukie. Thank God. I'm sorry. Thank God you're there.'

'You want to fix a date for lunch now!'

'What? I don't know what you mean. Listen.' Amanda's voice sounded scratchy. 'I'm worried about Jerry. You know I said he was up in London tonight, to be in the City for an early meeting?'

'Yes?'

'Well, I'm really worried. I telephoned him because he'd seemed a bit – I don't know – restless today. I didn't tell you, probably because of Peter, but Jerry has a heart condition. That's why he gave up smoking. I can't understand why he doesn't answer.'

'Perhaps he's out?'

'At three in the morning?'

20

'Or asleep?'

'He's a light sleeper and there's a telephone beside the bed.'

'Certainly not asleep, then.'

'Sukie, now you're awake . . .'

'Yes?'

'Well, could you go over there?'

'What?' She ran a hand through her hair and propped herself on one elbow.

'Just to see he's all right. I'd be grateful for ever.'

'But . . . how do I get in?'

'You've got keys.'

'Oh, God, so I have.' She was sitting on the edge of the bed, pyjamas rucked up to her knees.

'I knew they'd come in useful one day.'

'Night.'

'What? And let me know the instant you get there. Promise.'

'I promise.'

It did not occur to Sukie that she would be prevented from fulfilling Amanda's simplest request.

# Chapter Two

The same jeans, gym shoes and holey sweater, but with a navy coat on top. The square was deserted, only street lamps, a couple of yellow windows, and the moon. The moon adrift, cloud dredged. A rushing overhead as Sukie ducked into her car.

In the Brompton Road, there was the occasional taxi, a noisy young group kicking an empty Coca-Cola bottle, a couple kissing in a doorway. It was good to know that not everyone was asleep. Good too to whiz over wet surfaces of usually sluggish streets, her black Renault 5, eight years old, still lively, until they neared Knightsbridge and intuitively its pace slowed.

Jerry and Amanda's flat was in a sheer, red block in Pont Street. Sukie parked, turned off the engine, and sat for a moment or two, staring at the windscreen. Then she took a deep breath, got out, locked the door, and approached the building.

As well as the keys, Amanda had given her a plastic security card with which to gain entry from the street. There was a click and she moved inside, the door shutting behind her. The hall was dimly lit, dark wood, red stair-carpet, glass lift. Sukie was about to enter it, had her hand on the lever, when she changed her mind and made for the stairs. Their broad tread looked more trustworthy than the lighted lift, waiting.

Gliding up the hushed well, energized, she could have been flying. Is that the swish of the lift called to overtake? A race to the fourth floor. Again, dim lighting, as in a hotel or hospital: Flat 11, round the corner on the left, just past the lift at her right shoulder. Is that a quiver of wires behind the cage?

Sukie pressed the bell, primed for a sound behind the door, immediate, alarming. But the ring came from deep within the flat, hardly enough to disturb a sleeper; she pressed again. No movement. A third time. Nothing. Keys jangling against the wood, first the Chubb, then the other.

There was a strange smell.

Not strange in that it was unfamiliar. Strange that it should be there. Cigarette smoke. Strong. And drink, mixed in ... there'd been a night of it ... And scent ... Giorgio was it?

And, 'Jerry,' she called, very quietly. 'Jerry, it's me, Sukie. I'm sorry to intrude,' stepping through the hall, moonlit from the kitchen window, knowing the bedrooms are to the left, as in her own flat, the sitting-room to the right. The bedrooms were in darkness, both doors a little open. The sitting-room door was shut, a line of yellow along its lower edge.

'Jerry,' she called again, giving the door of the master bedroom a little push. It swung inwards, still dark but with just enough shine of silk to show bedspread sloping to pillows, undisturbed. The smaller bedroom likewise.

Her hands were sweating as she approached the sitting-room, fear rising, of embarrassment perhaps? She knocked on the door, knuckles close together. No one inside could have failed to hear it. She tried again, and knew no one would answer. Slowly, she turned the handle, firmly so that it should not slip.

They had been playing games. There was a backgammon set on a low table, a pack of cards splayed and untidy, some fallen to the floor. There was a square ashtray filled with stubs, and two empty glasses beside two empty bottles of champagne. But the games seemed to have got out of hand. Carpets were rucked. A brandy bottle lay on its side, leaking into a brown stain on the floor, and the sofa was at an odd angle to the armchairs. It was a large room, the sofa and armchairs at the far end, forming an intimate corner round the fireplace. Sukie approached the sofa, with the intention of straightening it, probably; at least she put her hands on the back.

And then she stopped. Not because the sofa was in her way, but because everything stopped at that moment. Everything inside her. Everything outside. She was unable to breathe, unable to move, unable even to gasp or scream. She wanted to. She wanted to do anything that would move time forward. Or back. Oh, yes, certainly back. Back as far as it would go, as far as it would take, to change what she now saw.

Think back.

Jerry was lying on the fur rug wearing an expression that was familiar and an old school tie. He wore it in the usual place, round his neck, screwed up, knotted tightly, and nothing else. Unless he could be said to 'wear' the string that tied his legs and ankles together, one arm behind his back. The other arm was flung outwards towards his pile of clothes, as though he had had the sudden hope of getting dressed. But in his hand was a knife, the same little paper knife that she had seen him take from his pocket at Newmarket.

. . . The third occasion.

Sukie was leaning all her weight on the back of the sofa. Then her legs started to shake. That knees should knock had always seemed an exaggeration, but now . . . her legs shook so violently and with such precision that she could hear her heels drumming on the floor.

There was an eerie shine to his body, some of which spread to the black pile of the rug. She shouldn't be looking at his body, wanted to apologize for having found him like this. She did not want to have noticed how narrow his shoulders appeared without the skills of his tailor, how his girth rose in a ridge from his wasted abdomen, nor the untidy trail of grey hair, sticky and viscid like the rug. She did not want to imagine Amanda with him. And she did not want to recognize that expression; the one she had seen on Peter's face before he died.

Sukie believed that she crawled to the telephone in the bedroom. At least, it was sitting on the floor that she spoke to the woman who answered to 999. She also crawled to the bathroom where she was sick, then rinsed her mouth with toothpaste, using a finger vigorously around each tooth, before composing herself on the closed lavatory seat to wait.

When the police rang the bell it was outrageously loud. It took Sukie a while to understand what it was. They rang again when she was on her way to answer it, which made her cross.

'In there,' was all she said, flinging out an arm, as though they had come to collect some piece of faulty equipment.

Now a policewoman was making a cup of tea and she was sitting at the kitchen table. She tried to lift the cup but it felt very heavy and seemed to be battery operated so that tea looped on to the floor. Sukie pushed it aside, put her arms on the table, her head on top of them, as they had been told put their heads on desks as children. She yawned. She was so sleepy. And the light in the kitchen was so bright.

Someone was talking to her. A policeman sitting opposite. Sukie blinked up at him, forehead aching. 'Yes?' Her mouth was bitter. He was asking questions, writing down her answers. All quite straightforward, explaining why she was there, how Amanda had telephoned her. God, Amanda!

'Oh, my God, I said I'd phone her. Oh, God, how awful of me. I must do it now.' She started to get up.

But they don't want her to. They are pushing her down, calmly, very firmly. They will make all necessary calls. Now.

'How well did you know Mr Wearing?'

'What? He was an old friend. Married to one of my oldest

25

friends. Amanda and I were at boarding school together. In Oxfordshire.'

'Yes?'

'Well?'

'Was there possibly anything more between you and Mr Wearing than just friendship?'

She was about to reply, when he continued.

'It seems pretty likely that he died of a heart attack.'

Now she couldn't reply. Those two words. The coldness that again took hold of her, as though she too had died. There in the next room, Jerry. The crushing pain between the shoulder-blades, and nobody with him. No touch of kindness. No help. No hope.

'It also seems pretty likely that someone was with him when this happened. We just need to know the facts. No blame. This sort of behaviour is not as rare as you might suppose.'

'It's rare to me!' Her shrillness vibrating amongst the cups and saucers. The policewoman has put a hand on her arm. 'Are you suggesting that I was his mistress?'

'We're not suggesting anything,' the woman said. 'Just asking.'

'For Christ's sake, do I look like a mistress?' Sukie plucked at her jumper, her jeans, lifted a gym shoe that also had, she now noticed, a hole in the toe. 'Do you really think someone would buy champagne for me, looking like this?'

'We come across all sorts.' A look passed from the man to the woman.

'Well. I'm not one of them. And I want to be sick again.'

After she had signed her statement they drove her home. Even helped her into her coat which they found curled up in a corner beside the lavatory. Did she think she needed a doctor?

'No thank you. I just need to be left alone.'

'I just need to be left alone. I do. I thought I told you.'

The phone again, ringing and ringing out of darkness. Only it wasn't dark. Sun flattened the foot of the quilt, fading oriental

26

birds to sandpipers. It lurched up a section of the wall, drawing a charcoal line down the corner.

Sukie lifted the receiver. 'No, I do not want to make a lunch date. I just want to sleep. I could sleep for ever.'

'So could I.' The words, without expression, were the most expressive she had heard Amanda speak.

'Oh, God. Oh, God, I'm so sorry. I was asleep. I didn't know what I was saying.' Sukie sat up, fast breathing, panic flashing into the morning.

'That's all right. Listen,' her voice was a dry whisper, 'I'm coming round. I'll be about half an hour. There's something you have to do for me.'

Amanda walked straight into the sitting-room and sat on a high-backed chair by the french windows, averting her face to look out at the square.

'Can I get you anything?' Sukie hovered, still in her dressing-gown.

'Scotch. Large. Unadulterated.' She gave an edged laugh.

Sukie poured two Scotches of differing sizes.

Amanda took the larger one. 'So. Here we are. I suppose I'd better get on with it.'

'If that's what you want to do.' Sukie went to sit on the arm of the chaise-longue.

'I expect it is.' She sniffed and began to study a piece of moulding, high up to the left of the curtains. 'Well, obviously they think sexual jinks were involved.'

'It was a heart attack?'

Amanda shrugged one shoulder. 'Now they want to crawl around and find out who the playmate was. Who, when the fun ran out, ran out with it. Left him to die. Without even calling an ambulance.' She stopped; stared out at the square, eyes stretched against the light, then continued as if there had been no pause, 'I gather they think he didn't actually get to the point

– if you know what I mean – so he even missed out on that. Forensics, no doubt, will be pleased to tell me. What the hell?'

Sukie felt unable to reply.

Amanda looked so alien; narrow and high-shouldered like the fruitwood chair, legs straight down, knees together, slap of sunshine across her face.

'Unless, of course, they think it's you,' she said.

'What?' Sukie took her first sip of Scotch.

'You.' Amanda did not move. 'That might make sense to them. It would give us time, at least.'

'Us?'

'So, that's what I told them. Or didn't, if you see what I mean.' She turned round, conspiratorial, almost gay. 'I told them that I knew nothing about the telephone calls you said you had from me. About the keys I was very vague.' She was actually smiling. 'If they think it was you, they won't go sniffing around to find out who was really there.'

'I don't believe this.' Sukie put her glass down on the floor between them. 'You intend to drop me in serious trouble?'

'It's only temporary.'

'*And* serious embarrassment?'

'Until we find out.'

'*We?* Find out what?'

'I'm not sure.'

Sukie stood up and reknotted the tie of her camel dressing-gown very tightly. 'I'm going to get dressed.'

'I've had enough of them tripping over carpets, taking snap-shots, assigning me to a teenage wardress with a caring look she'd learnt at psychology classes.'

'I know the one.'

'I gave her the slip. But not before telling her that things aren't always what they seem.' Amanda sniffed her whisky and twitched her nose. 'Are you sure this isn't Irish?'

'Quite. There were signs . . .'

'That all was not straightforward? Oh yes. I also told her that I knew Jerry a lot better than they do, for all they caught him at a bad moment.'

'Like him not drinking champagne, and giving up smoking.'

'Exactly.' Amanda looked straight at Sukie for the first time since she had arrived. 'But, of course, I'm just some pathetic wife who can't face what her husband was up to.'

'Did you mention any of this?'

'What do you think? Also, that Jerry never did anything he didn't want to do. For anybody! And I know what they think about that too.' Amanda gave another edged laugh. 'They think if the woman was young enough and attractive enough, and had given him what he wanted enough, he'd have been willing to do anything. I suppose I *do* find that hard – to face.'

'I would like to help,' Sukie said to her glass.

'But the worst thing. What I really cannot face at all, what – *hurts* – me, is that Jerry never showed any sign of being interested in *bondage*. Never ever. Not at all! And if he did like it . . . then why didn't I *know*? And why didn't he want to do it with *me*?'

They each took a large gulp of Scotch.

'I must tell you, Amanda, I am most reluctant to become Jerry's mistress.'

'Don't be such a prude.'

'And how do I get out of it? And *why*, anyway?'

'You get out of it because I own up. Jealous wife, hysteria, terrible shock, etc. And "why" is because I want you to get into his office before they do.'

'What!'

'Jerry's office. Big law firm in the City. Lots of plants.'

'I know that. And if you weren't my friend, I'd call this blackmail.'

'It is blackmail.' Amanda opened her latest Hermès bag. 'I shall continue to pay the school fees. Here,' she took out some keys and placed them in Sukie's palm. 'These are Jerry's second set.'

Sukie's palm remained open. 'What's this about school fees?'

'Well, Jerry *was* paying them, wasn't he? For Alexis?'

Sukie's fingers curled. 'I didn't know that you knew.'

'I saw a bill. Jerry was secretive about quite unnecessary things.'

'He was doing it for Peter. That's what he said. That Peter would have wanted Alex to go to his old school. I couldn't possibly have afforded it.'

'Jerry could be kind, you know. He was kind to me.'

'Of course, I do know that ... I do.' Sukie's hand closed over the keys.

'He was twitchy about some client who was also a friend. Don't know why. Know nothing about his clients. Not sure now about his friends.'

'You're thinking that may have something to do with his death?'

Amanda shut her bag and stood holding it by its handles, swinging it.

'Of course. But then I'm a pathetic wife who can't face what her husband was up to.'

# Chapter Three

'Barnie?'

'I know that voice. Don't tell me. So posh I felt I should be paying double. So posh, I felt you should be paying me. Sukie, my favourite flower, how are you?'

'Flourishing. How's business?'

'Busy. Don't tell me you want to come and work for me again?'

'Well, no. Sort of. For a day.'

'A day! What sort of a deal is that?'

'A week?'

'A week. Not much of a deal.'

'The usual patch. Including Wearing, Sutcliffe and Montague.'

'But you never did that one. Mr Wearing was a friend, you said. You thought you'd embarrass him. Some friend.'

'I've changed my mind. Is there any chance of my doing the plants there soon?'

'Maybe. Why?'

'I need the money.'

'You always did. But you still liked to miss out your friend.'

'Oh, that. For a bet. A joke.'

'So. For a bet – or a joke? Which is it? You want me to help you win a bet or play a joke?'

'A jokey bet. A bet made for a joke. I can't explain.'

'OK. You need help with your bet, I need help with my plants. But no comeback. I don't want any complaints from your Mr Wearing.'

'There will be no complaints from Mr Wearing. I can absolutely promise that.'

'Tomorrow, then. You want to pick up your kit tonight? I'll put the usual girl on to another job. Lots of new planting. Dirty hands. You never cared for that.'

'I'm sorry.'

'So, what do I care? You don't work for me any more.'

When Barnie had originally introduced her to his indoor gardeners' uniform, Sukie's eyes had widened and they had both known she would never wear it. This morning, however, approaching the security booth at the rear of the City block which contained Wearing, Sutcliffe and Montague, the green pinafore was in place.

He was very tired, the young man behind the glass; his soft skin shadowed, his eyes drained of colour like the sky at that hour. He took Sukie's letter of authority, shaking his head, not looking at it.

'Nobody's told me about this.'

'It explains it in the letter.' Sukie nodded encouragingly. 'I'm just doing the plants for today.' She lifted up her basket from which poked trowel, misting spray, canister of plant food.

'You can't leave your car there.' He continued to shake his head at the Renault parked humbly close to a wall.

There was a clang, the strum of a bell, laughter, as the lift opened into the lobby to release a troop of cleaners at the end of their night shift. They all crowded round the booth, joking, fastening their coats, ready to sign out and in no mood to be kept waiting.

The young guard swivelled the book round to Sukie, slapping down his biro, looking towards the empty lift. He peeled off a dated sticker and handed it to her, calling over the heads of the women, 'Go with her, Josh, will you?'

The doors of the lift closed and Sukie found herself alone with a despondent man in navy uniform. 'The other girl usually starts at the top.' His hand fidgeted over the buttons then he stepped back and gazed skyward.

They surfaced with a jolt into a dark corridor under a drooping ceiling with visible pipe lines. Josh immediately indicated the cloakroom and waited while she filled her watering can. 'There's only two plants up here. This is one.' He unlocked a door almost opposite to reveal a dejected *Dracaena marginata*, then led the way down an entire hundred yards of shabby brown carpet to another dragon tree, in a worse state than the first. 'Let me know when you've finished the top three floors. I'll probably be on the one below by then.'

She would have to work quickly. The tree had obviously been overwatered; it had a bad case of alopecia. Sukie got down on her knees to gather up yellow strands, stuffing them into a plastic bag, returned to the lift area to deal with its fellow, then down to Floor Eight.

Wearing, Sutcliffe and Montague: the smooth grey carpet reeled back under her feet, a moving walkway, she with hand luggage of basket and watering can. Wearing, Sutcliffe and Montague.

Jerry's office, hessian walls, mahogany furniture, was more as the wrought-iron gates at the entrance had promised. Soft mushroom carpeting spread from reception into private rooms. Palms in white pots rippled with health. But in spite of the furnishings there was a bleakness; seaside stance of uninterrupted light, high wind all around that ceaselessly worried and whined.

Jerry's door was the only one that was closed, but it wasn't locked. Sukie faced the solidity of his leather-topped desk, his armchair twisted sideways. And behind, that expanse of white sky, propped by the spire of a nearby church.

Moment over, she glanced round: a wall of law books, another of cupboards and drawers, an alcove with a coffee machine. She put down her watering can and basket and walked round to the other side of the desk.

An appointments book in the centre, dark green leather, a tray of pens and paper-clips, to one side a computer, to the other a large coloured photograph of Triumvirate, sun reflecting from his flanks.

She turned away. What twist was in her that she should be so touched to find the horse on his desk rather than his wife? She withdrew from her kangaroo pocket a pair of fine rubber gloves and smoothed them on to her fingers.

'What am I looking for?' she had asked Amanda.

'Anything,' Amanda had said. 'Anything you can find. I don't know.'

Drawers were where people kept things. Locked drawers. Only two were locked. The others contained writing paper, envelopes, more paper-clips. She found the key that fitted the deep locked drawer. It was full of documents, impossible to read and leave undisturbed, impossible to read at all in the time. Lawyer's business. The shallow locked drawer was personal. A new form book for the coming flat season, a set of dog-eared playing cards and underneath a pile of snapshots. Taken over the years, in different gardens, on holidays in sun and snow, pictures of Amanda, and of Simon right back to when he could only just stand, smiling under a blue cotton hat.

Had she been wrong about Jerry? Had Peter?

An address book was at the back of the drawer, dark green like the appointments diary. This was the sort of thing, handwritten, scraps of paper inside the cover. She slipped it into the kangaroo pocket.

Some client who was also a friend . . . Now for the clients.

Alexis had recently given her lessons on his computer. 'You need them, Mosie. You can't go on living in the past. I insist that you join the twentieth century.'

'It's nearly over.'

'Exactly.'

Now, feeling rather proud, she switched on the one on Jerry's desk, found the documents on the hard disc and, startlingly easily, his list of clients. Switching to 'print' command, for some reason she clicked to '2' for the number of copies then, while the printer did its work, began to do hers; spraying the palm and squeaking the leaves clean with a J-cloth.

Was that high-pitched whistle a vibration along the pipes? Or was it the wind? Sukie paused, frond between thumb and finger, trying to hear above the hum of the printer. A muted whistle. Not the wind.

She darted into the reception area. Behind her, the printer hiccuped and hummed as Josh put his head round the door of the main office.

'Thought you might care for a cup of tea?'

'Oh, how terribly kind of you.' She began to pull off the gloves, snapping the rubber, advancing on him, forcing him to back into the corridor.

'Surprised you can feel to do the plants properly in those,' he nodded at the gloves. 'The other girl never wears them.'

'Oh,' Sukie flapped them about. 'I just hate getting my hands dirty.' She took the mug with a smile.

'Funny job to choose, then.'

'Well, one just has to take what one can get nowadays.'

'That is very true.' He nodded again, standing there with her, drinking his own tea. 'Take this, for instance. Very lonely job, this.'

'I can imagine.' She could now hear a reassuring absence of sound. The printer had done its work. 'Well, I'd better get on. Lots to do.'

'Oh. I'd have thought you'd have finished up here now? The other girl's much quicker.'

'I mean, I've done all the others. I've just got to finish this one.'

35

'Oh, all right, then.' He held out his hand for the mug. 'Funny you should be working on that one just now.'

'Oh? Why?'

'Gary downstairs just had a phone call. Chap who works in that office was found dead yesterday morning.'

Behind her there was a loud hiccup. The printer switching itself off.

He looked over her shoulder. 'What was that?'

'I didn't hear anything.'

He sniffed. 'Wind plays funny tricks in this building. Well, see you on the second. There might be another one waiting for you,' he raised her mug in a jaunty fashion. 'You never know.'

Without separating the copies, she gathered the list of clients from the printer, rolled them up and slid them into her kangaroo pocket with the address book. Then, not waiting to clean any more of the palms, she filled their reservoirs with water so that the plastic indicators bobbed like floats on a line, and made for the stairs. When she reached the seventh floor, she could hear the sound of the lift, moving upward, and then the clunk as it stopped.

That sound was like a string being plucked in her mind; floor to floor, building to building, City to the Euston Road. And the leaves of the plants, their tension squeaking through her fingers, a materialization of that memory. A strumming note. Registered, then ignored. Because she had other things on her mind . . .

Driving home into the square, still in the pinafore under her coat, exhausted, mind blank . . . Sukie knew what it was.

The lift. In Pont Street. In the corridor, on the way to Jerry's flat. There had been a sound. Someone leaving? She had said nothing to the police when they had questioned her. Hadn't remembered it. And now that she had, she wasn't sure she had heard it at all.

\*

36

There were four messages on the answerphone: one from Alexis who had seen of Jerry's death in a tiny paragraph in the *Evening Standard*, one from Jemima whom Alexis had telephoned, one from Amanda telling her to call, and one from a girl friend asking if she could do a directors' lunch the following week.

Sukie turned on the bath, having immediately phoned to say 'yes' to the directors' lunch, now wondering how on earth she could fit it in amongst all the plant watering. Alex would be home tomorrow. Jemima would call again. She untied the strings of the pinafore and laid it carefully on a chair. Amanda would have to wait.

An hour later, warm and guilty in pyjamas and dressing-gown, a large glass of Muscadet to hand, Sukie settled herself on the sofa with the address book and list of clients. She smoked a cigarette as well, which made the process slow, but her feel racy. A friend who is also a client ... By the time she had finished, dusk was filtering through the room, and three names had emerged: Officer, Rosamund Joyce; Graham-Jones, George; and Whippet, Henry – who, while he could hardly be included as a friend, was in the private address book.

She went to refill her glass. The room was quite dark when she returned, so she drew the curtains and turned on all the lights. Beside the address book were the few scraps of paper that had been inside its cover. One was a scribbled fax number for one of the names inside, two were betting slips. The other, folded in half, was a training bill, rather a burly one, made out to Jerry, George and Rosamund, and there was something scribbled on the back. She turned it over. It was a London telephone number.

Perhaps it was the wine, but a moment later she had the receiver in her hand and was dialling the digits. The ringing tone only sounded three times, then there was a click as the answerphone came on, followed by a woman's voice, efficient and inviting:

'Hullo. You have made contact with the White Tie Escort Agency. We are so sorry not to be able to speak with you just now. Please, do leave your name and a telephone number so that we may return your call. If this would not be convenient, although we are always discreet, please try this number again on Monday when there will be somebody here to speak with you personally.'

Sukie replaced the receiver, but not before she had heard the tone prompting the caller to leave a message. It sounded like an alarm, a warning that if she proceeded, there would be messages she would not want to hear.

# Chapter Four

Saturday morning eleven-thirty and Sukie, still guilty in pyjamas and dressing-gown, sat at the kitchen table making lists for the directors' lunch. She had found it hard to wake up. The *Sporting Life* remained on the mat. How much simpler to leaf through pages, savoury and sweet, to make plans within the circumscribed safety of a menu.

And then the phone rang.

'How could you do it to me, Sukie?'

'What?' For a moment she couldn't think who it was.

'How could you? That joke you wanted to pull. That joke was on me.'

'Oh no, Barnie, no. It wasn't.'

'The man was dead, Sukie. How are you going to pull a joke on a dead man? He's not around for the pay-off.'

'I'm sorry. Look, I was doing it for his wife.'

There was silence.

'I didn't do any harm. I did the job all right, didn't I?'

'Oh, you did a good job. There's a *Ficus benjamina* on Wearing's floor pegging out in sympathy. No good will come from spying on a husband dead or alive.'

'I wasn't spying.'

'So what does it matter? One dead *Ficus benjamina*. What the hell? The man's dead too. So, what the hell too? Both dead. What difference does it make what either of them was up to?'

'It wasn't that sort of thing.'

39

'I said no sort of thing. What a *Ficus benjamina* gets up to is its own affair. I don't care. And neither should you.'

'Barnie, I'm so sorry for deceiving you. And I'll pay for the plant.'

'Forget it. Forget I called. Forget it all.'

'And next week?'

'Next week, you show them proper respect. We have a deal, remember?'


'So, how is Amanda, Mosie?'

'Hard to tell. She seems ... It's not fair to judge people in these situations.'

'No. I found a dead curry in the oven.'

'Help!'

'Don't worry, I disposed of it with dignity.' Alexis was standing over his mother in the kitchen, hands in his pockets, the sleeves of his school shirt rolled up, tie loosened.

Sukie put the wooden spoon down, turned round and gave him a hug. His arms round her felt surprisingly muscular. He smelt of fresh air. She went back to stirring the bolognese sauce.

'But I don't want you to feel that any of this has got to affect you. Weekend, just the same. Football on the television.'

'I don't mind, really. Uncle Jerry was very good to me.'

She stopped stirring, rested the spoon on the edge of the saucepan, just touching the surface of the sauce. 'Amanda wants to go on paying your school fees.'

'Oh, Christ!' He flopped so that his chin almost reached his chest, then straightened up, pushing back his hair with one hand. 'That's such a relief! You can't believe what a relief that is. I was really worried. I know it's selfish, but when I heard the news, the first thing I thought was that I might have to leave school.'

'And that worried you?'

'It certainly did. It's so selfish, I know, but I just couldn't help it.'

Sukie shook her head. 'I'm just glad you like it there.'

'Oh, I do. But even that went out of my mind when I saw the tabloids.'

'Of course, the tabloids have got hold of it.' Amanda's elbow rested on the metal table. Her fingers crawled over her mouth as she spoke. 'Not front page, but all the details.'

Sukie looked up from the menu, but Amanda was busy chewing a thumbnail. They were in a tiny basement restaurant in Beauchamp Place. It was rather too crowded, but the bustle gave a spurious privacy.

'Everything. Can you believe it?' Amanda took the thumb out of her mouth and studied it. 'Even down to the old school tie. Anyway – ' picking up her menu and using it like a fan – 'it was certainly natural causes so at least we can have a funeral.' She hoisted a smile as though at the prospect of a good bash. 'Did I tell you about the oil?'

'No.'

'He was all covered in oil. Obviously they'd been having a slick time.' She yawned. 'All terribly boring. Let's choose lunch.'

Sukie studied her menu again. 'Do you want to hear what I found out?'

Amanda frowned. 'Ooh, I like the sound of this. "Turbot *Quenelles* with Lobster Sauce and Samphire Vol-au-vent".'

'I have a print-out of the names of all Jerry's clients. I also found this.' She leant down to her bag on the floor and held the address book above the table. 'I think he can only just have started it. It's not very full.'

'It's just like his one at home.' Amanda put out a hand, flicked through it: 'Just like.' She dropped it into her own bag. 'I think we should both have the *quenelles*. I'm paying.'

'There were three names that were common to both.'

'Right. *Quenelles* for two.'

'Do you want to know who they were?'

41

Amanda was smiling about for a waiter. 'I'm not sure that I do, quite honestly.'

Sukie shivered. She had meant to wear her cobwebby cardigan, but Jemima must have taken it off to Bristol. 'You sent me into Jerry's office to look for names.' The stone floor made her feet cold, the metal table. 'I was taking quite a risk.'

'So? What difference does it make now?'

'You said you needed to know what really happened.'

'Yes . . . well . . . if that's what I told you.'

'You certainly did. You also said that this place would be warm.'

Amanda glanced at Sukie's folded arms, her cinnamon satin shirt, was about to speak, but looked up instead.

Their waiter stood beside them with notebook and pencil. 'Ladies?'

Amanda gave the order, asking his advice about wine, tweaking a shoulder of her Starzewski jacket. When he had gone, she leant forward, hands clasped on the table.

'So, you didn't come across any evidence of a secret life?'

There was a brief pause before Sukie said, 'No.'

Amanda appeared not to notice it. She sat back, pushed both hands through her hair. 'All right. You're dying to tell me. The three names.'

'There were two men and one woman who were apparently both friends and clients: George Graham-Jones, Henry Whippet and Rosamund Officer.'

'Ha!' Amanda leant even further back, tipping her chair on to two legs. 'Rosamund hardly counts as a woman.'

'I didn't think that was the point.'

'Didn't you? Well,' Amanda let her chair come down with a bump, 'if I'd told you I was curious about bits on the side, you wouldn't have gone.'

'Too bloody right. Blackmail or no blackmail.'

'What? Well, roger me. Don't tell me you believed all that.

Sukie, you're such a fool. You don't honestly think I'd tell lies to the police?'

'Only to your friends, apparently.'

'Come on.' Amanda sniffed. 'Come on, let's decide what we'll have for pud. I think widows get dispensation from dieting, don't you?'

Sukie could not speak.

'Mmm. *Marrons Chantilly*. Perfect. I shall have that in Jerry's memory. He loved *marrons*. They were listed in the contents of his stomach.'

'*Quenelles* will be plenty for me.' Sukie had taken the rolled-up list of clients from her bag and held it out across the table. 'And, since I'm no longer Jerry's mistress, you can take your information and put it wherever it most pleases you.'

Amanda's fingers closed on the cylinder of paper. Not looking at it, she said, 'Oh, I wasn't making it all up. I wouldn't do that to you.'

# Chapter Five

It should have been easy to concentrate on form for the Whitbread Gold Cup, the final big chase of the season to be run the following Saturday, but it wasn't.

From the sunny sofa in the sitting-room Sukie could hear Mrs Tribe relentlessly driving the vacuum cleaner over that patch of rucked carpet in the bathroom. And across the room in her desk was the list of Jerry's clients and the training bill with the number of the White Tie Agency on the back.

Every time she thought she had worked out a good form line, calculating pounds and lengths, she was distracted by the existence of those other bits of paper. She gave a sharp sigh, and underlined a particularly crucial '6 lbs', forgetting instantly wherein their cruciality lay. What were the names of the horses, what their connection?

The names in the desk were all she could recall. And what was so crucial about them? Sukie put the paper down and took off her spectacles. Through the half-open door into the hall, she could see the flex now lashing her delicate Pembroke table like an angry tail. Jerry dead. Inquest opening tomorrow. She wouldn't be going to the Whitbread anyway.

She was about to get up and shut the door, but didn't have the will. This week did not exist. It was simply a space. Jerry might not have died. The non-existent week was as long as a piece of string, and as insignificant.

The roaring in the bathroom had ceased. The flex cracked

once and was still. Mrs Tribe backed into the sitting-room in her turquoise track-suit.

'No work today, Mrs Buckley?'

'I only had one office to water this morning, and I did it at six-thirty.' Sukie took her feet off the sofa. 'I've got some cooking to do in a minute.'

'That carpet doesn't get any better.'

'No. But then things don't, do they?'

'I beg your pardon?' Mrs Tribe leant down to push the plug into its socket. She was a big-boned woman with a noble nose and a mouth that shrank into her face as though resisting pressure to speak its mind.

'Well, they're not like us. We either get better or we die. Carpets don't even die.'

Mrs Tribe stood up straight. 'I'm a tired woman, Mrs Buckley. I've been a tired woman all my life. Now these,' she approached the ivory silk curtains and gave them an affectionate brush with her hand, 'now these are beautiful.'

'Oh, they are. But that was when I was working for that letting company with the Arab connection; they who paid over the odds.'

'Smooth as butter.' Mrs Tribe pulled the cord a little way, then pulled it back and carefully rearranged the marmoreal folds. 'If only the rest of this establishment ran as smooth as these.'

'Oh, I know, Mrs Tribe, I know. And if it wasn't for you things would be even bumpier.'

'I don't doubt that. But all the way over here, once a week for two hours . . . It's not as though we need the money, Bill says. And you going out at the crack of dawn so's you can pay me. You'd do better to do the work yourself and spend the money on some carpet.'

'I know that too. But that's women's economics, isn't it, Mrs Tribe. And, well, we've been together a long time.'

'That's what Bill says too. He says, things can't be easy for you just now. Stirring up memories. Cup of tea?' And she went out to the kitchen, leaving the vacuum cleaner in the middle of the room.

The week passed, but not time with it. The end of the piece of string had not been reached. Sukie thought she could see it, as she drove home late on Friday afternoon by way of Kentish Town. She had handed over her gardening kit, and untied the green pinafore with such relief that she really thought she had escaped when she got back into her car. But the piece of string still stretched ahead. It was a trail dragged before her through the streets. A trail that would finish in frayed ends and the burning of fingers when she tried to break it. The sun was out in the square, and a waft of spring flowers, but she didn't care. All she cared about was a bath and a large drink.

As she unlocked the door to the flat, she heard a noise. Somebody was moving about in the sitting-room. Then, in a draught, the front door slammed shut behind her, and Jemima came out into the hall.

'Puddles! Dear God, you gave me a shock.'

'Sorry.' Her daughter looked at her as though she were a little crazy. 'Where have you been? You look awful.'

'Thanks.' Sukie went straight through to the kitchen with her basket.

'What have you been doing?'

Sukie was bending down to the fridge. 'Plant watering,' she muttered, making a lot of noise with ice.

'You swore you'd never do that again.'

'I know.' She made for the sitting-room and unscrewed the gin, pouring herself a large double into the tonic.

'No wonder you're drinking gin. No wonder you look awful.'

'There's no need to go on about it.' Sukie took her first

mouthful. 'I was doing it as a favour. I shan't be doing it again.' She was now serene. 'What about you? You didn't tell me you were coming.'

Jemima flopped on to the sofa. There was criticism in her look. 'I'm here for the funeral, of course.'

'The funeral?' Sukie suddenly felt quite frantic.

'Uncle Jerry's? Remember?' Fingering the trail of black skirt she was wearing.

'Of course. Of course I remember. But I don't know when it is. Nobody's told me.'

'That's because you're always forgetting to leave your answerphone on. That's why I couldn't let you know I was coming.'

'I'm sorry.'

'That's all right.' Jemima's head was on the cushions, straight dark hair falling from her pale face. She looked at the ceiling as she spoke. 'Anyway, Simon left a message for me. And for Alex, I gather. It's next Monday. There's probably a message for you too. The green light's on, but I didn't check it in case I got one of your lovers.'

'I haven't got any lovers.'

'Only joking. Of course you haven't.' Jemima arched her back on the sofa.


Cooking dinner, *fritto misto* of vegetables, Jemima's favourite with a light mayonnaise, there was a sense of luminous peace. Outside was darkness; and their little kitchen a lantern held up against it. Jemima sneaking discs of vegetable as they drained on paper, dipping them into the sauce, getting a pot of Mexican relish from the fridge and trying that, licking her fingers. They should have more time together without Alex.

'It's more than Uncle Jerry, isn't it, Mosie?'

'I suppose it is.'

'More than actually finding him, which must have been awful.'

'More than that.'

'Is it . . . is it anything about Daddy?'

Jemima had adored Peter, had felt herself, Sukie now saw, excluded.

'I don't know. Yes. Yes, of course it is. But that isn't all.'

'What else?'

Alex, coming later, had found his place waiting; so young when his father had died, he had grown to take that place as of right, the women remaining at either side.

'The whole thing's wrong. Of course it's wrong, I don't mean that. There are circumstances that aren't right. That don't make sense.'

'You don't think he died of a heart attack?'

'Oh, yes. Yes he did. But not like Peter. I was there when that happened. I called for the ambulance. Was in it all the way to the hospital. I was with him at the end. He was Peter, but I'd have done the same if it had been a friend. I'd have done almost the same if it had been an acquaintance, someone I'd seen on the street – anybody. Do you see?'

Jemima put the top back on the Mexican relish. 'But this was different. Not the sort of situation most people would want to be found in.' She put the jar back in the fridge.

'True. But just because someone's a tart doesn't mean they have no kindness. She'd at least have called a hospital, even if she did spend time wiping her fingerprints off everything first.'

'Is that what was done?'

'Apparently. And the cigarette stubs; only Jerry's were found.'

'So what are you going to do about it?'

'Why do you ask that?' Music playing from the sitting-room, Sukie paused, lifting the last of the vegetables out of the wok to listen to it.

'Just a feeling.'

Corelli. Sukie slid the vegetables on to paper, put a dish in the middle of the table.

48

'Don't forget, I've known you nineteen years.' Jemima had taken out a bottle of Pouilly Fumé she had brought home, and shut the fridge door.

'That's disturbing.'

'Nineteen years?'

'No. That I'm going to do something about it.'

# Chapter Six

The funeral was somewhat of an imposition on the tiny Cambridgeshire village. Glossy cars were parked the length of the High Street with casual disregard for yellow lines; many with their wheels on the pavement, so that mothers had to bump their pushchairs down into the road.

Sukie, arriving only just in time, abandoned her car on a muddy patch in a distant side street facing open country. They had to run to the church in their smart clothes, apologizing to shoppers and dodging off kerbs.

Jemima strode ahead in her black skirt and Sukie's expensive cobwebby cardigan, accepting all stares as admiration. Alex was embarrassed and unusually sullen. Sukie watched her feet. She had the dislocated feeling she was going to the races: same black patent shoes, black tights, faithful Chanel bag clamped to her side.

Under the lych-gate, and the path was spotted with blossom. Blossom drifted across the churchyard from almonds growing at its edge. The grass among the graves was uneven, rising in waves over the stones, falling into troughs where nettles grew. A light breeze blew along the ground. The sun came and went between clouds.

The church was full. Simple and white, its walls glimmered, only just holding their form against the grandeur and substance of the congregation: the windows, fissures in its structure, the air misted. Scent overpowered incense. There was no more room in the pews, but rows of chairs had been placed at the back, where Sukie, Jemima and Alexis managed to find three together.

The organist began to play 'Jesu, Joy of Man's Desiring' and Amanda, her hand on Simon's arm, progressed up the aisle in a dress that clung like soot, eyes burning holes in her veil.

As expected, the occasion was upsetting. Sukie concentrated on the order of service, frowning to see without her spectacles, only occasionally glancing up at the coffin. Displacing her thoughts was the way to contain unseemly grief, anywhere rather than here: to the bathroom carpet, and a leak she suspected in the roof. The coffin was covered in lilies, achingly innocent – until one recalled that Jerry was inside it.

Afterwards, outside, the sky had cleared and the sun shone steadfastly as Simon handed his mother into the car behind the hearse, to a volley from press photographers. There were tears blinking behind Amanda's veil, but Sukie could not forestall a sudden vision of her throwing it back and inviting kisses from them all. Then she slid out of view, and the door slammed, sending blossom bowling along the road after her.

The three of them walked, heads down, back through the quiet of the lunchtime village. Passing, Sukie saw many faces that she knew, some socially, others as images from the racing pages and television. Just ahead of them, Henry Whippet was ducking into his Porsche.

'Who was that?' Alex frowned.

'That was Henry Whippet.' Jemima lifted her hair from the back of her neck.

'Why?' Sukie asked him.

'Oh, it was just the way he looked at you as he went by. A bit odd.'

'How odd? I didn't notice.'

'As if he knew you. Or something.'

Sukie shrugged. 'Well, we have met, I suppose.'

'Where?' Jemima gave her hair a final flick with her fingers.

51

'Oh, very briefly. In paddocks.'

'Oh. Well, that's all right, then.'

Henry Whippet was not at the cemetery, but then neither were the majority of the racing professionals. They were in fast cars or helicopters off to Kempton, Haydock or Nottingham.

At Tancred House, there was already a party going on. They were given champagne by Maria in the wide panelled hall, then encouraged through to the drawing-room and on to the terrace where Jemima tripped straight down to the lawn to speak with Simon.

'We don't have to stay very long, if you don't want to.'

Sukie and Alexis stood holding their glasses looking out over the garden. Alexis nodded. 'Just long enough to let her know we're here.' He lifted his champagne, eyes narrowing at the people laughing and chatting in their little groups, the two Labradors wagging their way between them. 'Isn't all this just a bit odd?'

'A lot of people nowadays like to look on funerals as a celebration.'

'Of what?' He hadn't yet tasted the drink.

'The person's life.'

'Oh.' He looked about him, then tipped his head back, almost finishing the glass. 'They don't look as if they're talking about Jerry.'

'Probably not. Celebrations are rather for the living than the dead.'

'Too bloody right.' He was scowling. 'I don't remember Daddy's funeral very well. It wasn't like this?'

'No.'

He took another gulp of his drink. He was still scowling, his face, unshaven, fine as a boy's. But the hand that held the glass, raw-boned knuckles, was that of a young man.

'Do you know,' he still had the laughing groups in his sights, eyes slit against the sun, 'I really didn't like Jerry very much.' He turned to her. 'That sounds awful, doesn't it?'

'No.'

'Well, it makes me feel awful. Now. But there's no point pretending, is there? I always felt, whenever we met, that I was being bullied. Somehow. He used to question me. Try to catch me out, I felt. See if I was worth his money, I always worried.' He shook his head. 'Funny. But I still don't feel like laughing now.'

'No. But some people just want to be cheered up.'

'I suppose you know most of them?' He said it as though he disliked her.

'No. Only their racing friends. And not many of them are here. Rosamund's here. And George and Nicola Graham-Jones – ' she looked vaguely about – 'and Bob, I suppose . . .'

'And that's another thing.'

'What? Here, have some of mine. I've got to drive.'

He held his glass out, not looking at her. 'I know it'll upset you, but I don't really like racing much either.'

'Oh, that really is awful.'

'You don't mind?'

'Mind? Where else am I to escape being a mother?'

Down the slope of lawn, Jemima was talking to Simon Wearing under a rose arch, head tipped back, one foot extended, hand plucking at a leaf.

'I didn't know Jemima was so friendly with Simon.'

'She went out with him occasionally, a couple of years ago. God, I'm starving. Do you suppose there's anything to eat?'

'I'd try inside. Follow your nose; it's sure to find some smoked salmon.'

Beyond Jemima, on a circle of stone round a sundial, Amanda was at the centre of a small group. Sukie began to walk across the grass towards them. As she drew near, Amanda raised her head to stare at her without recognition for a blink, before smiling and drawing her in.

'There you are. And you've got a drink.' She seemed surprised.

'Needs topping up.' That was George Graham-Jones, looking almost distinguished in a charcoal suit. He held out a bottle.

'We were talking about the horses,' Amanda included the group. Her hat had gone and her hair, like her eyes, was a little wild. 'What I'm going to do about them? They were Jerry's darlings, never mine. I just went along for the clothes.'

'A clothes-horse, you could say.' George's laugh was a sniff gone into reverse.

'And I think I'd rather not.' She held out her glass to him, which he solemnly refilled. 'It's just . . . Sukie, you'll understand. I just can't face taking an interest in them at the moment. Did you feel the same?'

'We never had horses.'

'Yes, but you know what I mean.' She had taken Sukie's arm. 'Sukie's husband, who died, also of a heart attack, was Peter Buckley.' She looked round at the group. 'The most respected racing correspondent of his day.' They all nodded respectfully and uneasily at Sukie.

'Well . . .' Sukie discovered a tip of mud on her patent shoe. 'I did find it a little difficult for a while.'

And trying now to identify with Amanda, all she could remember was that with two young children there had been no time. And then how expensive racing is, the memberships, the travel, the clothes. There had been no question.

'Don't you worry.' George patted Amanda's shoulder. 'Marcus'll look after the horse end of things. Good man, Marcus. Jerry's fag, after all.'

'I always thought Sylvia had more to do with the actual running of the yard.'

'Did you, now?' Rosamund Officer had come up behind them. At her throat was an enormous diamond brooch, in her hand a very small clutch-bag.

'No, no, no,' George swivelled round to acknowledge her. 'No,

Amanda, Sylvia may be good with the actual horses. You know, what one might call the pastoral side, but when it comes to the business – forget it.' And he wandered off with the empty bottle.

'Hmm. I'm not so sure.' The group had closed round Amanda again, leaving Rosamund with Sukie on the outside. 'I got a whole load of bumf from Sylvia Irvine the other week. Marcus couldn't manage without her, that's my impression.'

'Sorry?' Sukie was looking around for Jemima and Alex.

'A whole load of bumf, she sent me. I just handed it on to Jerry. George is supposed to deal with it really, but Jerry didn't mind. Me – that's what I have a secretary for.'

Alex was coming towards them from the house, awkward, with Nicola Graham-Jones hanging on to his arm.

'Don't you ever feed this handsome young man?' She released the arm with a squeeze. 'I've never seen anyone eat so much. He was absolutely starving.'

'No, no,' Alex was saying. 'Really, I just got up too late this morning.'

'But you're so thin. He really is thin.'

'I wish I was thin,' Amanda wafted past, pressing a hand to her clinging stomach. 'He's like Sukie. She's thin. Always has been.'

'You ought to come to Atalanta's.' Nicola began to open her bag.

'Whose?' Amanda pulled up.

'My health club. If you're worried about your weight.'

'I don't think I am worried about my weight, actually.'

There was a silence while they all looked about and enjoyed the sunshine.

'Oh, well,' Nicola had a card in her hand, '*you* might as well have it.' She handed the card to Sukie. 'Come and have a free trial session. You live in London, so you might make more use of it.' And she suddenly saw someone she knew at the far side of the garden.

Amanda smiled brightly. 'All been a bit much. All those photographers snapping at one's heels. Still, I've got plenty of reliable friends...' She threw out an arm towards the lawn of people. 'Dogs returning to the vomit.'

'She's drunk,' Alexis said as Amanda veered off towards the sundial.

'So are you.'

'Not very.'

'Time to go home.'

As they progressed back towards the terrace, collecting Jemima on the way, the sound of laughter was softened by the garden and the chinking of glass was like little bells. From each group, at some moment, someone would detach themselves and move to another. (Nicola had already taken Jemima's place with Simon under the rose arch.) In the scent of warm grass there was the memory of every summer they had ever known. And so the dance would go on.

'Hullo.' Bob was standing alone, elegant in the way only wealthy Americans can be. 'It's too bad that we have to meet again on such an occasion.'

'Yes.' Sukie had stopped while Alex and Jemima continued on up to the house.

'That day at the racecourse...'

'I know.'

'Might I? I know it's not the right moment but... Might I call you some time? To talk? I feel I may have said the wrong thing at that Sunday lunch where we first met.'

'Oh. Really?'

'Yes.' He straightened his spectacles with a precise finger. 'About your son.'

'Oh.' She shook her head.

'So, might I? Call you?'

'Yes.' She was already moving away. 'Yes, of course.'

# Chapter Seven

High above the heath a lark was singing: the sound, the sweetness in the air, the sting of the morning all one to Sukie, hands deep in navy pockets, waiting by a line of trees.

She was not alone. With her were five people whom she did not know. Nobody spoke. One man, a little apart, smoked a cigarette. The grass was awash with dew.

Then the lark-spinning sky was whipped away; horizon brought to earth by the rhythm of hooves. Heads turned. And the horses broke through. In spider formation they ran the rim; down the dark track diverging, heaving mist over their shoulders to draw level with the group in intimacy of straining leather and snorting breath. And then they were gone. Only the carapaces of their rugs still visible lifting from their quarters, leaving the air to silence.

'So, which was yours?' the man with the cigarette asked as they started to walk carefully back through the wet grass.

'None of them.' Sukie thought him vaguely familiar. 'I was watching one for a friend. Triumvirate, the second of those three. What about you?'

'Sweet Basil.' He threw the cigarette away, still smoking.

'He's rather good, isn't he?'

'Well, we're aiming him at the Wokingham this year. Just hope he doesn't get too much weight. He can't go with yours at levels. Looks like Triumvirate's a bit of all right. Going to ask the Whippet what he thinks?'

'What?'

'You did know he was on him, didn't you?'

'Of course.'

'Know that arse anywhere. All right for transport, are you?' He was good-looking in a battered sort of way, grey hair, humorous eyes.

'Fine, thanks.'

'Anyway I've got to get straight back to town. Give my love to Amanda.' He wandered off between the car ruts. 'My name's Millfield, by the way. Reggie Millfield.'

'Sukie. Sukie Buckley,' she called. 'Good luck for the horse at Ascot.'

He waved a hand without turning round.

As she got into her car to drive to the town for a quick cup of coffee, Sukie realized where she had seen him before. He had been in the little group surrounding Amanda by the sundial, after Jerry's funeral.

The Irvine yard consisted of two brick-built rectangles divided by a driveway. Marcus had accommodation for fifty horses and usually had about forty-five in his string. It was not a top Newmarket stable but had a certain reputation for fair treatment of animals and owners. And according to George, Marcus had been Jerry's fag, say no more.

Sukie was considering this, walking from the front of the house where a disc of gravel contained by bright grass was the designated place for owners to leave their cars, when Sylvia Irvine came up behind her.

'You want to speak to Henry Whippet.' It was an instruction, not a suggestion. 'Jerry always did.'

Sylvia had a saddle over one arm. She was a small woman, tough as thread, with white-blond hair and delicate features. She should have been pretty, but her hair was uncombed and her skin chafed from freezing mornings and soap.

She proceeded into the right-hand yard without looking to see

58

if Sukie was following. 'He's somewhere about. The horse is in there,' she jerked her head and continued on her way.

Sukie stopped on the clean, pale concrete. A single piece of straw fluttered past and she heard the sound of a broom behind her. The lad looked up then continued with his task. From the box came a gentle rustling. She moved towards it, to peer over the door into green darkness.

'Want to take a look?' The voice was right behind her.

'What?' She had not even heard a footstep.

'Want to take a closer look?'

Henry Whippet's arms were folded. He was in jodhpurs and a wind-cheater. His accent was West Country, which came as a surprise, although she must have seen him interviewed many times.

She took a step back. 'He's not mine.'

'I know that.'

'I just offered to come. Mrs Wearing doesn't know much about horses.'

'And you do, do you?'

'A little.'

'Well. He went all right.'

'Good. He looked all right.'

'Oh, yes?'

'Yes.'

'Of course, he was only going half speed.'

'I know that.'

'Oh.' He nodded. 'So you can explain all that to Mrs Wearing?'

'Yes. I will.' She nodded very fast, and was just turning away when he jerked his head, as Sylvia had, towards the inside of the box.

'So, you going to take a look? Mr Wearing liked to go into the boxes.' He opened the door and stood back to let her in then, once they were both inside, bolted it. 'Have to do that, in case the old horse decides he'd like a trot round the yard.'

Triumvirate turned his head to look at them from the far corner of the great airy space. Sukie approached him and put her hand on his neck. It felt firm and warm and very reassuring. The horse turned his head further to watch her, the whites of his eyes showing.

'He's a good old lad,' Henry Whippet said. 'In spite of being a bit of a nipper.'

Instinctively she withdrew her hand then, glancing at the horse's muzzle, put it back and continued to stroke his neck.

'You don't believe me, do you?'

'No. I don't think I do.'

'Quite right. I wouldn't believe me either.'

'He's gorgeous.' She smoothed over a piece of mane. 'Close up, even more so. I don't know why.'

'Don't you? But it's much nicer to touch, don't you think? Feel him breathe. Feel what he's made of.'

Sukie moved her fingers to the bristly bit of mane over the withers. 'Do you actually like the horses that you ride?'

''Course I do. Some of them are buggers. 'Scuse me. Anyhow, I likes them too.'

She took a deep breath and turned round to face him. 'I'm thinking of buying a horse.'

'Oh, yes.'

'But I need advice.'

She waited for him to speak, but he didn't.

'A two-year-old, I think. Like this. But I'm not sure.'

'Well, Mr Irvine would look out for something, if you asked him.'

'No. You see, I'm not really certain yet what I want. I don't really care to involve him at this stage. I need advice – without strings, I suppose.'

'Shall I take you out to dinner, then?'

'What?'

'Shall I take you out to dinner?' Henry Whippet's insouciant tone had not changed. His expression remained hidden as he stood with his arm along the door, daylight behind him. 'So's we can talk about horses?'

'Oh, I sort of thought I could talk to you now.' She cleared her throat. Jerry Wearing was an old friend of mine and—'

'Of course, you were there, weren't you? You called the police.'

'Yes.'

He nodded. 'Can't talk to you now. About horses. Got to get up to York. Next Saturday'd be good. Saturday's my going-out night.'

'Is it? Oh. All right. But I can't make it late.'

'Seven o'clock, then? I like an early bedtime myself.'

'Right.' She began to move towards the door.

Henry Whippet put his hand on the bolt, but did not give way. 'Haven't you forgotten something?'

'What?'

'I need your address, if I'm going to pick you up.'

'Oh.' She felt in her pocket for her purse and took out a free individually printed 'World Wildlife' sticker. 'Here's my card, such as it is.'

He nodded, as he read it. 'That's a good address, that is. Kensington. Very smart.' He drew the bolt and held the door open for her, watching her across the yard before calling, 'Saturday night, then. I'll be looking forward to it.'

Sukie decided not to call in on Amanda, even though she was desperate for a pee. She drove straight back to London as fast as the M11 would allow. It was panic, of course. As though, by putting a speedy distance between herself and the stables, she could escape the trap of dinner with Henry Whippet. It was all Amanda's fault. She had no wish to speak to Amanda.

Instead, she poured herself a dab whisky and telephoned

61

Nicola Graham-Jones, and the White Tie Escort Agency. On Rosamund Officer's number there was only the answerphone. She left no message. Then she fell asleep.

It was almost two o'clock when she awoke, cramped and shivering on the sofa. After half a bar of expensive cooking chocolate and a short sharp bath, she curled up on the sofa again wrapped in an enormous striped bathrobe.

The television was on, the *Sporting Life* beside her, her spectacles on her nose. The bathrobe had been Peter's, one of the few items of his clothing she had kept. Being much too big for her it had no use as a practical garment, but was just the thing when she felt the need of extra comfort.

The racing had already begun, but that didn't matter. She wasn't betting. Like the bathrobe, it was just part of the comfort. Seeing Henry Whippet in his proper place, framed, behind glass, put things into perspective. It removed him from her world, from any sinister imaginings, his bright silks against a Technicolor sky.

And the crowd looking so full of zest as it always does at York, the faces round the paddock, animated, optimistic, all except one. And she, the best-dressed woman there, is looking down at her race-card, flicking through it, kicking her heel into the grass, until her companion leans and says something close, into her ear. And then she laughs. Throws her head back and laughs in a way that makes her unrecognizable. And the companion turns to look at the horses again, while his hand remains on her arm. No wonder he had been in a hurry this morning. And no wonder he had made certain Sukie was going back to the stables. Amanda's companion is the owner of Sweet Basil – Reggie Millfield.

# Chapter Eight

Nicola Graham-Jones's health club was in Fulham. Parking could be difficult, she had said. They were negotiating to buy a disused warehouse next door, but for the time being it might be safer to leave the car a little distance away, then walk. Sukie secured a tight space just off Parson's Green and set off with a hand-drawn map.

Summer had arrived that afternoon, opening up the streets, bringing cafés tumbling out in check tablecloths with rickety chairs to scrape their livings on the pavements, while trees extended tender awnings over steaming roads. Let anxiety lurk: Sukie felt happy and full of hope.

Atalanta's was right down on the river, in a dark cobbled street, but raised within a golden-bricked complex, high above the watermark of silt and detritus where people did not have to exercise to stay thin. And today even the river, monolithic, inert, reflecting the carved wings of seagulls, was scalloped with light.

'Mrs Graham-Jones,' the receptionist whispered into an intercom, 'Mrs Buckley is here to see you.'

The high ceiling of the space suggested that this also had been a warehouse, but now given form by paint and credibility by pale wood.

'If you would like to go through?' the girl still whispered, 'Zana will take you.'

Zana, complexion of licked toffee, led the way to a hushed lounge where Nicola was waiting.

'I've organized a key for you,' she indicated one of the cubicle doors down the length of the room. 'If you'd like to get changed, I'll explain our various programmes.'

Sukie had only her black leotard which she had bought from a magazine offer. It had served as swimming-costume, underwear and, lately, as a 'body'. Today it would have to serve its true purpose: she hoped they were both up to it.

On the way to the gym Nicola, now effulgent in yellow and pink, glanced at Sukie sideways. 'So flattering to the stomach, isn't it, black.'

The gym was very different from the chilly, echoing building she remembered from school, with its whiff of perished rubber. This space was temperate and scented, with bright machines rather than daunting obstacles.

'Now, you could certainly do with some toning of those muscles. Definition is what we aim for.' Nicola stood in front of Sukie and stroked one of her own bronzed biceps.

Something disturbs. Not the contrast of the leotards. Or the bodies. Something in the gym. Something that makes Sukie feel a little sick.

The sheen on the bronzed arm. 'Very gently, of course. At your age it's essential you take things gently, and anyway, we don't want you ending up like Popeye.'

'Oh. No. But in one day . . . ?'

'Yes, of course. This *is* your free trial. But anyway, we'll work you out a programme.'

'That sounds fun.'

And it was. What with the vibration and the music, the lifting of weights like a periscope, beneath the warehouse windows on the sky. It felt like being in space. Not real space, of course, but the space of the movies, where everything is predictable and beautifully dressed.

After the gym there was the sauna where Nicola joined her, spreading herself out, so still, as though she had just come out of

64

the sea. And suddenly out of her stillness, 'I can't believe it, of course.'

Sukie lifted her head, wrapped in a white towel, dropped it back again.

'I can't believe it.' Nicola's eyes were closed. 'That Jerry's dead.'

She might have been alone.

'And all the things they're saying.'

The sauna was so quiet. Heavy with it. Sukie fancied that if she listened she might hear the water oozing from the pores of her skin.

'Things are not always what they seem,' she said, then wondered if it was she who had spoken. She lifted herself up on one elbow. And Nicola too had raised her head again. They looked at one another then sank back into separateness.

'Of course, I'm a lot younger than George.' Again the words came as though spoken for herself to hear. 'We've only been married a year.'

'So, you didn't really know Jerry well.'

'No. But he did some legal work for me, over this place.'

'How long has Atalanta's been going, then?'

'A year.'

They were silent again, considering that interval, letting it pass with whatever it meant to them.

'They used to come over.' Nicola lifted a leg, looking at the pointed toe, the peony painted nails. 'Drop in on us, some evenings. I'd sign things then.'

'They?'

She lowered the leg. 'Jerry and Simon. We live near Stevenage. On their way home.'

'Of course, Simon's with Jerry's firm.'

Nicola's toes curled. 'But he hates it. He told me. Jerry always decided everything for him.'

'I suppose Jerry thought it was for the best. He was successful; he wanted to pass it on.'

Nicola sniffed and sat up. 'He had all the right contacts. You know, the old-boy thing.'

'What about Rosamund?'

'Haven't a clue. She probably thinks of herself as an old boy.'

'The triumvirate.'

'You what?' Nicola screwed up her nose.

'The horse. The three owners.'

'Ah, yes, well, there you go. They asked her because they couldn't get another suitable man. An old school friend of Jerry's was supposed to have been the other partner, only he was killed out hunting.'

'There must have been others?'

'I don't think Jerry had many real friends.'

Sukie thought of the address book, the empty pages. She thought of the funeral, the packed church, the party atmosphere. Of course, they had been mostly Amanda's crowd.

'You may be right. When people are married, one doesn't know.'

'Marcus came up with a couple of people, I believe, but Jerry wouldn't consider either of them. So, Rosamund was the nearest to a man they could get.'

'And George?'

'What about George?' Nicola swayed towards her, almost touching.

'I don't know.' The heat, that had been building gradually, seemed abruptly to have been cranked up. Sukie could feel a break of sweat over her entire body. She was breathing water. She sat up, shaking her head free from the towel. 'I've forgotten what I was going to say. This is an amazing place. You must have pulled all the stops to get it going.'

Nicola's face was totally blank. It looked as though it were about to melt in the heat. 'Well, of course.' She got to her feet, turning to take Sukie's hand, 'Come on.' The towel fell from her body. 'I think you've had enough of this. What you get now is the cold water treatment.'

When Sukie stepped out of Atalanta's her bristling skin was met by a chill in the air. Over the river, the silhouette of a tower block stood against the sinking sun. The cobbled street was empty, as had been the reception area when she left. The whole place almost empty. Even when she had arrived. Now, there was only Nicola in her office doing paperwork, the sauna cooling, the whirlpool still.

Sukie was walking away, turning left out of the door instead of right. Away from the direction of her car, recognizing a reluctance to go home. Young people were gathered on corners, sharing cigarettes, laughing. Some walked hand in hand, rounding suddenly to look in a window or study a menu. And so Sukie walked, half a mile of pavement, a frozen smile, until she turned into a boutique and bought herself a white 'body' for far too much money. Then she scurried home.

The kitchen was in shadow as she poured the wine, the glass so cold it hurt her hand. But outside the sitting-room the leaves of the lime were blasted with gold and birds were still singing. She wanted to go somewhere, anywhere. To a pub or a restaurant, to stay out all evening drinking wine until there was only darkness and the scent of flowers. Scent. She could smell her own, on her wrist with the glass, in her hair when she turned her head. And in the gym? Not at all. In the gym not smelling of rubber. And in the sauna. There too, the same scent. As Nicola had leant towards her, from her skin as she had let loose her towel. A scent to sicken, like dying flowers. A scent of death. Lingering in Jerry's flat when she had found him, anointed and ready . . . Giorgio? . . . Ready for what?

# Chapter Nine

'You're looking very sleek today, Mosie.'

'I went to a health club yesterday.'

'Christ on a bike, what on earth for?'

'I wanted to feel fit.'

'Fit for what?'

'I don't know. Anything.' Sukie watched herself in the art nouveau glass that hung over the fireplace.

'You make a perfectly serviceable mother.' Alexis threw himself on to the sofa and picked up the TV section of *The Times*.

'Get your great filthy feet off there.' She snatched the cushion from under them and began to spank it. 'I saw it as a challenge. It is a challenge to be fit, the kind of circles I move in.'

'It's a challenge not to be, the kind I move in.' He slouched over the television and switched it on. 'Round and round the yard on punishment runs.'

'Don't tell me.' She replaced the cushion. 'That's why you all sport packets of Marlboro in place of hankies.'

'Usually *because* we do. Anyway,' he had found some football and was watching it without sound, 'I know why you went off to get yourself all refurbished. It's in aid of this bloke you're going out with tonight.'

'It certainly is not. And I am not "going" out with him. I am just going out. On business.'

'Mosie, you haven't got any business. Unless you count cooking and plant watering.'

'I certainly have. You know nothing about it.'

Alex came and put an arm round her shoulder. 'You really mustn't think I mind. I'm not like Puddles. I'd like you to have somebody nice.'

'Well, this person is not nice.'

'You shouldn't be going out with him, then.'

'I've told you. It's business.'

'All right.' He lifted his hands as though testing a door, then went back to the television. 'I like that T-shirt, by the way. It suits you, sort of shows your shape. Very cuddly.'

'It's called a "body", and I think I'd better change it.'

'Too late.' He had got up again and was peering down into the square. 'Your date's here. He's just driven up. In one hell of a car.'

'Alex, do stop looking out of the window.' She marched across and pulled the cord, seeing the curtains slide silently, seamlessly together, so that the only light in the room was from the flickering football pitch.

Immediately, there was a sharp buzz from the entry-phone and she rushed out into the hall. 'I'm coming straight down,' she spoke into it.

Back in the sitting-room, Alex was standing looking at the screen, his smile and the hollow of his shirt caught in its light. Sukie glanced at the curtains, about the room enfolded in their security, wondering if, for a moment, she had understood what they meant to Mrs Tribe. Then, pressing her bag to her hip, she turned to go. 'Don't worry, I won't be late.' But he did not hear her, for just as she spoke he had stooped and turned up the sound.

Henry Whippet was waiting by a pillar at the top of the steps when Sukie came out. He was wearing a double-breasted pinstripe suit with a silk tie. 'Hullo,' he said, and strolled down to open the car door.

It was a particularly beautiful Porsche, dark green, the inside fresh as the wind. 'Right,' he said, swinging away from the kerb, 'I've booked at Butler's. I hope you like it.'

'I've never been there.'

'Well, I still hope you like it.'

Familiar streets slid away through the side window. The glass, faintly smoked, and the insulation from sound so complete that the journey had the lingering, heightened perception of a film. It could have been seductive, if the other half of the two-shot had not been Henry Whippet.

'Here we are.' He looked over his shoulder and the car drifted into a space.

They were in a leafy street of dignified houses. Through a wrought-iron gate was a courtyard with a striped awning and tubs of flowers. Henry Whippet lifted the latch and held the gate open for her.

'Good evening, sir. A very good evening.' An Italian voice. 'Not every day you land a twenty-to-one double.' A tall, heavily built man came forward to greet them.

'You were on them, were you, Ricardo?' Henry Whippet continued on to his table without need of direction.

'Of course I was on them.' They had arrived at their table, and Ricardo pulled back Sukie's chair. 'Each at long odds for a small trainer. Now, what can I get you to drink? On the house.'

They were both looking at her.

'I'll have a gin and tonic. Thank you.'

'Mineral water for me, as usual.' Henry Whippet pulled out his own chair. 'Fizzy.'

Sukie rested her arms on the white cloth and looked out at the courtyard. 'I saw one of those races on television this afternoon.'

'Oh, yes? You should've come. Just down the road from you, Kempton.'

'I never go on a Saturday. My son comes home from school.'

'Oh. Good thing it was Kempton and all.'

'Why?'

'Would have had to break the speed limit a bit to make it this early from Doncaster.'

'I thought you boys always used helicopters.'

'Oh, yeah, come down with the pigeons in Trafalgar Square.'

A waiter brought their drinks and menus.

'What are you going to have to eat, then?' Henry Whippet looked up from the wine list, no whites to his eyes.

'The asparagus, I think. And the sole.'

'Right. I'm having the sole too. We'll have a nice white Burgundy for that. A nice Côte de Beaune. Does that appeal?'

'Yes.' She knew that she sounded startled. The evening did not feel as she had expected.

'Number twenty-one,' he handed back the list, watching her.

And although it certainly did not mean that Henry Whippet had style, it might mean that he knew what style was. The idea was discomposing.

'I also thought you broke the speed limit as a matter of course.'

'Oh, you did, did you? Well, maybe round Newmarket. Got a few friends in the Old Bill round Newmarket. But out on the open road – there I'm just another punter.'

The asparagus was perfect, fat with purple tips. Henry Whippet was having *oeuf en cocotte* which he set about delicately with his little spoon. He had asked for the wine to be left. As he poured some into her glass, he said, 'So, why did you agree to come out to dinner with me?'

'I wanted to talk about horses, remember?'

'Oh. You're sticking to that, are you?'

'What do you mean?'

'You couldn't afford a horse. Not a flat racer. Not even an old jumper at Bangor-on-Dee. I don't know about a pit pony. I hear they give them away. But you'd have to have a field.'

She put down a piece of asparagus and dipped her fingers into the bowl of water. 'If you thought that, why did you ask me?'

He laughed, and rested the base of the bottle on the table, still holding the neck. 'Because you're ever so pretty. And I likes older women.'

71

'You are unbelievable.' She dried her fingers on her napkin.

'Well, you aren't thirty-one, are you?' He began to fill his glass.

'No. I am not thirty-one.'

'So, you're older.' He smiled.

'All right. I'll tell you why I came. How well did you know Jerry Wearing?'

'That sounds like asking, not telling.'

'Jerry Wearing. Who was found dead.'

'Who *you* found dead. Quite well enough.'

'What do you mean?'

'That's my answer to your question. I knew him – quite well enough.'

'But what do you mean by that?'

'I rode for him. Sometimes. That's all.'

'He wasn't a friend?'

'He didn't have friends amongst the jockeys. He was quite old-fashioned like that. I wasn't at public school.'

'It never occurred to me that you were.'

He held her gaze for a moment, a little frown on his face; then he turned away.

Sukie looked beyond him at the petunias in their tubs outside. A slant of light caught their frilled edges, making them transparent.

Their second course arrived and Henry Whippet was asking after the waiter's son who had just had a football trial. On Sukie's plate, the fish was beautifully arranged, white and pink and green.

The waiter left them. Henry Whippet picked up his knife and fork. 'Not that I wouldn't send a son of mine to one.'

'I'm sorry,' Sukie said.

'Why?'

'I don't think I'm being very nice.'

'Oh, you're all right, doll. You can't help it.'

72

She also picked up her cutlery. The fish appeared complicated. 'Would you really send a son of yours to public school?'

'Course I would. Better than Newent friggin' comprehensive like where I went.'

'You did all right.'

'Yeah, well that's me, isn't it.' He began, most efficiently, to fillet his sole. 'So, what's all this about Jerry Wearing?'

'His wife isn't happy about the circumstances of his death.'

'Well, she wouldn't be, would she?'

'So, I'm just, well, asking around a bit.'

'What's it got to do with you?'

'I'm her friend.'

'What's it got to do with me?' He was busy eating his fish.

'I'm just talking to people who knew him.' She stared at her plate, cutlery poised, not knowing how to continue. 'I was there that day when he threatened you with a knife.'

'That was no big deal.'

'What was it about?'

'Well, he'd missed out on a punt, hadn't he?'

'Nothing else?'

'No.' He looked her straight in the eye. 'Here,' he noticed her plate with disgust, 'you've made a proper dog's dinner of that. Give it here.' He reached over, picked it up and began sorting out her food. 'Bondage is no big deal either. He just got found out, that's all. Not my bag, though.' He handed back her fish, the backbone lifted and all the bits of skin and prawn whisker tidied to one side. 'There, get that down you. No, I like things natural.'

They continued to eat in silence. Neither of them finished. When their plates had been taken away, she picked up her glass and began to glance round the restaurant at the other diners.

'I'll bet you don't eat pudding.' Henry Whippet was watching her. 'Which is just as well, because I don't eat it either.'

'Why is that "just as well"?'

'I just thought you might feel shy sitting there, ploughing your way through on your own.'

'You're fond of your assumptions. Like, I can't afford a horse. Like, I don't eat pudding.'

'I'm just observant. I've seen your car; it's eight years old. And you're ever so slim. Not room for much pudding in there.'

She stood up. 'I ought to be getting back.'

'Aren't there any more questions you want to ask me?'

'No.'

'Not tonight, anyway.' He caught the waiter's eye for the bill.

Outside in the courtyard it was now quite dark except where honeysuckle extended its bracts to catch the spill from the awning. Beneath it the petunias were ruffled by a draught, but the air was filled with scent.

Alex was waiting for her when she got home, a glass of vodka in his hand. 'Of course. I understand now.' The curtains were still drawn but had been disturbed.

'What do you understand? And you shouldn't be drinking that.' Deftly she removed the glass.

He appeared not to notice; his fingers remained in their holding position. 'The car. Of course, I'd seen it before.'

'Wine yes. Spirits no.'

'At Uncle Jerry's funeral. You've been out with Henry Whippet.'

'I have not "been out". I have had a business dinner.'

'D'you know,' he came towards her, 'I never took you for a snob, Mosie, but you are.'

'And you are pissed.'

'I mean, you should be proud. He's famous. I asked around at school, after I saw him that day. And everyone, but everyone's heard of him.'

'Yes, well that's only because of his ridiculous name.' And she tipped the remains of the vodka down her own throat.

# Chapter Ten

Racing from Newmarket was on the television. It was not at all easy to see. Sukie had to stand on tiptoe and stretch her neck at a painful angle. There was a queer silence. The screen went blank.

She climbed down from the swivel-chair and picked up her watering can. In the inner office racing took second place to the telephone. Outside, she proceeded on to the next weeping fig and shook it smartly. A litter of leaves fell to the carpet. Far too many. She felt the soil. Barnie had been right.

'I can't trust them,' he had said, 'these girls. The ones I've taken on to handle the extra work. They take their money, but the plants are not happy. Go to them, Sukie, stroke them. Tell them a few jokes.'

'Like last time?'

'Last time never happened. And Ella says you're to come and eat one night. What do you say?'

So here she was on her knees, sweeping up dead leaves, and once again wearing the despised pinafore.

It was not for authenticity this time that she wore it. This time it was to keep herself clean. The black crepe trousers, the white body, the flamboyant silk shirt round the passenger seat of the Renault, had all been carefully chosen for an appointment. An appointment at which she wanted to look her best.

The White Tie Escort Agency was suitably accommodated in Mayfair, in a dark mansion block close to Berkeley Square. A gilded lift transported her shakily towards the top floor where, along the corridor, in a tiny office, a man sat between two telephones filing his nails. When he saw Sukie he quickly slipped the file into his breast pocket and ushered her into a much larger room.

Anne Marriot was younger than Sukie had anticipated, but dressed with gravitas: a close-fitting brown suit, crocodile shoes, flesh-coloured tights – or possibly stockings? Her amber hair was loosely swathed up on to her head, and she appeared to have no need of makeup. Her smile knew that she was beautiful, successful, and young.

'Do sit down.' She retired behind her mahogany desk and leant forward, hands clasped in an interested pose. 'How may we help you?'

'Well.' Sukie looked at her own hands. There was earth down the side of a nail. 'I need an escort.'

'A special invitation?' Anne Marriot twinkled.

'Well no, not really.' Sukie frowned. 'It's just that I like to be taken out sometimes.'

'Don't we all?' Anne Marriot's nails were a tender pink, only the thinnest coat of varnish had been applied; or maybe they had simply been buffed.

'I like to go out in the evening. To a restaurant. You know? I can't exactly do that alone.' The fingers of her right hand were pressed tightly round her wedding ring, trying for some reason to obscure it.

'I understand completely.' Anne Marriot plucked a gold pen from a pot and slid a pad in front of her. 'You would need someone rather special. Someone sophisticated, amusing, some-one who could really appreciate you.' She made a gay little squiggle on the pad then reached into a drawer. 'This is our standard questionnaire. If you would like to fill it in?'

Sukie pulled in her chair to where the form rested on the desk. Filling in her various particulars: age, interests, et cetera, writing 'none' under qualifications, it was as though she were under the eye of an invigilator.

As she handed it back, she said, 'There are two questions I found it rather difficult to answer.'

'Oh?'

'Yes: "brief description of ideal escort" and "purposes of introduction".'

'Ah. Well, just give the age, height, colouring perhaps, of the sort of man you like, and then what you hope to achieve through the friendship.'

'But this isn't a marriage bureau?'

Anne Marriot laughed, 'Oh, no. But if two people like each other . . .' She swivelled the questionnaire round to her own viewpoint, pen poised. 'Now, let's see, you're quite small.'

'Yes, but I like them to be tall.'

'Oh. Shall we say five feet nine and over?'

'I prefer them at least six foot.'

'Yes, well . . . Hair?'

'Absolutely.'

'What?'

'Well, I don't want anything bald. Or ginger.'

'Right.' Two little exclamation marks formed between Anne Marriot's pencilled brows as she continued rather too quickly, 'Well, that brings me to age, shall we say forty-five and upwards?' The pen was already writing.

'Absolutely not.' Sukie slapped both hands on to the desk. 'I did not come here in search of a seventy-year-old in a wig. I had something considerably younger in mind. I'm sure you know what I mean?'

'And I am not sure that I do.' Anne Marriot glanced down at Sukie's wedding ring. 'Forgive me for saying, but perhaps your requirements are beyond the brief of this agency.'

'No need to forgive me, but would you have said that if I were a man?'

'I most certainly would.' Anger brought water to Anne Marriot's eyes.

Sukie stood up. 'I hope you're not suggesting that I have asked for any services beyond that of a straightforward escort?'

Anne Marriot was round the desk like a knife. 'Of course not. But we have to be so terribly careful. Of course I can arrange for a younger man. But it might take a week or two. Please,' she held out the form with an almost wistful expression, 'if you'd just fill in your name.'

Sukie accepted the form, and the little gold pen, then, leaning on the wall so that Anne Marriot could see over her shoulder, wrote: 'Amanda Wearing. Marital status – widow.'

As she handed it back, she looked into the young woman's eyes, but they remained liquid and steady. Nonetheless, she avoided the lift, running down and down the spiral of narrow stairs, tugging all the while at her wedding ring. When she reached the street, she held it up to the evening light, then dropped it into her pocket.

She was not driving straight home. Sukie didn't know why. Eventually the car stopped in a meter space so she turned off the engine. It was early evening but still brutally hot. The low sun slashed her vision no matter how she turned her head to avoid it. Her silk shirt was creased.

Anne Marriot had shown not a blink of recognition at the name of Wearing. While the three names collected from Jerry's office had held no significance for Amanda. And Jerry had died of natural causes. It was all nonsense.

That Jerry had written the number of the White Tie Escort Agency on the back of a training bill, that Henry Whippet had not admitted to being a client of his, that Nicola used Giorgio, hardly added up to anything more than coincidence... Why then, when she would much rather be home, was she now sitting slumped in her car, just across the road from the mews where Rosamund Officer lived?

Because whoever had been with Jerry, who had left him without summoning help, must have wanted him to suffer, be humiliated, dead.

Sukie undid her seat-belt, got out and walked under the shadow of the stone arch leading to the cobbled slope of the mews. Her silk shirt stuck to her back and she pulled it free with a satisfying sting. Rosamund's door was to the left, white with a black number five on it. Above, jutted window-boxes of pink geraniums, and silver helechrysum. Sukie shut her eyes. Suppose she were to go to sleep? Like a horse, standing up, in a mews. She opened them again. Just this one call. Then she could forget. Amanda seemed to have forgotten already. And there was always the chance that Rosamund would be out.

As she approached the door, a sound made her halt. An irregular but rhythmic tapping. Sukie looked up and immediately saw what it was. Water was dripping from the bases of the window-boxes. Hope that Rosamund would be out trickled away.

She was just about to ring the bell when another sound, from within, made her dart back and take cover behind a conifer in a tub outside number three. Then the door of number five opened and Rosamund emerged on a gust of laughter, her elbow supported by a ravishingly handsome young man. Pale as a statue, Rosamund's cheeks, her eyes; statuesque in proportion but not in beauty, she tottered amongst the cobbles, feet tightly bound with gold straps. Her precarious posture: chest leading, behind never quite catching up, was defined by a hand holding together the edges of her green silk coat. But the young man too was laughing, with his arm in fond gesture about Rosamund's shoulders as he guided her into the passenger seat of her Mercedes Sports.

*

Sukie drove home with all four windows wide. That was it. She would wash her hair, slip into some loose silk trousers and listen to beautiful music. Smells from the restaurants that she passed made her hungry for something more and, after reaching the top of the stairs with her basket and canvas bag, she felt sure something exciting was about to happen.

'Where on earth have you been?'

This was not it.

Jemima's face poking at her from the darkness of the hall.

'Working. What else?' Sukie tried to lose the bag and basket amongst a stack of Alex's sports equipment.

'Well. You might have been out with Henry Whippet.' She had put a cigarette in her mouth and advanced on Sukie, shaking a match. 'Was that when you decided to chuck the wedding ring?'

'I took it off just now, actually.' Sukie felt in her pocket and produced it on the palm of her hand. 'It felt uncomfortable. And I thought you gave up smoking a year ago.'

Jemima wafted past her. 'You've been at it again, haven't you? Plant watering.'

But Sukie was off to the kitchen, ripping into the neck of some Muscadet.

'I saw you with that great big bag.' Jemima leant in the doorway. 'That's why you're in such a foul mood.'

'So?' Watching wine sparkle into the glass. 'So, I've been plant watering. I owed Barnie a favour, and other people money. More to the point, you're not due home for three or four weeks.'

'I know.' Jemima's lovely face, so smooth, so secret, was like an egg hit with a spoon. 'I'm here because I'm so miserable. I've split up with Nick.'

'Oh.' Sukie refrained from lifting the glass. 'Oh, Jemima, and you were so fond of him.'

'Was I?'

'Well . . .' She tried to keep the look of concern in her eyes.

80

'I thought *he* was fond of *me*.'

'Ah.' She picked up the glass and took a quick sip.

'He said that when he first saw me he thought I was *so* beautiful. That it made me unfathomable. But now ... he says he's ...'

'Fathomed?'

Jemima nodded violently, 'Yes. And *plumbed*.'

'Oh, Puddles.'

'And found me *shallow*.' She lifted her head, hair streaming like water. 'Is that the phone?'

It was. As she put the receiver to her ear Sukie saw across the square a young couple getting into an open-topped Golf. He gave her a quick kiss on the cheek before starting the engine.

'Sukie? This is Bob. Bob Teichgraeber? I said I'd call you a couple of weeks back. Sorry it's been so long.'

'Oh. That's all right.'

'I've been back to the States for a bit. But, how do you feel like coming out for some dinner tonight?'

'Tonight?' There was a urgent rustling behind her.

'Yes. It's such a lovely evening. I like the idea of driving off somewhere, watching the sun go down.'

Jemima, with a tumbler full of wine, was pulling tissues out of a box.

'Oh ... I'm sorry. I really would love to but ...'

Jemima waiting, watching, ring-eyed.

'... there's something else I have to do.'

'Oh. Too bad.'

'Some other time, perhaps?'

'Perhaps. Yes, goodbye.'

'Goodbye.' She took extra care rearranging the flex, before turning round.

'So?' Jemima stood at bay. 'Who was that?'

'Some American. Friend of Jerry and Amanda's. Well, sort of.

81

I gather Marcus introduced them. He's looking out for some horses for him, apparently.'

'And he wanted to take you out?'

'That sort of thing.' She went back into the kitchen for her wine. 'So what do you want to do this evening?'

'I don't know,' Jemima called. 'I suppose I might as well work. Take my mind off things. Use it.'

'That's the ticket.' Sukie wandered back. 'It's nice to see you anyway. Could you cope with music, if you worked in here?'

'I might. I'm just going to read and make notes for an essay: Jealousy, Psychology of, etc. Ha!'

Rosamund's crossed toes touching the cobbles as she lifted one foot to get into the car, the young man's fingers brushing her shoulder. The young couple getting into the Golf where she and Peter had used to drive off for the evening. The American's horn-rimmed spectacles, his grey flannel suit.

Through the french window came the sharp call of a blackbird; the clucking as he swooped into a tree. In the darkening room their smiles were mysterious. Jemima went to collect her books and Sukie switched on a lamp.

'Were you and Father ever jealous?'

Sukie looked up from her book. It was dark outside. 'Never got round to it.'

'It must have been hard for you when Father died.'

'I was spoiled. I didn't know anything. But one learns. The worst thing, I think, was that I lost the person he allowed me to be. I liked that person. They don't exist any more.'

Jemima shook her head. 'It was ten years ago, Mosie. You wouldn't be the same anyway.'

'What would have happened, then?' Sukie tried to distract from the anxiety in her eyes with a smile.

Jemima smiled back. 'I don't know. You'd probably just have got fat like most happily married women.'

'I sometimes feel like I've disintegrated . . .'

'Not you.'

'. . . like ingredients in a blender.'

'That's not disintegration. That's rearrangement. Into something more stable if you're a good cook. Which you are.'

'What if someone's not a good cook?'

Jemima had shut her books and folded her arms across them on her knees. 'Then the mixture can break down.' The reply seemed to resolve something for her. There was optimism in the tilt of her chin.

'Separate. Curdle, even?'

'We all want to prove our uniqueness in some way. It's often the threat to that uniqueness, to effectiveness, that triggers serial killers. They *do* feel themselves disintegrating.'

Sukie also shut her book. 'Mug of cocoa?'

'Please.' Jemima curled her feet up under her, tapping her pen against her teeth.

In the kitchen Sukie heard the phone ringing. Heard it answered, as she was pouring the milk, then Jemima's voice, 'It's for you,' the tone a little shrill.

'Hullo?' frowning out at the square, trying to shut the french windows against the darkness, the receiver a little way from her ear, so that the voice, hoarse, breathless, panted her name into the soft night. 'Yes.'

'So sorry. So late, I know, but I can't get hold of Amanda. I wondered if you knew where she was?'

'No. No, I don't.' The doors banging together, failing to close.

'I only get the answerphone, you see. It's Rosamund, by the way. Sorry.'

'Yes. I expect she's asleep.'

'Yes, yes, of course. I just wanted to check she was all right.'

'Why?' The doors clicked to. Sukie turned from the ghost face in the pane. 'What's happened?'

'And to warn her.'

83

'Why?' She looked round in alarm, at Jemima holding two mugs.

'Well . . . so silly . . . but I've just been attacked. Outside here, in the mews. Hit over the head with something.'

'But that's terrible. Have you called the police, a doctor?'

'They're on their way. Look, perhaps it's just as well as it is. No point in worrying her. I probably misheard it. Ah, that sounds like someone now. So sorry to have bothered you.'

'What did you think you heard?'

'Oh, nothing. I thought I heard them say her name. Something about "getting her too". Best forget it. All right? I was pretty groggy at the time. Lot of nonsense. I'm just talking nonsense. Last thing we want to do is to frighten her.'

# Chapter Eleven

'You're up and about very early.' Mrs Tribe barred the way with her Hoover attachment.

'Yes.' Sukie slid into the hall and shut the door.

'I haven't seen you come home so early for a long time. Not since . . .' she gazed up at the light fitting, holding the attachment like a wand '. . . what was his name?'

'William. And it was nothing like that, I'm afraid. I was taking Jemima to Paddington. She came home for the weekend.'

'Your phone's been ringing a lot, for all it's so early.'

Sukie was taking her mac off. 'How many times?'

'Just the once. But it was ringing a lot. You forgot to put that machine on again.'

'Oh, Lord. Well, I must get cooking. I've got three lunches to do this week.'

Cutting out little discs of pastry, Sukie tried to separate and place in order the events of the last few weeks. The attack on Rosamund on Friday night had changed everything. She lifted the discs and patted them into dinky pans with her finger, then put the trays into the fridge while she made the fillings. Spinach, tomato, mushroom, smoked salmon, always popular; stick to what you know.

Chopping onions, eyes streaming, and the phone is ringing. Sukie pushed back her hair with a wrist, wiped her hands. Mrs Tribe was in the sitting-room so she took it in the bedroom.

'Sukie? This is Bob Teichgraeber again. Let's go out. Wednesday. Seven o'clock.'

'I'm not actually doing anything on Wednesday.'

'That's what I hoped. I look forward to it.'

On her way back to the onions she met Mrs Tribe in the hall.

'Was that it?'

'Was that what?' The onions had made her dizzy.

'The one who tried earlier?'

'I don't know. No. Absolutely not. This one wouldn't have waited so long for an answer.'


'You didn't enjoy it?'

'I was rather cold.'

'I'm sorry. I'd forgotten how chilly English summer evenings can be.'

'I can't get into things when I'm cold.'

'All I wanted was to give you little a piece of America.'

'I prefer this piece.'

They were eating salt beef with gherkins and potato salad in a spacious but energetic American deli. Lights reflected from marble and chrome and the cheerful murmur was regularly topped by shouts to the kitchen.

'You looked to me a sporting kind of girl, I thought you'd take to the ball game.' Bob licked a streak of mustard from his finger.

'I'm not exactly dressed for sport. You should have warned me.'

'I thought of it. I thought of suggesting you change, but I couldn't bear to lose the shoes.'

'Ha. They're probably ruined now, hiking across the park.' Sukie stretched out a leg from under the table. There was dried mud around the spike of heel.

He reached a hand down under her ankle and lifted it, examining the foot for a moment. 'There's no damage. It'll come off with a brush. Are you sure you won't have a beer?'

She drew her leg back. 'No, thank you. I know it offends with this sort of food, but I'll stick with the cat's piss. You'd have got on with Jerry. He was just as happy with beer as wine. Actually preferred it to champagne.'

'Is that so? I heard he'd been at the champagne when he was found.'

'Yes.' Her hands rested over her plate and the noise in the restaurant receded.

'I'm sorry,' he was saying. 'That was pretty insensitive of me. Of course, it was you who found him.'

'You heard that too?'

'Pretty common knowledge.'

She shook her head. 'I'm sorry too. I know I must get used to it. That's probably why I mentioned him. Just sometimes . . . It was the lack of privacy. I felt I shouldn't have been there. That the only decent thing I can do is forget. The last decent thing I can do for him. And yet . . .'

'And yet?'

His head was on one side, and behind his glasses was a look of concern. It made Sukie feel terribly upset. She smoothed her napkin out on the table and began to pleat it in neat clean lines.

'I don't think Jerry's death happened the way it appeared, you see.' He wasn't disagreeing with her but she continued. 'And Amanda doesn't either.'

'What exactly are you saying?'

'I don't know. There's this agency, the White Tie. It looks like Jerry was being "escorted" when he died.' She screwed the napkin up into a tight ball and laughed. 'I don't know.'

'Are you saying you think it was murder?'

'No. Of course I can't be saying that.'

'Why not?'

'I don't know.' She shook the napkin out again and arranged

it on her lap, picking up her knife and fork. 'So. Tell me all about you. Your hopes and dreams. Tell me the story of your life.'

He remained watching her, elbow on the table, fingers pressed to his mouth. Then he lifted his head, curled the fingers. 'You don't really mean that.'

'Don't I?' She had begun to eat.

'I don't think so.' He broke a roll in half. 'You're just acting fey. To get yourself out of a conversation you find uncomfortable.'

'Then you should act gallant and let me out without comment.'

'OK.' He put a small piece of bread into his mouth. 'How's the horse?'

'By the horse, I presume you mean Triumvirate. He's rapped himself. But you'll know that anyway. You're in contact with Marcus.'

'They're aiming him at Ascot, I gather. Do you know, is Amanda going to take over Jerry's share permanently?'

'Why? Are you looking to buy in?'

'Absolutely not. Marcus has orders to find me four horses. They may not have the class of Triumvirate, but they'll be my own.'

'Hmm.' She watched him spear a small gherkin down the spine and convey it to his mouth. 'You must be a hard man to work for.'

'I don't think so. I choose my people carefully. I trust them. In England . . . that could be difficult?'

'You don't like England?'

'I love it.' He lifted his eyes, his face. 'That's why I've come. And particularly for the horses. The racing, the hunting – it's just not the same in the States.' He returned to cutting up his meat.

'And when your company's set up with people you can trust, you'll go back to America?'

'I guess I'll commute.' He was active now, cutting, arranging, chewing his food all at the same time. 'Not difficult.'

'No. No, I don't think Jerry was murdered, but . . .'

'But what?'

'There are things I need to chase up.'

'Why?'

'For me. I found him. Hell, that sounds dramatic.'

'Could it also be because he died in the same way as your husband?'

'Oh, I'm sure. Yet so differently. It makes me sad.'

She looked into his spectacles, her own eyes glazed with tears.

'Are you asking my permission, or what?' His tone was harsh.

'I don't know what you mean.'

'I think you do. You have children.'

'I'd never involve them.'

'No? How do you think they'd feel if something happened to you?'

'Oh, come on.' She took up her knife and fork again, pushing her food to one side. 'Now it's you being dramatic.'

'Perhaps. But also perhaps, you are preoccupied with a dead husband to the avoidance of living children.'

She let go the cutlery so that it fell off the plate. 'You have no reason to say that.'

'No. I don't. And I'm sorry.'

'It's all this stupid boarding-school thing again. Isn't it? No good telling you that Alex is very happy there.'

'No good telling you that you're the last person he'd tell if he wasn't. Again, I'm sorry. What can I say?'

'Nothing, preferably.' She swiped her napkin on to the table and scraped back her chair.

*

The city, as they drove back to Kensington, existed in one of those velvet nights of early summer when scents from all the hidden gardens rise in such fusion that any glimpse of loss is sharpened by hope.

With the window open, Sukie leant her head towards it, absorbing the smell and listening to all the sounds that came from outside the car, the swish of tyres, the throb of music, the odd shout. Within, was silence.

When they reached the square and stopped, she said, as though they had just been introduced at a party, 'What is it you do, actually? You have a company, but what sort of line is it in?'

Without moving his hands from the wheel or looking at her, Bob replied, 'Emergency Communications.'

'Ha!' She flung her seat-belt aside and was out of the door, elated that he couldn't see the joke.

The elation lasted up the stairs and into the sitting-room to glancing down and seeing he had gone. She drew the curtains. It wasn't yet eleven. She poured herself a gin and tonic and phoned Amanda.

'What do you know about this Bob character?'

'Not much. American. Divorced. Rich. Why?'

'He's a real prig.'

'Did you say prick?'

'No. But I should have done.'

'Have you been seeing him?'

'Not to speak of. Not to speak of at all.'

'Jerry met him through Marcus. Marcus thought he might put up a third share in Triumvirate, but he wasn't interested.'

'So he wasn't one of the two oiks that Jerry rejected?'

'Oh, no. They were both people from school.'

'They can hardly have been worse than Bob.'

'What's got into you this evening?'

'Nothing.'

'Perhaps that's the problem?'

'Don't be gross.'

'Just testing.' Amanda transferred the receiver to her other ear. 'The original idea was that Jerry and his two closest friends should own a horse together and call it Triumvirate, which is what they'd called themselves, rather mawkishly in my opinion, at school.'

'But one was killed in a hunting accident.'

'Yes, Dick. Dick Manningtree. That was awful. And the other one was posted to the Far East.'

'What other one?'

'Rupert Fabian. He's a diplomat. He was in Europe, which would have been OK. But the Far East, well it just wasn't on. He'd never have seen him run.'

'So how did George get into the plate?'

'Oh, George. He just happened to be there. When Jerry and Dick were looking round desperately for a substitute.'

'And Rosamund?'

'Jerry had already laid out. With Dick dead, he'd got to find someone quick. The best he could get at that late stage.'

'A woman, even?'

'Sukie, I'd just put some AHA cream on my face and it's come off all over the telephone. Do you think it'll eat into the plastic?'

'Probably.'

'Why the late call? Have you just come back from being out with him?'

'Bob? Yes. He took a fancy to my shoes.'

'You sound pissed. I'm going to bed. Derby, Saturday week. You going?'

'I never go on Saturdays. You know that. What makes you think I'd decide to change my plans just because they decide to change the day of the fucking Derby?'

'Only asked. I *am* going to bed. You too, I suggest.'

'Oh, do you?' Sukie said to the looking-glass, after she had poured herself another gin. 'Oh, do you really?' Then she lay on her back on the sofa and raised one leg, looking along the line of it to the foot with its delicate splay of bones, to the ankle within its circle of black patent and, without knowing why, saw the world to be full of possibilities. And then the phone began to ring.

Sukie couldn't think what it was, but anyway put the glass down and crawled across the carpet to it. She lifted the receiver and the noise stopped. There was silence. Then a whisper, 'Amanda?'

'No.' She tossed the receiver back on to the cradle, watching it. When it didn't move, she lifted it and laid it on the floor, hearing the dialling tone and then the prim voice telling her to replace it, again and again, until she reached her bedroom and shut the door.

# Chapter Twelve

In the morning, two hours after the alarm, a second tumbler of cranberry juice at the ready, Sukie sat at her Davenport with an exercise book and pen. She was making a list, pausing between each item. It took a lot of thought. It was not a list of ingredients.

It was headed, 'Suspicions':

1. Was Jerry having sex with someone provided by the White Tie Escort Agency?
2. Was there any connection between the problems he was having with a client who was also a friend, and his death?
3. Nicola – smells of Giorgio, the scent that was in Jerry's flat. (Why not?)
4. Amanda – at York races with Reggie Millfield, who had been keeping an eye on me on the gallops. (Again, why not?)
5. Who phoned in the middle of the night, asking for Amanda? (And why?)
6. Rosamund – who attacked her?!? (And why?)
7. George – does he know he was desperate substitute?
8. Henry Whippet – generally unpleasant, and why did he not admit to using Jerry as a lawyer?
9. Bob – also generally unpleasant. (Is it me?)
10. Did the lift move?

Sukie put her pen down and looked at it. The list gave neither the satisfaction nor the enlightenment for which she'd hoped.

She flipped it into the drawer, then went out to the kitchen and washed her hands.

As she jointed several chickens, feeling for the bones, slipping the knife between them, cracking them apart, one name came out on the tip of the knife each time. But how to proceed?

She heated some butter with oil in a heavy pan, browning the chicken pieces in batches, turning them with tongs, carefully, so as not to pierce the flesh, laying them on a large plate to await the second stage. One couldn't just hold someone down and investigate them with pointed questions.

In another pan she melted some more butter with oil, gently this time, adding the onions from the food processor quickly, putting on the lid to let them sweat for a while. One could, however, calmly continue in the natural sequence, step by step, after all.

At the end of the day, food all tucked up, ready to appear fresh in the morning, Sukie flopped on to the sofa with the telephone and without a glass of wine. She dialled Rosamund's number and waited, expecting, half hoping, to get the answerphone.

'Hullo?' Rosamund said.

'Oh. Hullo. It's Sukie Buckley. I tried to phone you last week to ask how you were.'

'How kind. I'm fine. No after-effects, as far as I can tell. You didn't tell Amanda?'

'No. I saw no point in worrying her.'

'Agreed. But I got some flowers from the American the very next morning.'

'Well, I didn't tell him.'

'Of course not. Listen, my dear, there's someone at the door. I must go. Call me at the office one day.'

And Rosamund rang off without giving the name or number.

*

The invitation to the fashion show arrived on the Monday after Derby Day and had been posted first class. On the bottom Nicola had written: 'Amanda says she'll break a fetlock to be here! Do come.' The careful, rounded letters did not disguise the fact that Sukie was an afterthought – it was for the following evening.

And Atalanta's was transformed. The deserted, even derelict, street was now jumping to loud music. Equipment vans were parked outside, and cars everywhere, anyhow. Through the open doors a pool of faces, shadowless, young, glistened in the overflow of lighting from the gym where the show was to take place.

Guarding a cocktail that fizzed with health but was depressingly free of alcohol, Sukie pushed her way between hard-trained bodies, keeping a lookout for Amanda. But she had evidently thought too much of her fetlocks: she was nowhere to be seen.

A catwalk had been built down the centre of the gym with chairs on either side, while over the equipment hung swaths of muslin like fog across boats at harbour.

Sukie found a seat and watched the gathering faces. Here, with the light now intensified on the surface of the catwalk, they were illusive, smoky, and for a flicker she thought she saw one she knew, but then the house lights went down leaving only a flarepath.

And it was fun: models of both sexes showing off leisurewear with charm and humour. Every now and again, she peered between loping legs, thinking again to see that face, but behind the flash and swing of lights not even darkness was constant.

When the show was over, the audience was thanked (much reciprocal clapping), and informed there would be going-home bags of cosmetics and health foods to be picked up at the exit.

As Sukie waited in the queue, she looked about for the face which might now be recognizable. She was distracted by a hand on her arm.

'So glad you could make it.' Nicola wore a Tahitian style dress with bright pink flower in her hair. 'Zana's going to run out of those bags soon. Outrage and chaos. Why don't you come up to my office.' Her fingers now pulling at Sukie's sleeve, she dodged between caterers and men carrying handfuls of gilt chairs. 'I've got some real bubbles up there.'

Her office, reached by a spiral staircase, was a small room overlooking the river, with no desk or computer visible, only white wall cupboards and a telephone on a table. A bright striped rug lay in the centre of the floor around which were rattan chairs with cushions and a coconut palm in an oriental pot ... the smell of Giorgio ...

Nicola switched on the light. It had been raining on and off all day and the sky across the water was a threatening lime green. She then opened one of the wall cupboards, inside which was a fridge.

Watching her twist the bottle away from the cork, Sukie said, 'You want to talk to me about something?'

Nicola looked up. A puff of mist rose from the bottle. 'Yes.' She sounded surprised. A smile flicked up the corners of her mouth as she poured the champagne into two flutes. 'Cheers. Do take a seat.'

'Thank you.' Sukie took a very small sip, watching Nicola.

She had turned away to the window. There were blinds but she did not pull them, just stood there, hand on the frame, looking out. 'Amanda said you were investigating Jerry's death. Is that true?'

'It depends what you mean by "investigating".'

'It is true, then?'

'Amanda didn't believe that Jerry could have been playing away. I've just been, well, sort of tiding her over.'

'Tiding her over?' Nicola had turned round, eyes like dropped flies.

'Just asking around, in case there could be some other explanation. For the situation in which he was found.'

'Of course, you found him, didn't you?'

'Yes. Don't worry, it's common knowledge.'

Nicola's head drooped and she poured more champagne into her glass. 'I'm just so frightened, you see.' She took a gulp then went over to where she had put her bag on the table. 'This arrived on Saturday.' She withdrew an envelope with a card inside. 'Read it.'

Sukie did so. 'I did know about her being mugged.'

'I'm really frightened.'

'But Rosamund's fine. I spoke to her on the telephone. Even if she didn't feel up to your show. She's pretty tough.'

'Oh sure, but is George?'

'George?' Sukie was about to drink, but thought worse of it.

'Yes.' Nicola's tone was rising. 'First Jerry, then Rosamund – well it's obvious who's going to be next, isn't it?'

'Next. Why has somebody got to be next?'

'It's obvious. It's the horse, isn't it? And who owns the third share?'

'What does George think?'

'He thinks I'm being ridiculous. He says there's absolutely no reason to think the two things are connected.' Nicola sat down and refilled her glass which she had put on the floor, then handed the bottle to Sukie. 'Two violent incidents like that. One after another.'

'They were hardly alike.'

'It doesn't feel right.' She had begun to shiver, leaning down to hug her knees so that the moulded top of her dress came away from her shallow breasts. 'Nothing feels right at the moment. What's the horse for? George never even has time to watch it on the gallops.'

'I hear he deals with all the paperwork.'

'Oh, tell me about it. Time is money, he's always telling me. And he never has any time.' She looked up at Sukie as if she had asked a question. Receiving no answer she looked down again. 'Nothing but problems. Sylvia giving him hell, screeching at him down the phone. And the mistake was certainly hers.'

'What mistake?'

97

'Christ almighty, don't ask me. Not worth discussing, George said.'

Sukie was studying the bottle. 'They'd known each other a long time, after all.' She handed it back to Nicola, who topped up her glass.

'Had they? He was at school with Sylvia's brothers, but he didn't get to know them well. Not like Jerry did. Yet he talks so fondly of the place. Even insisted on taking me there once. Great hulk of a building high up on the coast. Freezing even in summer. But you know what they're like with all the old school tie nonsense.'

'Funny . . .'

'All that male bonding. No wonder it leads on to bond*age*.'

'No. I meant the words "old school tie". It only just occurred to me. We usually take them to mean "old-school-tie", but they could equally mean "old school tie". Do you see what I mean?'

'You what?'

'Well, they're different, aren't they?' Sukie was sitting very straight. 'I suppose what is usually meant is the first version: a special old boys' tie that is bought on leaving school. But it could mean a frayed bit of striped nylon worn since the first year.'

'Anyway . . .' Nicola was wandering about with the empty bottle.

Sukie stood up. 'Well, thanks for the drink. I'll tell Amanda she missed a really good show.'

'I didn't honestly expect her to come.' She waved the bottle. 'I'm exhausted.'

Sukie went over to put her glass on the table. In her other hand she still held Rosamund's card. 'Could I possibly take this with me? She asked me to contact her at work, and this has the address and number.'

Nicola waved the bottle again. 'Feel free.' She was being waved away.

*

98

Downstairs, the caterers and furniture hire people had gone. Outside it was completely dark, except where the lighted office slewed a diamond across the cobbles, and then the blinds came down. Now there was only the lapping of the river below the wall.

In the distance was a bright street with restaurants and pubs and groups of young people drinking outside, where Sukie had left her car. As she began to walk towards it she heard a movement behind her and, turning, saw a shape darker than the darkness dissolve into the substance of the building. She froze, half in courage, half in fear, nerves bristling all over her body. But once more she could see nothing but darkness, hear nothing but the shifting of the tide. And then she began to run, covering the wet ground with flying ease until she felt the smooth pavement beneath her shoes and the street about her was lit bright as the catwalk.

'Amanda?'

It was morning and Sukie had not slept well. She sat on the edge of the unmade bed in Peter's bathrobe, hair unbrushed, a mug of cocoa beside the phone.

An unhealthy smell had pervaded the night. It criss-crossed with another smell, a scent, sweet as sleep, as death, seeping into her privacy. As she turned from side to side, neither asleep nor awake, her thoughts lost their direction, became dirty, harsh, cutting her, binding her to the bed. And still it continued to rain. Now, under the window was a large damp patch where the sprigged paper was peeling away.

'Yes?' Amanda's voice was sleepy, although it was past ten o'clock.

'Sukie here.'

'I know.'

'I want to ask you something.' She picked up the cocoa and took a sip.

'Go on.'

'Well, have you any idea which of Jerry's school ties he was actually wearing?'

'You found him.'

'I know. But I didn't actually notice. It wasn't, you know, the most obvious thing. At the time. You once said that the O.E. and the prep were very similar.'

'I did? I did. So, which tie was he wearing . . . ? Hang about – forget I said that – I think they had it in a plastic bag.'

'Yes?'

'And I told them to dispose of it as they thought fit.'

'Oh.' Sukie took several sips of cocoa.

'But look, something might come to me. In the bath. I'll ring you back.'

Sukie took her empty mug through to the kitchen and put it in the dishwasher, then she went back to the bedroom and phoned a man about the damp patch. Amanda would be at least an hour.

Rosamund's card was still in her bag, half under the curtains in the sitting-room, with a glass. How it had got there . . . ? She drew them back, shivering, and saw the french windows still open, and the brandy bottle, without its top, on the balcony. That was how.

She picked it up and brought it inside and shut the doors. The bottle was cold, and gritty after the rain. It felt just like she did.

Rosamund's card: she took it out. Thick, vellum coloured, printed with both her home and office details. She dialled the office number. Miss Officer was in a meeting, the receptionist said, but if she would care to leave her name? Sukie did so. The office was in Victoria, some sort of recording company? That was fine, but something bothered her. It was when she looked at the card. Something she just couldn't catch . . .

*

The next day Sukie left very early for a large directors' lunch in Blackfriars. When she got home, and had made three journeys up the stairs with all her bits and pieces, there was a very red letter from her bank, a note from the damp man saying he'd been 'unable to obtain access', and a message on the answering machine from Nicola asking her to call 'as soon as possible'. She went straight to the kitchen and ate four roast potatoes left over from Sunday lunch before realizing today was Thursday. She tipped the rest into the bin and poured herself a glass of wine.

This was no good. It would butter no parsnips, let alone rancid roast potatoes. All this interfering in other people's lives was interfering in her own: costing her money. And next week was Ascot.

# Chapter Thirteen

'I had a most extraordinary phone call this morning.' Amanda slid her tray on to the white table and edged herself into her chair.

'Oh?' Sukie looked up from unloading an array of dishes. 'In what way, extraordinary?'

'Some young woman offering me the services of some young man.'

'Are we talking stud duties?'

But Amanda was frowning at the brilliant sky. 'Some bastard's taken our umbrella.'

They were in the enclosure of the seafood tent at Ascot, crammed into a corner, sun curdling the mayonnaise.

'Nicola did telephone and invite us to join them and their hamper in the car park. I was quick to decline. Was I precipitous?'

Sukie repositioned her hat. 'She'll certainly have an umbrella.'

'I was also quick to decline the other offer.'

'You didn't ask for details?'

'I was shy.' Amanda coaxed a forkful of crab out of its shell. 'It all smelt terribly fishy.'

'Yes. Well. It would. They thought they were nominating me.'

'Oh, Sukie,' Amanda paused in her investigations, 'I could have fixed you up, no fun no fee.'

'No, no, no.'

'Bob's a classy type. All that fresh American blood. How about it?'

'Absolutely, no.'

'Sadly he's not on parade today. Too late to apply for the Enclosure.'

'No. That's not it. I gave them your name, you see. The agency. But with *my* phone number.'

'Why?' Amanda paused, crab about to enter her mouth.

'Because I didn't want to upset you.'

Amanda's eyebrows lifted and the crab disappeared.

'Inside Jerry's address book, you see, was a piece of paper. A bill, with this telephone number written on the back.'

'Yes, a training bill. I saw it. How's your salmon?'

'Fine.' Sukie picked up her knife and fork, then put them down again. 'You saw it? When?'

'Oh, I don't know. At home, a few days before . . . Jerry took it out of his home address book and said he was taking it to the office. He always put urgent bills in his address books. I presumed he'd paid it.'

'But the number on the back? I dialled it to find out who it was. Why Jerry had written it down. It turned out to be an escort agency, the White Tie. So I went along as a client and gave them your name, to see if it would mean anything to them. Sorry.'

'You didn't have to do that.'

'I am sorry. Anyway, they didn't react in any way to the name of Wearing.' Sukie took up cutlery, at last, to look into her salmon.

'Well, they wouldn't. Idiot. Seeing as that wasn't Jerry's writing.'

'Not?'

'I haven't a clue why he even had the bill. Jerry never paid Triumvirate's training fees. George did.'

'I knew he did the paperwork . . .'

'Makes him feel important.' She pushed her plate away and lit a cigarette. 'Anyway, Jerry and Rosamund paid their whacks to him and he paid the total. Your White Tie effort, could it possibly be wishful thinking?'

Sukie sat with her hands in her lap, facing her probed salmon.

Amanda was on to her strawberries. She paused, considering the flavour, before replying. 'Better to leave things, don't you think?'

'You don't want to know any more? You don't mind?'

Amanda lifted another strawberry in her spoon, studying it, serene. 'I don't care.'

Sukie nodded to a waiter to take her salmon away then drew her own strawberries towards her.

Amanda looked over at the fruit, as though she had designs on them. 'Don't worry. I'll still pay the school fees.'

'I didn't realize that was . . .'

'A quid pro quo? It wasn't. I'm such a shit.' She put her spoon down. 'I just want to have fun again. I'm no good at grieving.' She hauled the champagne from amongst the ice and began to untwist its restraining wires. 'Look what we've forgotten.'

'Well, well, well, if it isn't the beautiful Mrs Wearing.'

'Reggie. And Sally!' Amanda turned to a stolid freckled woman standing just above them on the steps beside the paddock. 'Sukie, let me introduce you to two very dear friends: Sally and Reggie Millfield. Sukie Buckley: we were school chums.'

'We've met.'

'Oh, yes.' His glance slid away to the empty paddock as he replaced his top hat.

'At Newmarket. On the gallops.'

'So it was.' He peered at her name badge, then returned his glance to Amanda. 'So how is Triumvirate? Expect him to win?'

'God knows. I might not have come but I'd already ordered the outfits.'

'And bloody marvellous you look too.' He leant towards her.

She was wearing pink, a burning pink like the heart of a flame;

a short curved suit that scrunched as she moved, and a black hat with feathers and veil.

'Jerry always liked me to be easy to spot.'

'Amanda! *Here* you are!' Nicola and George were struggling up the steps. 'I wanted to see the Queen, but George insisted he had to get a bet on.' Nicola edged herself near to Sukie. 'Look at my shoes.' She lifted a high and complicated sandal fringed with grass.

'Yes, well I always wear a medium heel for Ascot.' Amanda concentrated on the paddock. 'It's such a scrum these days. All the extraordinary people they let in.'

'Where?'

'At lunch, someone actually half-inched our umbrella.'

'But when you're out of the sun it's really quite chilly.' Nicola leant round to her. 'Look.'

'What?'

'At my chest.'

'Oh, I thought you were showing me the brooch.'

'Goosepimples!'

'Oh, I thought you were showing me your tits.'

'Did I hear you mention umbrellas?' Reggie shouldered between them. 'That's funny, because Sally heaved one at lunch-time.'

'People shouldn't bag tables.' Sally drew a line through the name of a skittish mare that had just flounced past.

Reggie moved down the steps to clap George on the shoulder. 'So Triumvirate's going at six, I see?'

George rocked on his heels. 'We think it's the right distance.'

'If he wins I'll be a bit churned. Jerry offered me a share, you know.'

George stopped rocking. 'When was that?'

'Oh, last back end. When that fellow got chopped out hunting, was it? Or when the other one sailed off into the rising sun? Yes, that was it.'

'I think you must be mistaken.' George levelled his eyes at the rear of a chestnut colt.

'Can't think why I didn't take it up.'

'Because I wouldn't put up the pennies, wasn't it?' Sally was looking over his head.

'No, no, no,' George flapped his race-card. 'You've got it wrong. I came in when Fabian got posted to the Far East. Jerry had wanted me in all along but there wasn't a pitch. He must have asked you after Manningtree kicked it.'

'I haven't seen Simon yet. You'll be meeting up with him, I expect?' Nicola had attached herself to Sukie. She kept looking over at her race-card although she had one of her own.

'I don't know. Amanda said he'd be with Froggy's crowd. She's not sure he'll want to detach.'

Nicola inclined closer so that their hats touched. 'I really did want to speak to you, you know.'

'I'm sorry. I'm not always good about returning calls.'

'It is actually a bit urgent.'

'Well, I'm in tonight.'

'I'll see. It's not always that easy.'

Below them, Reggie and George appeared to have made peace over a copy of Uncle Ernie's System. 'So what do you reckon to Cecil's in this one?'

George was rocking again. 'I'd say he looks a bit hard trained.'

'Darling,' Nicola stepped down to insert a naked brown arm through his, 'you always say that, as if somehow it's cheating.'

'Time to be getting along.' He lifted his wrist without looking at his watch. 'We've arranged to meet some people in their box. 'Bye, Amanda. See you in the paddock before the big one.'

Reggie stared ahead, morose grey eyebrows jutting under his brim. 'Ghastly fellow,' he said.

'Wherever did you meet him?' Sally was marking her card. 'He was never at Harrow.'

'Good God, no. City. Old Etonian tie made in Hong Kong caper. Bet he even gets his bloody gee-gees run up on the cheap.'

'So that's what you think of Triumvirate?' Amanda kicked him on the ankle. 'Just 'cause you turned down a share.'

'Ha!' Sally shut her race-card, put it in her handbag and proceeded down to grass level. 'Come along, Reggie. I want you to put two pounds for me to win on Swan Song.'

Caught rubbing his ankle, Reggie hesitated, then limped down the steps after her impervious hat.

Amanda looked at Sukie and gave an exaggerated shrug. 'George couldn't cart an O.E. tie. He lacks the vitals.'

Triumvirate looked even better than he had at Newmarket. Bigger, yet no longer burly. The muscles in his quarters had designs on magnificence. Watching him, alone, from the paddock rail, Sukie thought he really was the pick. But the Coventry Stakes would take some winning. There were others with stronger claims than his narrow defeat in April.

Amanda also stood out in the paddock, where she had arrived with George and Nicola, and Simon who had claimed her just in time.

It was very hot. Sukie's willow-green suit was wilting. Six years old Armani, she had shortened the jacket and wasn't sure now about the proportions. Hotter than she could remember.

She looked up, aware that a great tree that had given shelter over the years was no longer there. In rain and sunshine that tree had been part of the sky. Now, everything had shifted. There was a new alignment that left her exposed.

And then the jockeys appeared, scattering colour through the setting, among them Henry Whippet; he in vermilion silks, clashing with Amanda in her pink. Amanda hardly looked at him, was considering instead Sylvia's Ascot effort of navy suit, cream boater and shoes.

Marcus talked to Henry Whippet, watching the horse, fingers

on chin, other arm folded across his chest. And Henry Whippet too watched Triumvirate, passing in front of Sukie now, blocking the group from her view. When he moved on, his great swaying quarters leaving a gap, she saw that Henry Whippet's eyes had not moved on with him. They were still looking in the place where the horse had been. They were looking at her.

Then the bell rang and all the horses were swinging into the centre and she became part of a general movement towards the stands.

The only person who seemed to be concentrated on the race was George. He had let it be known that he had had a serious punt. Everyone else, Sukie included, was taking it far too lightly. They had all laid down more than a yard of champagne. And the race was such a short one. Sukie yawned. It all seemed to be happening to someone else. There, within her binoculars, in a silent world, fourteen horses were giving of their substance to entertain a befuddled crowd. 'All except the Arabs,' she thought out loud.

'You what?' Nicola was always beside her.

'Arabs don't drink.'

'Oh, Christ,' Nicola said.

The horses were in the last furlong. Triumvirate had struck the front, striding out like a good thing, but he was being headed. Henry Whippet was riding a whirlwind but the favourite on the outside was surely overhauling them, inch by inch, reaching out his neck like the experienced horse, reaching it out to the line, and over.

'Oh, Christ!' Nicola said again. She had turned to look at George, but he was nowhere to be seen. She ran up the steps and through the exit door.

Standing in the second's enclosure again, Amanda looked happy. Marcus and Sylvia greeted her with rare smiles. It had been a stout performance, better than expected, considering he was a lazy horse at home and needed the race. But, as Marcus lifted the reins over Triumvirate's head and Henry Whippet jumped lightly to the grass, Sukie, watching from the terrace above, was aware of a shadow. A shadow, the shape of Jerry's shoulders, blocking out the light. Jerry, cut out of the picture, leaving a great dark shape, dominating them all with his absence. Winning was all that mattered.

. . . There'll be some bloody ones coming up in a moment.

And then Henry Whippet was passing directly beneath her feet as he ran down the steps into the weighing-room.

'Too bad Rosamund couldn't make it.' Amanda appeared beside her on the terrace with Sylvia Irvine in tow.

'Yes,' Sukie said, then knew she had not meant it.

She was seeing the evening mews, the maroon sports car, the laughing young man. It brought goosepimples to her skin. It was as though the shadow cast in the mews had somehow lengthened to touch her here.

'Yes, too bad,' she said.

'We thought we'd go and have a beer.' Amanda looked a little feverish. 'In Jerry's memory.'

'I prefer beer anyway.' Sylvia Irvine led the way to the escalator. 'Comes from having brothers.'

Amanda pushed on to the step behind her. 'Have you noticed how many women have forced their legs into sausage-skins this year?'

'Yes.' Sukie was gazing upwards. 'Curious also how they take on the shape.'

'It's the gleam.' Sylvia leapt off at the top, clapping a hand to her boater.

'Men don't have these dilemmas. Good thing, uniform.' Sukie bumped into Amanda who hadn't picked up quickly enough on the dismount.

Amanda was having difficulty with obdurate morning suits.

'Yes, but God, these as sure as hell are all hired. They have a look. And what a slum they make of it up here. If I were Betty I'd only issue vouchers conditional on a tailor's reference.'

'They have their ties.' Sylvia leant rakishly on the counter.

'True.' Sukie looked round, feeling that Nicola was with them.

'Oh, that reminds me,' Amanda was signalling impatiently with a tenner. 'On the subject of ties. I think you'd better come over one day. I've discovered something rather odd.'

But Nicola wasn't there, of course. It was the scent: Giorgio. Criss-crossed with other scents, it was everywhere.

# Chapter Fourteen

'So, was Ascot a success?' Alexis was at the drinks cupboard, squinting at something in a glass.

'Yes. I think so. I only went on the Tuesday.' Sukie eased off her shoes. 'Triumvirate was second.'

'God, I bet you were out of it. What a terrifying thought. All those women in hats, batting down the M4 at the end of the day.'

Sukie sniffed. 'We had beer, actually. What are you doing?'

'Don't tell me. It has to be Amanda being sentimental.'

'It was actually rather sad. Jerry would have been so proud.'

'Not as proud as if he'd have come first.'

'Alex, you're so cynical. What are you *doing*?'

'Nothing. Of course I'm cynical. Somebody doesn't suddenly become a wonderful human being just because they've died.'

'I know that. But Jerry could be kind. He was always kind to me.'

'That's because you're no threat.'

'I shall take that as an insult. What have you *got* there?'

She had moved a step towards him when the phone began to ring. They both started, Alex spilling some of a violet liquid he had just measured into a tiny glass.

'The answerphone's on.'

But she had already picked up the receiver. 'Hullo?'

There was silence, an intake of breath, then the voice whispering very close to the mouthpiece. 'Amanda?'

'No. My name is not Amanda. Who is this?'

'Amanda? I know that's you. Don't bullshit. What are you doing?'

'What do you want?'

'What do *you* want, Amanda? Let me guess . . .'

Sukie slammed down the receiver. 'Heavy breathers!'

'He phoned earlier.' Alexis wiped his fingers on his school trousers. 'While you were out shopping. Asking for Amanda?'

She nodded.

'He got quite abusive when I said she didn't live here, so I just put the answerphone on. I tried the number recall but it was a public box.'

'How many times did he phone?'

'I'm not sure. I haven't checked it.'

Sukie knelt down to play it back. There were four messages from the whispering caller. The first one angry, demanding that Amanda turn the answerphone off, the second frustrated, tense; the other two wordless, breathless and short. And then there was another message.

'Hi, Sukie. This is Bob Teichgraeber. We don't seem to be too good at mind meeting. So I'm going to suggest another sort. With an intermediary. My first horse. She's much nicer than I am. And much better looking. Give me a call.' He left a number which Sukie did not write down.

'You see, he knew who you were by your voice on the message.' Alex had been writing down Bob's details. 'But it's odd. Last Saturday, I forgot to tell you, some woman phoned from some agency and asked to speak to Amanda too. So I just gave her the number in the country. It didn't seem to matter then. But what if the two are connected?'

'I suppose I'd better put a new message on, with my name.'

'But don't you think you should warn her?'

'I'm going over there on Tuesday.'

*

112

Amanda was playing with the dogs on the lawn, throwing a ball into the yew hedge, a stick held high in her other hand. She was twisting, laughing, running away, then growling back when one caught the stick, tugging and refusing to let go. She wore black jodhpur trousers and a lime-green shirt. Her feet were bare.

Then the dog retrieving the ball saw Sukie watching on the terrace and the two of them came pounding towards her, barking and wagging their tails.

'Shut up,' Amanda shouted, coming towards her. 'Belt up, you stupid animals.' She followed the Labradors up the steps. 'We'll go into the drawing-room. It cows them.'

'So you've not been propositioned again?' Sukie leant back on the mushroom sofa overlooking an expanse of pale, spotless carpet.

'What? Oh, no. I was pretty damn sharp with the hussy. There you are.' Amanda presented her with an exuberant Pimms. 'I made it specially. Sorry I can't do lunch. Reggie's whisking me off to Newhury for two o'clock.'

'That's all right. This looks marvellous.' She took a sip. 'Where's Sally, then?'

'What makes you think she won't be coming too?'

'Just a feeling.'

'She's at some shareholders' meeting.' Amanda looked at her watch. 'I'll have to get changed soon, so I'll just get them.'

She went to a walnut tallboy and took from a drawer a small Harrods bag which she put between them on the sofa. 'There. Jerry's school ties. And they're all there.'

'You mean that none of them is missing?'

'None. That's what I thought was odd. All labelled too. Take a look.'

Sukie put down her Pimms and slipped her hand into the bag to withdraw a packet of carefully folded tissue paper. 'Were they all together like this?'

'Yes. Sentimental old thing. I found them on a shelf in his wardrobe. Not the bag, though. I put them in that.'

'You don't mind?' Sukie began to open the paper.

'Go ahead.'

Inside was a collection of ties, neatly rolled like eggs in a nest.

'I thought I was being so clever, you see.' Amanda looked indulgently at the ties. 'I thought that if one of them was missing, we'd know which one was around his neck. But,' she shrugged, 'as you see. I don't actually understand it. Do you?'

'No.' Sukie fingered each of the coiled ties. 'Not yet. But it was clever of you. It does tell us something.'

'What?'

Sukie shook her head. 'I'm not sure.'

'Of course, it wouldn't have been that one.' Amanda pointed at the Eton tie. 'It certainly wasn't a little black bow, was it?'

'No. And it wasn't any of those.'

'Oh. The sports ties.'

'No. Much too bright. It could have been the Old Etonian.' Sukie had unfurled it, running it through her fingers. 'Or one of the preps. They are all much alike. Will you introduce me?'

'Well, the very new-looking one, black with double narrow blue stripes, is the one he must have bought when he left. The black with the broad silver stripe is his prefect's tie. And that little screwed-up bit with the single narrow stripe is the one he must have worn most of the time he was there.'

Sukie picked up the scrappy piece of fabric. It so lacked substance that it hardly unrolled, the narrow end that had been inside remaining curled. Stitched to the seam, which was coming apart to show the interfacing, was a name-tape: JEREMY C.S. WEARING in upright blue letters. There was something infinitely pathetic about it, the tiny stitches around the edge worked with such care. She could see his mother, basket beside her, peering at those stitches under the electric light, sadness and hope in her heart.

114

'This was the one,' she said. 'One like this.'

'Are you sure?'

'Yes.'

'Why? It's very like the O.E.'

She coiled it in on itself again and put it back amongst the others. 'If it had been the Old Etonian, I'd have known it, immediately, in spite of the circumstances. It would have registered. Like this does now.'

Amanda put her hands out to the tissue paper and gently held it together around the ties. 'I'd rather it had been the O.E.' She opened the Harrods bag and slid the package inside. 'And I wish you weren't doing this.'

'I wish I wasn't doing it either.'

'You don't have to. And not because of what I said at Ascot. It's more ... Well now I actually wish he had been having it off with some tart.'

'Yes.'

'Because I'm beginning to believe that something much nastier must have happened. Aren't you frightened?'

Sukie had got up to stand at the window and look out at the sunny garden. 'I think someone's been following me.'

'Where?'

'In London.' She turned back towards the room. 'After Nicola's show the other night, there was someone waiting as I came out.'

'You didn't see what they looked like?'

Sukie didn't reply instantly. 'No.'

Amanda ran a hand through her hair. 'God, I must go and get changed.'

'I'll be off. Thanks for the Pimms. By the way?'

'Yes?' Amanda was behind her at the door.

'You said George never wore an Old Etonian tie. Why not?'

The Harrods bag nestled within her hands. 'Well, George was never at Eton. You surely never supposed that he was.'

# Chapter Fifteen

'So sorry, my dear, to have left you dangling. Most inconsiderate of me.'

Rosamund Officer bustled down the couple of stairs from the control box above her small studio. The lights in the studio went out as two young men with clip-boards also emerged into the corridor.

'Well done.' Rosamund turned to them, patting one on the shoulder. 'Nearly there. Shall we say ten past two sharp, boys and girls?'

She took Sukie's arm and guided her up towards daylight. 'How about a turn in the park? Get some fresh air. Unless you need to eat? I think I've got some – ' she rummaged in her large handbag and produced a screwed-up paper bag – 'bread. Jolly good.'

'I'm fine, really.'

'For the ducks.' Her swivelling gaze rested for a beat. 'You do like feeding ducks? Jolly good.'

They walked towards St James's Park without speaking, but not in uncomfortable silence. All the while Rosamund made little clucking sounds as she hobbled along, taking in with benign interest the passing world.

'Pochards, those are the fellows.' They had reached the lake. 'Like teddy bears. Here you are.' She handed Sukie some bread.

Sukie watched her hurl a crust to a nervous bird on the outermost ripple. 'I'm glad to see you looking so well.'

'I went to stay for a few days with my father in Solihull. Stone deaf, poor darling, so he doesn't ask questions. Very restful.'

'You've still no idea who attacked you?'

'Nope.'

'But his mention of Amanda means he couldn't have been a complete stranger.'

Rosamund continued aiming bread over the lake as if she had not spoken.

'Could it have something to do with the horse?'

'The horse?' In directing her pale eyes on Sukie, irritation was revealed.

'Nicola thinks it'll be George next.'

'Good heavens.' She resumed feeding the birds. 'The triumvirate? Well, well. Did I tell you I had some flowers from that American?'

'Bob. Yes.' Sukie had been crumbling the bread; gritty and grey it fell from her fingers.

'A huge bouquet, all done up with cellophane and wires. Took me half the morning to break into it.'

'I wonder how he knew?'

'It's a small world.'

'Racing?'

'That's not what I meant. My dear,' Rosamund leant to pop a pellet into a thrusting beak, 'it's very good of you, but quite unnecessary, to be so jumpy.'

Sukie gave a little laugh. 'The last I heard was your voice in the night saying you'd been attacked.'

Rosamund's head was tilted back, stretching her receding throat, as she gazed across the surface of the water. 'But that's no reason to start thinking anyone would want to attack George.'

There was a movement at Sukie's feet. A sparrow had hopped on to one of her loafers and was pecking up crumbs. She kept very still. 'I've been having some strange phone calls. Asking for Amanda. I also think I've been followed. Seems unlikely to be coincidence.'

Rosamund speeded up her feeding of the ducks, getting rid of the bread as quickly as possible. In the background was the arc of noise from traffic in Victoria Street. She wiped her hands off each other.

'That's enough, I think.'

They began to walk back.

'My dear, most of us, you know, have something to hide. Secrets. It can be something big, but usually it's something quite petty. We are all so open to embarrassment.' She looked at her watch. 'I can only answer for myself. But I know of no reason anyone would want to attack me. If I hear anything to the contrary, you shall be the first to know.'

'Perhaps you think I've been intrusive.'

'No, no, no, my dear. Disingenuous, I'd say. If you know what that means. Or even if you don't.'


Newbury evening meeting: sun slanting across hoof-worn track, splitting the roof of the Hampshire Stand with eye-watering beam. The contented murmur of the crowd, shouts of bookies hanging in heavy air, the smell of trampled grass.

Sukie wandered down to lean on the rail, alone, to watch the horses canter to the start. Then she strolled back to the stand. She was enjoying herself, not placing any bets, not drinking, or talking to anyone, forgetting with each moment why she was here.

Henry Whippet had a double. He looked over his shoulder at her as he jumped down for the second time in the winner's enclosure.

After the last race, she loitered in the stand, watching a mist that had begun to roll across the course in front of a line of trees, then she made her way round to the part of the paddock nearest the weighing-room. When his hand touched her shoulder she turned and followed him towards the car park.

'I'm staying over this way tonight,' Henry Whippet said. 'Not going back to Newmarket. Got a couple of two-year-olds to ride at Lambourn before I go down to Salisbury in the morning.'

'You have brought it with you?'

'Of course. What d'you take me for?'

She didn't reply.

'It's quite a nice hotel, the one where I'm staying. I thought we could go there. Want to follow me in your car?'


Hinton House Hotel, in a small village just outside Newbury, was really very nice. It had the dilapidated comfort of a private house, with dark panelling, heavy faded curtains and bookcases full of books. Sukie and Henry Whippet sat in cumbersome chintz-covered armchairs in the empty lounge with drinks on a small table between them. Everyone else was at dinner.

'Mind if I smoke?' He was already taking a cigar out of a leather case.

She shook her head.

'Didn't think you would. Thanks anyway.' He clipped the end of it, lit it and shook the match.

'My father used to smoke cigars.'

'Dead?'

She nodded.

'Mine too. Or that's our information. Did a runner when I was seven.'

They sat for a while in silence, watching the smoke drift through the room, drawing it about them with its scent. Then Henry Whippet took an envelope out of the inside pocket of his light jacket, holding on to it, narrowing his eyes.

'So, what're you up to?'

Sukie's hands were folded in her lap. 'Why should I be up to anything?'

'Oh, you're going to muck about, are you?'

'I wouldn't dream of it.'

'No? Well, perhaps I'd better give you a lead anyway.' He

slipped the envelope back into his jacket and picked up his glass of mineral water. 'I likes this hotel. Nice and restful. Not too full of the racing crowd. I brought my mum here once. She liked it.'

'Ah. Mrs Whippet.'

'No. Milligan.'

'I knew it wasn't your real name.'

'My mum married again.'

'Are you going to show me what's in that envelope?'

'Don't you trust me?'

'No.'

'Well you're wrong there. You should. I brought this – ' he lightly touched the breast of his jacket – 'just on a phone call from you yesterday. Don't I deserve some trust?'

'You'll get my thanks. When you decide to let me see it.'

'Oh, that's nice.' He took out the envelope and tossed it on to the table. 'But I don't think I'd better take your thanks. Might leave you feeling a bit skint.'

Sukie flushed, but picked up the envelope and opened it.

He was watching her as she took out the piece of paper. 'Is that what you wanted?'

'Yes.' She looked up briefly. 'Thank you.'

She opened her bag and withdrew the training bill. She turned it over and held it beside the letter in her other hand; handwritten from George to Henry Whippet, dashed off in a hurry, about the payment of a percentage. She looked at them both, at the formation of the figures, for a full two minutes before laying them on the table. 'Oh, well.'

'No good, is it? It's not what you wanted.'

'Oh, it is. It is what I asked you for. But it doesn't help, that's all.'

He swivelled the pieces of paper round so that they faced him. 'Well, they're definitely not the same writing, if that's what you was hoping.'

'No. Wouldn't your agent normally deal with fees and things?'

120

'Yes, he would. So why did you think I might have a sample of George Graham-Jones's writing?'

'It was just a chance. I didn't want to involve his wife or Amanda. I was going to try Sylvia after you.'

'Lucky, then, weren't you?' He blew a perfect smoke ring towards her. 'Whose phone number is this anyway? Do you know?'

Sukie was sipping her gin and tonic. 'Oh, some agency, called the White Tie. An escort agency.'

'Is that like – a euphemism?'

She looked up, startled. 'I believe so.'

'Ah, well I can guess what scent you're following.'

'Pretty obvious.'

'Yeah, well if it's all so obvious, what're you doing sniffing at it? What a man likes to get up to when he's on the loose is nobody else's business.'

'Even if it kills him?'

'Except perhaps his wife's.'

'Yes, well it was she who wanted me to look into it.'

'So you said. But you don't seem to have been exactly reluctant.'

Sukie put down her glass, misjudging the edge of the table, so that the drink slopped over her fingers. 'Why didn't you tell me that you used Jerry Wearing as a solicitor?'

He became quite still. Smoke rose between them. 'I don't have to tell you anything.'

'That's true.' She looked round for her bag, for a tissue.

'I expect I've got my reasons.' He picked up her hand and lifted it to his mouth, putting the tips of her fingers between his lips. 'Gin and tonic, very nice.'

She pulled her hand away. 'You are totally gross. Didn't anyone ever tell you?'

'No.'

121

'So,' finding the tissue, rubbing violently at her fingers, 'why did you say that you only knew Jerry through riding for him?'

'Because it's true. That was how I knew him. He wasn't a friend. But he acted for me as a lawyer, just the once. I wanted to buy some land abroad. Not his speciality, but he'd bought some himself quite recently. And he owed me.'

'Oh, yes, the house in Spain.'

'Yeah, well mine was in Portugal. Wouldn't catch me investing in Spain. Don't like the way they treat their animals.'

'I've heard that you hunt?'

'That's different. And you know it. Anyway, that was that. Don't have much call for lawyers. Accountants, now . . .'

'What do you mean, he "owed" you?' Sukie had picked up her drink again. She leant back and crossed her legs.

'Well, I found the horse, didn't I? Triumvirate. I'd heard he was looking for something a bit special and I told him about this yearling I'd seen. No money involved.'

'But you expected to ride it?'

'Yeah, well I'd be daft otherwise. So would he.'

She began to wipe the wet patch on the table, round and round with the crumpled tissue. 'Were you aware of the complications going on about the ownership of the horse?'

'I knew one of them died. Killed, wasn't he? And there was lots of scrubbing around to find people to take the third share. The other had gone abroad. I didn't involve myself with all that. Mr Wearing had laid it out. It was his problem.'

'What about George Graham-Jones?'

'Well, he was a surprise, wasn't he? Didn't seem quite Mr Wearing's type. But I gather they'd turned down worse.'

'Like who?'

'I don't know. People he'd hardly known coming out of the woodwork. He only took on Graham-Jones when he was really up against the plaster.'

She nodded.

'You're quite upset by all this, aren't you, doll?'

'I saw him.' She was looking at her lap. 'I can't understand anyone just leaving him like that.'

'Can't you? Not some floosie who wanted to get the hell out?'

She looked up at him. 'No.'

'No. Neither can I, as it happens. Neither do I think it was some floosie with him that night.'

'You don't?'

'I spoke to him, you see, at the flat, not long before he must have died. He said he had someone with him. He didn't say who, but it just didn't sound like he was in the middle of something. If you know what I mean.'

'Did you see him? Were you there?'

''Course not. On the telephone.'

'Someone was there. I heard the lift.'

'Well, it wasn't me.'

'Why didn't you tell someone? The police?'

'No one asked me. And I'm not going to start poking my nose. It was well known he and I didn't get on.'

'So, if it wasn't a girl, someone did that to Jerry on purpose.' She was leaning forward, arms on the table.

'Can't have got like it by accident. If that's what you was hoping?'

'Just now I'd rather believe he'd been enjoying himself.'

'Yeah, well.' He stubbed out his cigar.

'But why? Can people really be that malicious?'

''Course they can. Funny though, how when they are, other people often call them "animals". Wouldn't catch no horse doing that to another one.'

'No. Well, think of all the hooves.'

'What?' For the first time he looked disconcerted. 'You're a bit weird, doll. Did you know that?'

'Yes. It keeps me sane.' She stood up. 'I'd better go. I'm getting light-headed.'

He also stood, smoothing out his linen jacket. 'I'll give you dinner if you like. I'm not eating, myself. Got to do eight stone tomorrow. You shouldn't drive back feeling like that.'

'I'll be fine. Thanks anyway. I don't know why I'm always so rude to you.'

'Oh, I do. But I'm not going to tell you. Not now you're being nice.'

## Chapter Sixteen

'How much longer will lunch be?' Alex lay on the sofa in his pyjamas under the Sunday papers.

'If you got up earlier you might manage to take in breakfast.'

'That's not fair. It was incredibly late when I got to bed.'

'It's in the oven.'

'Yes, but how long will it actually be?'

'I don't know. And I'm not telling you anyway because you'd only keep looking at your watch.'

'That's a contradiction.'

'Tough. You've got all those papers to look at while you wait. And jolly lucky you are. They forgot to deliver and I had to go out and get them.'

'I know. I got woken by the phone. You never put that machine on. I had to get up and answer it.' He turned his head as there was a brisk ring at the doorbell. 'Oh, that's probably him now.'

'Who?'

'The American. Bob. That's who it was on the phone. He asked if he could drop round. I said it would be OK. I knew you'd be here cooking lunch.'

'For God's sake!'

There was another brisk ring.

'Well, go and answer it, Mosie. He'll wonder what's going on.'

'Good. And he won't be the only one.' She marched out into the hall and pressed the entry button without bothering with the intercom. 'You can let him in. And entertain him. Happily, I know my place, and I shall be in it.'

From the kitchen Sukie heard the front door open and close, the sounds of voices going into the sitting-room. She stood at the chopping board with a sharp knife and lined up beans and carrots to be sliced.

'Your son is an excellent host. Am I to put it down to his education?' Bob was in the doorway, a glass in his hand. 'Or rather to you?'

'I shouldn't.' She began to swipe the heads off the carrots.

He lifted the glass. 'Sherry. Alexis insisted. This one's yours.'

She took the glass and put it down on the table. 'He certainly shouldn't have expected you to bring it through.'

'He didn't. I insisted. May I return with my own?'

A moment later he did so, leaning now against the doorpost while she started on the beans.

'You didn't return my call.'

'No.' She took her first taste of sherry, then another.

He shrugged. 'That's OK. I just wanted you to see my horse. Marcus found her for me and she's in his yard now. I don't know that many people over here yet. Not many who'd appreciate her qualities anyway. I guess I'm like a child with a new bicycle and no one to play with.'

'Tell me about her.' She continued stringing the beans.

'Well, she's a two-year-old, called Atlantic Drift. Appropriate. And she's truly beautiful. Dark grey with an almost white mane and tail. She's had just the one run coming fifth behind some pretty decent horses at Nottingham, and she's due to go at Sandown week after next. I thought you might like to come see her.'

'I'm not sure.'

'Well, you've got plenty of time. I'm around until next Friday when I have to be in Scotland for the weekend. But you can call

126

me the following week when you know more what your plans are.'

'All right.' She put the carrots in a saucepan, went to the sink and turned on the cold tap. 'By the way. You sent Rosamund some flowers.'

'Oh, did I?'

'Some rather spectacular flowers.'

'They would be.'

'Wishing her well after she'd been mugged.'

'Well, I do wish her well.'

'Do you? How did you know about it? The very next morning?'

'I didn't.' He had hardly taken any of his sherry. He sipped it now and held the glass up to the light.

'I'm sorry, I don't understand.'

'You wouldn't.' He looked at her in the same way that he had looked at his drink.

She put the saucepan on the hob and turned on the gas.

He was smiling. 'My secretary, Margot, sent them. We have a contract with Rosamund's company. She trains some of our executives in media techniques. Pure chance, I couldn't make a meeting with her early on the Monday, so Margot called her on the Saturday morning to let her know. Of course Rosamund told her what had happened as she was cancelling all her sessions for the following week anyway. Margot likes to use my being American to indulge a dormant vulgar streak; and naturally the flowers were from me.'

'I see.'

'Good. How is Rosamund anyway? Did you see her at Ascot?'

'She wasn't there.'

'Catching up on the cancelled work, I imagine. I was sorry to miss it.'

'Next year, perhaps.'

'Yeah. England's still pretty much like a club, isn't it? With a very long waiting list.'

'There are reasons for it at Ascot.'

'I don't think I really mean that. Ascot has rules that at least one can understand. It's where there aren't any rules that the thing gets tricky. I think you may be a bit like that.'

'Me?' She was genuinely amazed. 'Gosh, I'm an open book.'

'Are you?' He drank from his glass again. 'What kind?'

'What?'

'What kind of a book?'

'Oh, gosh,' she pushed back her hair with one hand as she had seen Jemima do, 'I don't know.'

A sudden movement of air carried the scent of the lime tree from the open window of the sitting-room through into the kitchen as they both lifted their glasses, sipped, then swallowed in silence punctuated by the hoot of a car.

'It would be interesting to find out.' He said it as though inviting her to a joint investigation.

'I really don't think I'd be that rewarding.' Sukie took the lid off the saucepan and poked the carrots with the knife.

'You never know till you try.' He tossed off the remains of his sherry. 'Does Rosamund have any idea who did it, by the way?'

'No. Some yobbo, I expect. She's refusing to worry about it. Being afraid's a waste of time.'

'It can be a protection.'

'Not always.' She poured boiling water from the kettle into a saucepan ready for the beans, so that the steam stung her hand. 'Think of all those jockeys. If they were afraid of being injured, they'd be useless.'

'True.' He watched her put her hand under the cold tap.

'Are you just going to leave it at that?'

'Yes. And leave you in peace. I'm off house hunting.'

'Oh, where?' She bound her hand with a tea-towel.

'I rather thought Hampstead. I like the idea of Hampstead.'

128

'Handy for Newmarket.'

'And handy for my office. By the way, I'll give you the number.' He reached inside his jacket for a card. 'Please come and see the horse. You might even find you have fun.'

'I know it sounds dreadful but I'm actually having fun.' Amanda's tone was defiant, her demeanour decidedly pissed.

'You mean at the races?' Sukie was standing by the window, receiver in hand. Her tone was resigned, her demeanour decidedly pissed off.

'At the races? Salisbury. Of course, I haven't spoken to you since then, have I? And other things. Other occasions. But Salisbury was fun.' She stressed each syllable like an American film commercial. 'You've no idea.'

'No, I haven't.'

It was half past midnight. Sukie had been cooking all day. Cooking so that she couldn't eat. And Amanda had telephoned just as she was turning the lights out to go to bed, had stranded her in the sitting-room in her pyjamas in the dark, without even a glass of Muscadet inside her.

'You should try it.'

'What?'

'Fun. The little cur had three winners.'

'Henry Whippet? So?'

'Well. Saw him tonning off afterwards in his gorgeous car with his almost as gorgeous companion. All of sixteen, if one's being tactful. Amazing what money and a bit of fame can do.'

'Amazing.'

'Sukie, I wanted to speak to you.'

'I had thought that you were.'

'No. Simon sends his apologies.'

'What for?'

'For not waiting for you. He was most insistent.'

'Can you begin again . . . No don't.'

'After Nicola's show.'

'Oh?'

'Yes. He said he saw you there. Thought you'd seen him. But he had to dash. Something on with Froggy. Does that make sense? Anyway, talking about Froggy. I wanted to talk to you about that too.'

'Oh?' She was standing straighter now, finding the join of the curtains to divide them with a little light from the silent square.

'Yes. He really is determined. I mean, to go in with Froggy. And I know how much Jerry would have disapproved. What am I to do?'

'What are *you* to do?'

'You know what I mean.'

'Jerry's dead, Amanda.' The black leaves of the tree moved gently in the night, the street lamps filling each of their allotted spheres with a yellow glow. The square had not changed in ten years.

'I know.' There was a gulp, an intake of breath, then the sound of weeping.

'Oh, God, I'm sorry.'

'No, no, you're right. I'm a stupid, miserable cow and I'm going to bed.'

'I'm sorry.'

'No, no, no. No . . .' There was a click, the dialling tone, and under the tree, close to the railings that bordered the central garden, a shape darker than the darkness dissolved into the density of shrub and branch. Dissolved into such stillness that Sukie knew she must have been mistaken.

# Chapter Seventeen

The traffic on the A1 was heavy; a fast-moving jam leaving London for the weekend. Sukie did not want to be leaving London: she was determined to be back for the weekend.

Driving with the windows down, through a haze of dust and fumes, she felt cross and anxious. Her linen shirt stuck to her back and her espadrilles kept slipping on the pedals. She was not at all confident of finding the Graham-Jones house. It was in a village to the north-east of Stevenage within a switchback of twisting lanes. All that she could now remember was that she should look out for some roadworks just before the turning into the drive.

Nicola had phoned the moment she had walked into the flat that afternoon after covering in her friend Poppy's boutique in St John's Wood while Poppy met her married lover for a long lunchtime. It had been a pleasant job, and successful – Friday was always a good day for shifting clothes – and she had been looking forward to a favourite film on television and a glass or several of the champagne Poppy had given her to top up her wages. And then Nicola had phoned.

The car in front stopped suddenly and she hit the brake just in time. The whole line was at a standstill and the heat becoming intolerable, throbbing with sound systems all around. Then, like a Britannia penny, the first raindrop struck the rear window, followed in half a minute by another, then another. Faster and heavier they came until the view ahead was blotted out behind a screen of streaming water. Already Sukie's arms were wet as she wound the windows shut and turned on the wipers. Her flowered skirt hung limply where she had hitched it up above her knees. Over her head was a sound like coins being thrown into a tin can.

Nothing would have persuaded her to join the rush for the country on a Friday night, certainly not Nicola's whinings that she needed to talk to her. Nothing. Except those final words: 'Please, please, I'm all alone here and I'm frightened. You're the only person who might believe me, but I think I'm being watched.'

Slowly the traffic had begun to move again with much squealing of brakes on the wet surface so that Sukie was relieved when she reached the turn-off. There, from a large roundabout she swung into a minor road and, about eight miles on, into a narrow lane between lush hedges.

Immediately the weather changed. The sun came out. The rain stopped. Vegetation steamed in luxuriant contentment. She opened the windows again, to the warm scent of nettles and cow parsley and air rising with birdsong.

Still unsure of finding the house, it didn't seem to matter any more, she drove gently, letting the car's weight take it up and down the rambling gradients, enjoying the sounds and smells and the sweeping motion. And she must have come a creative route for it certainly took longer than Nicola had suggested and she seemed to have bypassed the roadworks altogether when suddenly, on her right, she saw the name Meadow View on a stone gatepost.

The drive was long, shaded between trees and ferns, and more rural in character than she had imagined. And when the house came into view about fifty yards ahead, it was plain and unrestored, standing on a scrubby bit of ground with roses on the façade but no garden. A mud path led up to it.

She left her car to the side of the drive and began to walk towards the house, stepping on to the grass beside the path, keeping in the shade of the trees. Then, turning her head, she caught a movement in the darkening wood. A figure, slipping ahead of her through the slender trunks, now veering away into the deepest part, noiseless except for the cry of a pheasant that flapped from its cover. She stood looking after him, wondering why he was there, why also he had not simply walked up the drive. It did not occur to her to call his name.

'Oh,' Nicola said on opening the front door. 'Come in.' Her expression was one of mild amusement.

'You *were* expecting me?'

'Oh, yes.' She stepped back with a light, shivering laugh.

'You did telephone.'

'I know. I know. Why do you say that?'

They were standing in the hall; too dark to determine its size.

'Well, you seem surprised. To see me, I mean.'

'No. Not at all. You're rather late, that's all.'

'Yes, I'm sorry. The traffic was terrible and then I came a long way round. I even missed the roadworks.'

'Oh? Well come into the drawing-room. The sun's in there. Would you like a drink?'

'Better not. I have to drive back.'

'You don't mind if I do?'

Sukie wandered to the windows, overlooking the yard, where the sun dazzled in horizontal lines, the puddles, the fences and fields. But here, inside the drawing-room, it was dark, the windows narrow. A red rose pecked at the pane. In spite of its size there was a meanness in the proportions of the house. And even on this hot evening there was a chill. Nicola, bending over the cocktail cabinet, wore a long fawn cardigan over her white trousers and tangerine polo shirt.

. . . A woman for whom it must always be summer.

'George still isn't here?' Sukie was looking out across what appeared to be farmland.

133

'No.' Nicola closed the cabinet and leant with her back against it, sipping her gin and tonic. 'He often isn't. Work. You know.'

'You phoned me because you were frightened. Because you thought someone was watching you.'

'Yes.' She swallowed too fast, coughed. 'That's true.'

'What made you think that?'

'I thought I saw someone.'

The sunlight had turned a deep orange, casting a shaft down the centre of the room. Sukie screwed up her eyes. 'Where?'

'Outside. Different places. All round the house.'

'So what do you think I can do?'

'I really don't know.' Nicola's glare was peevish. 'It's very lonely here.'

'Aren't you expecting George for the weekend?'

Nicola just shrugged and swirled the ice round her glass.

Sukie turned again to the window. The huge sun was sinking fast, levelling all before it with wasted colour.

'How does he seem, at the moment? Does he seem worried?'

'Yes. Yes, I would say that he does.' Nicola nodded several times.

The sun was sliding behind some trees now. Dusk gathered in the yard. It seeped from amongst fern and bramble, dropped from branches, concentrated in a shadow that withdrew to leave the space a little lighter.

'Perhaps I should have a look around?'

'Where?' Nicola looked about the room.

'Outside.'

'Do as you like.' She flopped into an armchair and stared at the empty fireplace.

Outside it was a little warmer, but Sukie wished she had brought a cardigan. The mud path broadened into a yard in front of the house, fringed with tired grass that gradually became fresher and longer as it reached back into the wood. The route to a garage was clearly marked by two parallel mud tracks round the side of the house.

It was built of brick but with a rumpled roof and a large padlock securing doors which did not fit together. Sukie peered through the crack. Empty. A shelf at the far end with a couple of oil cans and a clutch of dirty rags. Beside the garage, red and shiny, was Nicola's VW Golf; evidently the lock-up was reserved for George.

She turned away and crossed the open yard, sidestepping the occasional puddle that the storm had made. She leant on the farm gate and gazed across fields stretching to a sky left bruised by the fall of the sun. Higher up, the air was white and gauzy, and against it, at the edge of the first field, stood the bulk of an old barn.

Sukie climbed over the gate and took the path around the perimeter towards it. There were sudden rustlings at her feet, and overhead the cries of rooks. Although the grass was damp, the field seemed to have retained some of the heat from the day and she enjoyed the walk through the intense evening scents of hay and honeysuckle. A concentration of remaining light had caught the barn, lifting its red oxide to savage gold, and as she stepped inside, it was to enter the solemnity of a temple.

The door swung shut and Sukie stood in the soft gloom, at peace amongst comfortable bales, the flutterings of birds high in the roof. But there was another sound. Rhythmic, discordant, it rasped through the purring wingtips, insisting that peace was not to be found here.

Dividing the shadows, she could see nothing but steps of straw climbing the walls, open clerestories through which birds, or perhaps now bats, were flying. There was a creaking sigh as the barn settled to the night. Above the door a flap of corrugated iron rattled and a spray of water landed in her hair. Yet still the rasping dominated the place.

Sukie climbed on to a stray bale but could see little more than from ground level. Then she noticed that it was not stray. It was one of a number fallen like a child's building blocks across the swept floor.

The bales were heavy, and those about the walls so solidly stacked that it must have taken more than the wind or the movement of some small animal to dislodge them. She began to jump from one to another until she reached the place from where they had fallen. A deep shaft, reaching up into darkness, had been cut through the neatly stacked straw. The sound was coming from the top of the shaft.

Jumping off the bale, she manoeuvred another one on top of it and climbed on again. Then, carefully selecting a bale from the steps on either side of her, she raised herself until she could clamber on to the main structure beside the shaft. It was heavy work, and dangerous; several times the step on which she was standing rocked ominously, and the ones beside her swayed as though the whole edifice might start to collapse, taking her with it.

The bales were surprisingly deep. There was no question of simply climbing them like stairs. She had to clamber on to each one, using her hands, elbows and knees to drag herself onwards, upwards. While all the time the sound was getting closer.

There was a familiarity in its rhythm, an intimacy in its discord. But Sukie would not look up, used all her concentration for the climb. When finally she reached the top, landed on the broad platform of straw, she felt only contentment that she had arrived. The air was warm as in an attic, the smell of the straw strong, foetid even. Just above her head were the girders that supported the roof and the sound was very close now. It had drawn her up through the darkness to land at this place. The final responsibility was hers.

Think forward.

*

She looked up. The sound came from the girder immediately above the shaft and was caused by a metal hook large enough to bear the carcass of an animal. The hook had been hitched over the girder then linked into a ring from which swung a rope weighted at the end. It was the weight which made the hook swing on the girder to produce the rhythmic rasping sound. And the weight that hung on the rope was George.

. . . His jacket has the gleam of silk.

In life he had always appeared overdressed. In death he had surpassed himself. He wore a black morning coat, an emerald shirt and plus-fours. At his neck was a scarlet bow tie, on his head a Tyrolean hat with jaunty feather. And his feet were sheathed in chrome-yellow socks.

. . . His brogues insist that they are hand-made . . .

Sukie subsided on to one elbow, all sense of urgency gone. From the comfort of the straw she watched his swaying form, taking in all those details together with the bulging eyes and jutting tongue, the stain on the trousers, the smell. Above the stretched neck his face was livid beyond recognition. And yet Sukie had recognized instantly that this had once been George.

She felt so sleepy. She wanted to lie down and sleep. Why always this lethargy? It panicked her. But not as much as action. (When Peter had died she had wanted to sleep for ever.) Not as much as living. Sukie forced herself to sit upright, to stand staggering on the high platform so that her face was almost level with the dangling yellow feet.

Carefully, deliberately, she climbed back down the shaft of straw. When she reached the floor, she walked across it and with a pull, harder than was necessary so that she almost fell backwards, the door came open and she was outside in the misty field. Then running.

Running close to the hedge as fast as she could until she reached the gate, where she stopped, listening to the rasp of her breathing, clutching the top bar, seeing the lighted house ahead. Only then did she understand that she would have to tell Nicola.

# Chapter Eighteen

Nicola sat hunched in her armchair beside the cold fireplace. Sukie had returned to find her as she had left her, but the glass empty in her hand. Now, one and a half hours later, the glass was in the kitchen, the curtains had been drawn, police churned about the yard, and still she had not moved.

'I think I will have a drink now, if that's OK?'

Nicola just waved a hand.

'Can I get you anything? A cup of tea?'

Nicola shook her head.

She had been the same with the police, apathetic, removed. They had been patient. She had only stared in response to their coaxing, not a tear on her face. Shock, Detective Sergeant Crowther had said as she questioned Sukie tersely. What had Sukie been doing in the barn anyway?

Sukie poured herself a large brandy. It reminded her how cold she was. The sting in the throat, instant warmth, spreading to fingers and toes. And George was still dead.

Think forward.

'I've found him,' she had said.

Nicola had looked up, 'Where?' And when Sukie had told her, 'How? How did he do it?'

And after the phone call there had been no more need for decisions. Everything followed in logical order once the police were in control. Now a doctor was here, Forensics, and they were all in the barn, with their vehicles and a constable to keep watch at the house.

Nicola's back was to her now, head bent, arms stretched along the arms of the chair. The room was a hollow carved out of darkness.

'What did you mean, how did he do it?'

No response.

'You told me you were afraid he'd be murdered.'

'What?' Nicola's cheekbone angled up at her.

'When you talked to me at Atalanta's, you were worried he'd be next.'

Nicola turned round in her chair. 'Yes. Next. To be attacked. I never mentioned the word "murder".' She settled back in her original position, only now her head was not bowed, while Sukie moved warily about the room sipping her brandy.

'I think I will have that cup of tea.'

In the narrow kitchen at the back of the house everything was easy to find. The units, all new, unpainted, had very little in them. While Sukie set out the cup and saucer and waited for the kettle to boil, she thought of the figure she had seen slipping through the wood earlier that evening, of the shadow she had seen in the yard. There was a blind above the window but it had not been pulled down. She pressed her face to the glass but could see nothing. The kettle switched itself off and she poured water on to the tea-bag. Then she went to try the back door. It opened and a soft breeze drifted in, the rustling of leaves. She shut it and turned the key.

'I assumed that you didn't take sugar.'

'You assumed right.' Nicola took the cup and gave her a sweet smile.

Sukie sat down on the hearthrug and spread her skirt over her feet. 'Why did you say, "How did he do it?"'

'Did I say that?'

'When I told you I'd found him.'

'I can't remember anything I said. I've had a shock. How could I possibly?' She began to take little sips of tea.

'Nicola? Was there something worrying George? You mentioned him having a row with Sylvia Irvine.'

'Not a row. I didn't say that. Anyway, how should I know? He never talked to me.'

Sukie glanced about the room. 'No. But Simon did, didn't he?'

'What?' Nicola put her cup down with a clatter.

'Was he by any chance here this evening?' She began to rub her leg under her skirt.

'No?' It was a defiant question, while she watched the movement of Sukie's hand.

'I keep seeing him, you see. I think.' There was blood on her fingers. She lifted her skirt to find her legs covered in scratches. 'At Atalanta's, here, even in the square outside my flat. Perhaps it was he who was watching you?'

'No!'

'No?' Her arms were itching now, stinging. She began to scratch violently. 'I think then that perhaps he was here to see you.'

'No.' Nicola stood up.

'Or George?'

'What would he have to do with George?'

'If George was murdered—'

'No!'

'Well, I can tell you, it wasn't an accident. He didn't have a plastic bag over his head and an orange in his mouth.'

'For fuck's sake, have you got fleas?'

'I don't know.'

'Well, will you shut the fuck up scratching!'

'I'm sorry.' Sukie reached a hand down her back. 'The straw. It must have been the straw.'

Nicola shook her head and went over to the drinks cabinet. 'This tea's doing me no good at all. I need a gin.'

'I need a bath.'

'You'll itch even more if you do.'

'I know.'

'Sting all over as soon as you hit the water.'

'Yes.' Sukie followed her. 'Are you having an affair with Simon?'

'Yes.'

There was the sound of feet in the hall and they both rounded on the door as Detective Sergeant Crowther and a uniformed constable came into the room.

'Yes?' Nicola eyed them fiercely.

'Er, sorry to interrupt, Mrs Graham-Jones.' DS Crowther was a cool young woman, short dark hair, a touch of lipstick. 'We're taking him away now, your husband. Just thought you'd like to know.'

'Yes, of course.' She looked completely exhausted. 'Have you any idea yet how . . . ?'

'We'll know more when Pathology have seen him. At the moment it looks like asphyxiation due to hanging. But we can't be certain of anything. I can think of better places than a barn for Forensics and Fingerprints to do their stuff.'

'Like looking for a needle in a haystack.'

They all turned to the constable, who blushed. His pink and white skin had the bloom of rose petals.

'Right,' DS Crowther said quickly, 'well, try and get a good night's sleep, Mrs Graham-Jones. We'll talk to you again in the morning. You'll be staying then, will you, Mrs Buckley?'

'Yes.' Sukie took a step forward. 'Er – can you tell us, when? I mean, when it happened?'

'Can't be certain of that either. But it looks like he's been dead at least eight hours. That's all I can tell you. We'll be with you for a couple of days yet, I suspect, but I'm leaving PC

Spencer outside the house tonight, to keep an eye on things. That car by the way – ' she had turned to go – 'the red Golf. You said that was yours, Mrs Graham-Jones? Any idea where your husband's car might be? How he got here?'

'No. No, not at all. Maybe someone gave him a lift?'

'That happened sometimes, then, did it?'

Nicola shrugged and shook her head.

'I see. Right. Goodnight.'


'We were just two lonely people.' Nicola was in the armchair again, picking at a thread in the pattern. It was almost one in the morning. 'Trapped in our situations.'

'Yes?' Sukie failed to suppress a yawn.

'He still living with his parents. Me living with George. He was much too old for me.'

Sukie nodded against her knees. She was bone-achingly cold.

'And then we both had our own things. He wanting to train racehorses. Me with Atalanta's.'

'But didn't George put up the money for that?'

'Yes.' Nicola sniffed. 'But he wasn't interested. He wouldn't come to anything, bring any of his friends. And when I needed just a little bit extra help, he point-blank refused.'

'How's it doing?'

'These things take time. To build. I hoped Amanda would come. Bring in her crowd. It's all a question of image.'

'True. And Amanda's image wouldn't let her near anything healthy. She's like my son.'

Nicola placed her empty glass on the table. 'Anyway, it's very hard work. And Simon understands that. He insisted I took a day off. He even left his car in London to drive me back here, so that I could have a bit of a rest. He's so caring.'

'And how was he going to get home?'

'He was going to take my car on, put it in an outhouse where Amanda wouldn't see it, then come back on Monday and we'd

143

go back to London together. I could always tell George it was having something done to it at the local garage.'

'So why is it still here?'

'Because I got nervous. If George didn't turn up, I'd have been stranded without a car. So he was going to see if there was a bus he could take.'

'Was that when you phoned me?'

'Yes. Yes, it was. I got really frightened when he left.'

'Why not call for a taxi?'

'It's a long way. We'd neither of us got much cash on us, and he didn't want to ask Amanda in case she got suspicious.'

'He must have been away a long time, looking for a bus stop?'

'What do you mean?' She looked up, her eyes moving from side to side in jerky movements.

'Well, I saw him in the wood when I arrived.'

'Oh? Did you? Well, I don't think you can have done. Or maybe? We find it hard to say goodbye sometimes. Perhaps he'd come back because he was worried about me, then saw you and knew I'd be all right.' She was looking down but an indulgent smile lifted the flesh on her cheekbones. 'Poor darling, he doesn't know anything about all this. I'm dying to phone him, only I'd probably get Amanda. Do you think it's too late?'

'Absolutely.' Sukie stood up. 'At the top of the stairs and to the left, you said?'

Sukie had lain awake behind her eyelids for some time before snapping them open to find sun hot and bright as midday staring through the window, and birds swinging past with such a clatter of calls it seemed impossible she had slept till now. But it was still only seven o'clock.

She washed at the basin and dressed in crumpled clothes. The scratches on her legs and arms were now beady and red, and they hurt. Just as well, perhaps, that the bath had never happened. Downstairs all was silent, and the sun only peeped around corners. She went into the kitchen to make herself some coffee, then, while the kettle boiled, went to the front door.

'Good morning. Can I get you a cup of something?'

PC Spencer was watching a sparrow bathing in a puddle. 'Oh, thank you very much. I'd like a coffee, please. Milk and two sugars.'

When she returned with the two mugs Sukie said, 'I hope it's all right, I'm off back to London quite soon. My son finishes school at lunchtime and I have to be there to pick him up.'

His hand, as it curled round the handle, was pink and smooth, and he leant forward so as not to spill coffee on his uniform. He looked up. 'I've got no instructions to detain you.'

'No. But I'm a bit concerned for my friend. She may not wake up for a while, but I don't think she should be alone.'

'Is there someone else you can think of? Someone who could come?'

'Well, she has a sister, I believe, called Lisa. In Stevenage. You might find her in the address book beside the phone.'

'Right. I'll give her a call.' He bent over his coffee again.

'Thanks so much. Gosh, we rather put it back last night. I'm still feeling the effects. Would it be all right if I took a bit of a walk? Clear my head before I drive back.'

He stood to attention. 'I think that would be a very good idea.'

Having washed up the mugs, together with glasses and the cup and saucer from last night, Sukie took her bag to the car and locked it inside, then she left the path and entered the wood. Already it was so hot that the dappling was balm to her scratched skin. She stepped carefully amongst the undergrowth, occasionally looking up to the net of branches, to stop at the spot where Simon had changed direction and plunged away towards the main road. Then she continued, as he might have done, round to the back of the house.

The kitchen window was blind as it had been at night and

dusty grass wavered from cracks. Just beyond, on the other side of the building beneath overhanging trees, was the garage with Nicola's car parked beside it.

Keeping close to the wall, Sukie passed the kitchen, a dining-room, and round a blank unwindowed side to peer round the corner into the front yard. There was no sign of PC Spencer. Hopefully, he was occupied with the address book. She darted back to the grass and studied the tracks on the earth leading to the garage and the ground behind Nicola's car, looking from one to the other several times to be sure she had not made a mistake. But there was no mistake. Quite distinct in the shallow surface mud leading right to the garage doors were the double tracks of car tyres. Behind Nicola's car there were no tracks at all.

Nicola had arrived with Simon before the rainstorm when the ground was dust dry. The rain would have obliterated any flurry of marks her car might have made. But a car had certainly used the garage since the rain. And, as there was only one set of tracks and the garage was empty, it must have been parked before the storm and afterwards been driven away. In which case, Nicola must know about it and had chosen to say nothing.

Slowly she walked back towards the yard where the double tracks faded to nothing beyond the umbrella of trees. Looking up she saw that PC Spencer had taken up duty outside the front door. She gave him a little wave and continued on to the farm gate, unhooking the iron hoop to let herself into the field.

She wandered on a wide curve, into the centre of the field and then back, out of sight, on to the path that led to the barn. It was still wet and she could clearly see the marks of her own espadrilles, going in each direction, from last night. There were no other prints at all. The police here had evidently been careful, had walked over the grass. Unless his murderer had been careful and George too had walked across the grass, he had certainly died before the storm.

She looked up at the barn, now homely in the morning sun,

except where the bright police tape sealed its approach. She had no desire to approach it. She went back to the gate, then towards her car, waving again to the constable as she passed.

'Take care, now,' he called after her. 'Take it nice and steady now.'

Steadily, peering over the bonnet, along the drive Sukie watched the ground where, as it cambered into a made-up stretch, she saw some prints of mud that looked very like those at the garage. She could even make them out as she reached the exit, and then on the road where they swerved right. She turned and followed them until soon they faded into the tarmac amongst the confusion of lanes. At that point she wheeled into a seven-point turn and, discarding PC Spencer's advice, gave the accelerator some toe and headed home.

# Chapter Nineteen

'I knew you wouldn't mind.' Alexis was stuffing clothes into a sports bag. 'You always say I spend too much time in the smoke.'

'I probably mean the DIY kind. So Paton's parents will return you to school tomorrow night?'

'Correct.' He heaved the bag on to his shoulder. 'We intend to play croquet. You always say I should take up more gentlemanly pursuits.'

'I do?'

'You don't mind, do you?'

'Of course not. You'll need a tie.'

'What for?'

'For dinner. You'll need a tie at dinner. Unless they dress?'

'What?' He dragged one from his cupboard. 'We'll probably get our own dinner.'

'Nonsense. Does that one go with your shirt?'

'I don't know. I expect so. It doesn't matter.'

'I think that it does.'

'You live in the past, Mosie.' He put the bag down and took hold of her shoulders. 'You live life as how you want it to be, not how it is. You try to do it for me too.'

'I'm sorry.'

'That's all right.'

'Does it annoy you?'

'No, it just makes me uncomfortable.' He let her go and went over to the window to look down into the street.

'I'm sorry.'

'It's all right. You're such a snob, Mosie, that's your problem.' He leant against the frame, arms folded. 'I really find it amusing. I mean, look at you, crumpled old skirt, dirty canvas shoes and scratches all over your legs. You've got no money, no education to speak of – what have you got to be snobbish *about*?'

'Perhaps all I have got is my snobbery?'

'You've got me.'

'Ahhh.' She folded her arms in parody. 'Yes, and you'll piss off some day soon, and then where will I be?'

'My point exactly. I wish you had somebody, Mosie. I'd like you to have somebody.'

'So would I, actually.' She began to smooth out his counter-pane. 'And you know I have tried, once or twice, but they all seem to peter out.'

'Freudian slip?'

'What? Oh, very probably. Listen, there's the doorbell. You must go. 'Bye, darling.' She hustled him out of the room.

''Bye, Mosie.' He hadn't yet managed to get his bag on to his shoulder. He kissed her and was gone.

In the sitting-room the french windows were open but nothing stirred. Down in the square she heard a car drive away. She crossed to the cabinet and stood with a bottle of vodka in her hand but didn't take out a glass. She put the bottle away, switched on the television, kicked off her shoes and opened the *Sporting Life*.

One by one the races flashed past, all seven of them as she flicked between channels. Sun shone on the screen, blanking out part of the picture, but Sukie did not have the will to get up and draw a curtain. And in the blank space, between the parallels of jockeys' silks, a figure even brighter seemed to swing, distorted and dusty, as amongst motes in a barn.

She awoke to a low ray drilling into her eye. Football was on the screen, and the telephone was ringing.

'Fancy coming to Windsor tonight? I could go through the card.'

'What?' Sukie ran a hand through her hair.

'I thought you might like to come to Windsor. I'm off in the helicopter now.'

'You're better, then?'

'What? Oh, yeah, fine. Just a stomach bug. I'll even take you out to dinner after.' Henry Whippet's voice was so cheerful.

'I don't know.' She felt shivery and sick.

'You don't have to come, of course. I just thought it might buck you up.'

'What do you mean?'

'Well, you must have had a bit of a shock.'

'What are you talking about?'

'Graham-Jones. I'm talking about George Graham-Jones. Well, you found him last night, didn't you?'

'How do you know about it?'

'Small world, racing. So, are you coming or not?'

The air in the flat was difficult to breathe. The sliding sun had an oily gleam. Everything looked just a little grubby.

'I'm coming.'

'Well done, doll. By the way, how d'you know I was ill yesterday?'

'Small world, racing.'

'You're learning.'

'It was on the television, of course.'

'Yeah, missed three rides and all. Going to make it up tonight, though. See you in the members' bar after. OK?'

'I hate Windsor,' Sukie said and put the phone down.

'I meant it, I really do hate Windsor. This has to be the tackiest place.'

'Nice view from the stands, though.'

'Unless you actually want to see any horses.'

150

'Sun on the river, very pretty.'

'Especially when it hits you smack in the eye so that even when you get to the winner's enclosure you can't see what's won.'

'Those willows are nice and all. Romantic trees, willows.'

'I'd still settle for seeing the odd horse.' Grudgingly Sukie sipped her champagne. 'Everywhere smells like a burger bar.'

'Surprised you know what one of those smells like.'

'I have two children, in case you've forgotten.'

'I never forget anything.'

'Do you know, I believe that.' She sat rather too close to Henry Whippet on a high stool, but kept one foot on the ground.

'So, four winners. Not bad, even at Windsor.'

'You said you might go through the card.'

'Ah, well. Did you back me?'

'I concluded you'd have to ride a stinker to lose on any of them.'

'Even Up Town Girl?'

'Well . . . That one is known to be moody.'

'She's not moody. She doesn't like to be crowded, that's all. Now I've twigged it . . .'

'Where do you intend us to eat?' She tipped up her glass and emptied it.

'Hungry, are you?' He refilled it from the bottle. His mineral water had hardly been touched.

'A bit.' She took another sip.

'Not far from here. Somewhere we can sit outside. You'll have to give me a lift. We can't take the helicopter.'

He was so relaxed in linen trousers and a blue cotton shirt.

'You look remarkably brown.' It sounded like an accusation.

'Very wholesome, the outdoor life.'

His throat, where the button was open, looked young and vulnerable.

'That's what I tell my son.'

'Yeah, well, I was sallow as a ferret at his age. Let's go, then.'
He put down his half-full glass and stood up. 'Do you like
ferrets?'

'What?'

'Ferrets. Do you like them?'

'I like most small animals.'

'That's good.' He was on his way to the door.

Sukie tipped back the rest of her drink and went after him.
'Alex isn't sallow.'


It was a pub by the Thames: charming but not self-conscious,
with flinty walls and roses everywhere. They left the Renault in
the car park at the side and entered through the metal-studded
door. It was cool and dark with only the glow of bottles and
brasses to pinpoint its dimensions.

'We'll eat outside, Bill,' Henry Whippet called to the barman.
'Just taking her round the shed. All right?'

'Right.' Bill raised a hand.

'Come on.' Henry Whippet took Sukie's arm. 'You said you
liked small animals.'

The smell in the shed was strong. At the end of a gangway
between empty crates were several cages.

'Here we are. This one's called Sid. He knows me.' He undid
the catch, put his hand in and withdrew what looked like the
type of fur little old ladies used to wear round their necks. It even
still had the head on. 'There we are, Sid. Isn't he nice. Nice little
fellow. Want to stroke him?'

The ferret was pale cream with very dark eyes and teeth like a
tenon-saw. He slithered in and out between Henry Whippet's
fingers, whiskers aquiver. Sukie put out a hand to touch him.
His fur was soft yet resilient, his body muscular as a snake's. And
through his movements the fingers continuously wove, so sure
and delicate they might have been skeining silk. Very beautiful
fingers, slender and brown, the nails clipped and shining.

152

'He's my favourite.' Henry Whippet put the creature back and peered into the other cages. 'He knows me.' He jerked his head back towards the bar. 'They all do. I often come here when I'm round this way. I like it here.'

'You have all your regular little haunts.'

'You could say that.' He fastened the door of the shed. 'My name opens most doors. But I'm choosy about the buttons I press. They'll bring us some champagne and mineral water, unless you'd like a cocktail. Bill does good cocktails. In a proper shaker, not all whizzed up in a blender.'

They were walking along a brick path between beds of red and yellow roses. Before them a bright green lawn ended in a slope down to the river.

'Is Henry Whippet your real name?'

'That, doll, is something I tell to nobody, not even you.' He pulled back a chair for her at a wooden table.

'So, what's in a name? Not that you smell of roses. I don't believe that it is.'

'Don't you? Oh, well, you're welcome to your opinion.' He swung round to look up at the waitress who had brought the drinks and come to take their order. The menu was small, the girl helpful. It didn't take long.

When she had gone, Sukie spread her arms in front of her on the table's surface, clasping her hands together, and turned to watch the swans paddling by.

'So, do you want to talk about it?'

He had spoken out of silence and it took her a moment to comprehend what he meant.

'No. I'm not sure that I do. I don't really want to think about it at all.'

'No, well, that's my philosophy: forget what's past and move on. But I don't think it's yours, somehow.'

'Yes, well you don't keep coming across bodies.'

'True.'

'One can get a reputation. Soon no one'll invite me round in case I find them dead.'

'Oh, I'd always invite you. I'd say you're worth the risk.'

'Thanks, but you hardly count. Will dinner be long?'

'All in good time. Don't be so greedy. Drink up your champagne.'

'I haven't eaten all day!'

'So? Neither have I.'

Sukie crossed her legs and was just about to turn away when their chicken liver salads arrived. She grasped the pepper mill and ground with vigour.

'I'm not trying to upset you. I'm trying to cheer you up.' He waited patiently for the mill, which she plonked in the middle of the table. 'It must have been really nasty for you.' He gave it a couple of delicate turns. 'I think you're being very brave.'

'No, I'm not.' She bent over her salad, alarmed that she might cry. 'I'm dreading another inquest. Resent it, really. He was nothing to me.'

'He'd hanged himself?'

She nodded, then, 'Well, he was hang*ing*. Whether he did it himself or not . . .'

Henry Whippet had stopped eating. 'You don't think that he did?'

She stuffed a whole leaf into her mouth. 'He was wearing the most extraordinary clothes. All different colours. No co-ordination.'

'Well he always did that.'

'He even had a hat on. With a feather in it.'

'Crikey. It hadn't fallen off?'

'No. That's odd, isn't it?' She began rubbing one of her arms.

'In a barn. That's where you got all them scratches.'

'The straw. I had to clamber.' She put down her knife and fork, frowning at the remaining lettuce.

'You think it was murder.'

She continued to stare at the lettuce. 'The police do.'

'Who, then? Who do you think would have wanted to?'

'I don't know.' Swans, boats, glided by. Mist rose on the river. 'They're nothing to do with me, these deaths. I just keep finding them, that's all.' The river was beautiful, mauve air above it, fading down to white, to grey. 'Nicola behaved oddly. And then there were the car tracks.'

'What car tracks?'

'Oh, I don't know,' she let out a long sigh. 'I don't know. I really don't.'

'You're drunk.'

'Probably.'

'What about the car tracks?'

Sukie told him about the tracks, those from the garage, the lack of them behind Nicola's car. The mist on the river was now weaving amongst the reeds, like the ferret had woven between his fingers. Or had it been the other way round? And the calls of birds were drawing down the borders of the sky. She leant back in her chair, smoothing out her short white dress. 'Like you said, it's all in the past.'

'Yeah.' He had lit a cigar. Its smoke coiled towards the water's edge.

'All the dead men.'

'You're thinking of your husband.'

'Am I?'

'Peter.'

She lifted her head.

'Small world, racing.'

'Have you always known?'

'I used to keep his cuttings when I was a kid. I knew who you were.'

'I see.' She drew back from the fish pie as it appeared before her.

He smiled up at the waitress. 'Now that looks tasty.'

'Hope it's as good as last time, Henry,' the girl said over her shoulder.

'I'll let you know when I've tried it,' he called back.

The fish pie was tasty. Even so, he only ate half of his. The rest he cut neatly away and left at the side of his plate.

'Who told you about George?' Sukie asked when she had finally finished. 'About me finding him?'

'Can't remember now. I was riding work at Royston this morning. Heard it up there. So. Neither of us eats pudding. We'll have our coffee, then I'd better drive you home.'

'I suppose I should offer you a drink.' Sukie threw her bag down on the sofa, slipped off the light jacket she wore over her sleeveless dress, and opened the french windows.

'That'd be nice. I'll have a mineral water. With a slice of lemon.'

'You won't join me in a vodka?'

'Is that a good idea?'

'It's up to you.'

'You've already put back a pint or more of champagne.'

'So? I wasn't driving.' She tossed ice into his glass and proceeded to hack at a lemon.

'Careful. Here, let me do it. You'll cut yourself.' He took the knife and the fruit, paring with precision, floating frail slices on to both their drinks.

Sukie took hers and drifted out to the balcony to lean on the wrought-iron bay, looking out over the night. The air was so heavy. She could feel sweat at the back of her neck, inside her elbows. There was a glorious scent in the square. It seemed to bear her up, the scent of the lime. 'Thank you,' she said.

'You shouldn't have been left alone.' He put a hand to the side of her face.

'I'm not frightened.' She continued to look out over the square.

'A pretty woman like you, on a Saturday night.'

156

'Saturday nights are for teenagers.' She tossed her head.

His hand stayed. 'Smooth and healthy.'

'Thanks.' She turned round to look at him, swaying a little. 'But I really am not frightened.'

The hand moved round to the back of Sukie's head, steadying her, drawing her towards him. And there on the balcony Henry Whippet kissed her. He smelt like Alex, of fresh air, his breath clean as an apple. When his tongue flicked between her teeth, the shock, the pleasure were discomposing. His hand sliding down her hair, her neck, a gentle pressure so that she did not wish to get away. Brandy warmth spreading between her legs. He seemed to be waiting. Then he drew back. Still keeping contact, fingertips on her shoulders.

'You said you wasn't frightened.'

'I'm not.' Sukie could feel herself shaking.

'No need to be. I'm not going to ill-treat you. Unless that's what you want?' He tilted his head, eyes calculating. 'Not even then.'

'I don't know what you're talking about.' Sukie tried not to look at him. But his eyes were so beautiful, so dark in his face, so luminous against the night.

'I'm talking about sex. You know that. I reckon you'd like it.' One hand was feeling the bare bones at her throat; it slid lower to cup one breast, looking at it, looking back at her.

'Are you going to fuck me, Henry Whippet?'

'If that's what you want.'

'I think that it is.'

He gave a light sigh. 'You are, you know.'

'What?'

The other hand had also slipped from her shoulder. He was looking at both her breasts, bending to kiss them through the white crepe. 'Ever so pretty. Prettier than when you was young, I reckon.'

'*That* can't possibly be true.' The fabric had become transparent where he had kissed, her nipples showing through.

157

'Want to bet?' He lifted a strand of hair from her forehead. His eyes were dreamy. 'I'd reckon you'd have been a bit soft then. A bit blurred round the edges. Now, you look really sharp, I'd say. Do you know your nose turns over, ever so slightly, at the tip?'

'No. I don't know anything about it.' She squinted away at the stars, the moon flying high, a balloon pulling on a string.

''Course you do. Little beak at the mirror. It's ever so classy. I like that. I like classy women.' His eyes were treacle bright again, his hand pressing her abdomen down to the mount of bone, pointing the way.

'Think you can buy into it, do you?'

'I don't pay to ride in the Oaks. People queue up to pay me.' He took her drink from her. 'You don't need that.' He led her back into the room, through the hall . . .

'But there's mould in my bedroom.'

'That's easy to shift.'


It wasn't difficult. Not difficult at all. Even in the light. Within the lantern of her room, sliding through positions with the sleight of a single form. Henry Whippet was keen and confident. He enjoyed himself, delicate fingers weaving in and out, his tongue, his body stroking away the barriers of skin. His cock was silk on her lips, fruit-textured between them. His sweat had the scent of grass about it. And 'You just feel so *nice*,' Sukie said, licking his shoulder. 'You make me feel so good. So good inside. So really *nice*.'

And yet it was disturbing.

Disturbing, the force of the body of a boy. Not a boy, of course. But Henry Whippet has a sheen familiar as the flash of a mirror. The mirror of a son. Disturbing. A body that takes possession then slips through the fingers to be gone before morning. Sukie watched him kiss her breast. 'I have never been with a really young man before.'

158

'Not even when you was young?'

'No.'

He propped himself on his elbows and looked down at her. ''Bout time, then.'

'You're very firm, Henry Whippet.'

'I get plenty of exercise.'

'Your arms, your legs.'

'Well, they get plenty of exercise and all.'

'Now you're being gross.'

'Not after what we've been doing. You enjoyed yourself, didn't you?'

Sukie shifted underneath him. The freedom of nakedness. 'It was – pleasant.'

'First time you've had a good blow for ages, I'd say.' He ruffled her hair.

'You're just being gross again.'

'Don't you like that? It's my experience you posh women like to talk dirty.'

'I don't think I care to know about your experience.' Sukie reached out an arm to switch off the lamp.

'Here, don't do that. I like to see what I'm doing.'

'Don't you mean, who?'

'Now who's being "gross"? Come on, let's have a look at you.' He rolled on to his side. 'Now I'm not chafing for the off.' He ran a hand down her ribs, over her hip-bone. 'Very smooth, very nice – hey, you're quite firm and all.'

'I'm an "all-weather" type. I have to earn my feed.'

'All that running round London. 'Course you do. I said you looked sharp.' He trailed his lips over her thigh, between . . . 'Reckon it pays off.'

Without thinking, she reached down a hand and stroked his smooth head.

*

159

'Tell me, why do you like me, Henry Whippet?'

'What on earth gave you that idea?'

... What on earth ...?

'I likes cheering people up.'

'Don't you mean, "women"?'

'I have a preference for women.'

'Like the one at Salisbury?'

'Yeah. I did see someone at Salisbury. And your friend, Mrs Wearing, saw me.' He lay on his back.

'And did you cheer her up, the "someone"?' She was leaning over him.

'I hope so. I like to give of my best.'

'I believe you do.'

'You didn't think I was saving myself for you, did you?' Their eyes met in the night. 'You may be a bit special, doll, but I likes variety. Always will. Cor, them midges really had it in for me.'

... Decidedly ungenuine is Henry Whippet.

'Where?'

'On the ankles.' Raising the sheet into a tent as he scratched.

'I meant, where did they launch the attack?'

'By the river, of course.'

'Well, they didn't touch me.' Her own hand moved down her leg, feeling the dotted lines of scabs that the straw had made. 'It must be the way you smell.'

# Chapter Twenty

'This is a surprise. A nice one, but still a surprise.'

'Why?' Sukie followed Amanda through the hall, and down a narrow stone-flagged corridor.

'Well, it's Sunday.'

'And this is the kitchen.'

'Yes. Cosy, isn't it? But where's Alexis?'

'Gone to a friend's for the weekend. What are you doing in here?'

Amanda sat on a carpet-seated chair, swung her legs up on to the table and lit a cigarette.

'I discovered it. After Jerry died. It's my security blanket.'

'What about Maria?'

'I've made Sunday her day off. We don't have roasts any more. It suits us both very well. Take a pew.'

Sukie stepped out of her loafers and sat with her feet under her on a cushioned pew against the wall. The weather map had completely changed. Even a polo-neck sweater with jeans and socks did not keep out the chill. Rain had fallen in the night. Lying awake, she had heard it slashing against windows, running down gutters and drainpipes, while Henry Whippet slept silently on. And when, like dirty water, light had begun to seep through the curtains, he had opened his eyes, bright as brittle, and begun to get dressed: 'Riding second lot this morning over at Lambourn' – and, calling a taxi, he was gone.

'I'm sorry I phoned so early. I . . . I didn't sleep too well last night.'

How could he – the thought of his slight body – how could he give such a charge? And then again, the thought of what he could do with half a ton of horse-flesh coming up the straight.

'I'm not surprised.'

'What!'

'Well, after finding George.'

'Oh. Yes, that. Of course.'

'Why didn't you phone yesterday? You could have come then. Why didn't you?'

'I went to Windsor.'

'You hate Windsor. How was it?'

'Shitty.'

'Serves you right. Have some wine.'

There was already a glass out for her on the table. Sukie leant forward, hugging her knees, and took it as it was filled with a dark red. She had never been in Amanda's kitchen before. It was a huge, perfectly plotted Smallbone affair, with Belfast sink, Aga and pulley hanging with shining pans above their heads. On the floor the two Labradors lay in attitudes of watchful slumber. Outside, still the rain drenched down.

'I think it was murder,' she said.

'Windsor always was.' Amanda blew a flurry of smoke into the thickening air. She did not smile. 'I had a feeling that it might be.'

'Are you linking it with Jerry? Here, let me have one of those.'

Amanda threw her the packet. 'Hard not to.' Then the lighter. 'Though harder still to see how they're connected.'

'Nicola thinks it was murder too.'

'Well, she would.'

'Guilt. I suppose so.'

'No, not bloody guilt. The bloody insurance. Sukie, you are so persistently naive. She wouldn't get a penny if it was suicide.'

'Of course.' Sukie rested her head on her knees and put the cigarette to her lips, parting them with it, feeling the opening.

'I'm getting a bumper payout for Jerry. Surely you got something when Peter died?'

'Oh, yes. I don't know how I'd have managed otherwise.' She drew in a sharp taste of smoke. 'But Nicola must be all right, surely?'

'Why? What makes you so sure that George was sound?'

Sukie squinted up at her. 'Do you know otherwise?'

'I've seen it too many times.'

'Well, they always looked pretty spanking to me.'

'Mmm. More owing to their *arrivisme* than their soundness, I would suggest.'

'Maybe. But from the angle of one who's decidedly unsound . . .'

'Nonsense. You have class. And that has nothing to do with money.'

'Yes, middle. And money does have nothing to do with me. Their house is strange. It's not like the house of a successful married couple. Not just that it's unfinished, but . . . unwelcoming, shabby. She says he was mean.'

'I've heard that.' Amanda was pouring more wine into her glass, very slowly, holding the bottle at arm's length. 'What were you doing at Windsor? Here, "little top-up"?'

'No. Wine lowers my resistance.'

'You should drink more of it, then.'

'I don't think so. No. Absolutely not. Oh, God, I've got to tell someone, I've done the most ghastly thing.'

'Like what?' Amanda lowered the bottle to the table, uncharacteristic concern shadowing her face.

'I slept with Henry Whippet.'

'What?' The relief was explosive. 'Christ, how hilarious. Was he good?'

'It was the wine. And George's body.'

'Sukie, never explain, never apologize. Everyone's slept with Henry Whippet.'

'You?'

'No, not *me* . . . but one hears.'

'I feel totally humiliated.'

'Why? It's been over a year since you parted company with William. I admit I had been thinking more in terms of Bob for you, but now you've got your nerve back with Henry Whippet . . .'

'Nerve! Do you know, he even talked about Peter. How he'd admired him since he was a boy. I feel I've been star-fucked!'

'Really?' Amanda's glance drooped to her hand over the ashtray. 'You must have failed to notice all the jockeys' groupies these days. Most people would feel it was the other way round.'

'You always were a bitch, Amanda. Where's Simon, by the way?'

'Oh. Popped over to see Nicola. Took her some flowers yesterday. He's being unusually kind.'

Sukie finished her wine and reached for the bottle.

Amanda was watching her. 'What is it?'

'What?' Sukie opened her eyes wide.

'What is it? There's obviously something up.'

'Of course there's something up. There's lots of things *up*. Dear God, death, murder and bestiality amongst them.'

'It's something about Simon, isn't it? You haven't changed since school. Neither of us has. I've always been a bitch. And you . . .'

'What?' Sukie's eyes, unblinking, were level with the rim of her glass.

'You always got back at me. Found the soft spot.'

'Clever, wasn't I. You kept it well hidden.'

'Why should Nicola feel guilty where George was concerned? Was she having an affair?'

Sukie didn't reply. She dipped her mouth to her wine, hair falling forward.

'And the affair was with Simon?'

164

Sukie lifted her head. She licked her lips and sniffed.

Amanda had taken the bottle back. She swung her feet from the table and stood up. 'Did George know?'

'I don't believe so.' Sukie watched her cross the kitchen to a wine rack, take out another bottle, bring it to the table.

'And now she's free. Well, well, well.' She cut round the foil with a knife. 'Thank you for telling me. It was the act of a friend.'

'You reckon?'

'Not done with the best of motives, but what the hell? Do you remember the fun we had when I told you that chap you were madly in love with was going to be a priest? And you gazed into space and muttered my brother's name and then, a little later, that of a certain "uncle"?'

'I remember.'

'I'm still grateful when I think about it. We never really change, do we?' She twirled the corkscrew down into the cork.

Sukie concentrated on it. 'I didn't think George would be next. Not George.'

'Perhaps you suspected *him* of something?'

'Perhaps I did. No, we don't change. But then, has either of us tried?'


'At last. I've been trying your flat all day.' Nicola stood at her front door, holding on to the lintel, frowning as though the sun were in her eyes.

'I haven't been there. I've been lunching with Amanda. You were sort of on my way home, so I thought I'd see how you were.'

'Let's go into the kitchen.' Nicola stepped aside. 'Lisa's gone to get some fish and chips.'

'Your sister?'

'There's never any food in the house.' She sounded perplexed.

They stood with their cups and saucers, leaning on the rather

165

high units, the scant natural light only reaching the tops of their heads.

'They've found some letters. The police.' Nicola held her cup near to her mouth but did not drink. 'They were in his study. At the back of a drawer. They'd slipped underneath.'

'What kind of letters?'

'Blackmail. They think he was being blackmailed.'

'Have you any idea why?'

'No.' She took a sip of tea, eyes blank.

'You said George had seemed worried.'

There was a pause as Nicola finished swallowing. 'He was always making excuses not to pay for things. This, for instance.' She put down her unfinished tea to fling out an arm at the kitchen. 'Bare bloody wood. They were supposed to be hand-painting it. It's been here a year. And the garden. What garden? George was mean.'

'Perhaps he was short of money?'

'He always had enough for things he considered important. Club subscriptions. Trips abroad. Golf. Horses. Men's things.' Nicola turned on the tap and squirted washing-up liquid into the bowl. 'Men were what counted with George. Desperate to be one of the boys. Would have done anything for Jerry, anything Jerry said. Even married me to up his status. Got it wrong there.'

'Why do you say that?'

'Oh, come on. Jerry was a snob. So is Amanda.' She pulled on rubber gloves and held out a hand for Sukie's cup and saucer. 'Think I wasn't aware of the snide remarks at Ascot?'

'Am I included in this?'

Nicola began to scour the inside of Sukie's cup with a brush.

'OK. So why did you want to see me? Why did you want to tell me about the blackmail?'

'I . . .' Her hands floated for a moment in the foamy water, 'I wondered if it might be suicide after all?'

166

Sukie looked beyond her to where a crow had just flown past the window.

'Well?' Nicola's hands flapped, splashing foam over the sides of the bowl.

'I was just wondering. Why you should think that?'

'Blackmail. The blackmail, of course.'

'Ah. Of course. So, how did he get here?'

'You what?'

'How did George get here? To do it? His car was not here, if you recall. So someone must have brought him. His murderer, one had supposed.'

'Well, no.' Nicola turned from the sink. 'He could have hidden it somewhere.'

'Where?'

'I don't know. Left it in a lay-by or something?'

She turned back to the sink and tipped the water from the bowl so that the cups and saucers rattled against the stainless steel. 'Shit.' She began to pick them out. A handle had come off one of the cups.

'But Nicola, I saw tracks in the mud coming from the garage which meant that a car must have been driven out of there after the rainstorm. And as you were here at that time you must have heard it.'

Nicola licked her lips. 'I don't know what you're trying to say.' She was attempting to fit the handle back on the cup. 'There were tyre tracks all over the place. The police probably made them.'

'They didn't make those. And if I saw them, you can be damn certain the police saw them too, took photographs, so you'd better get your explanation sorted before they decide to ask questions.'

A loud ring at the doorbell made them both start.

'Oh.' Relief showed in Nicola's face. 'That'll be Lisa.'

167

Sukie followed her into the hall where a strong-framed girl in a dark dress stepped inside, shaking wet hair.

'God, it's still pissing out there. Hullo.' She smiled at Sukie. 'Have a chip,' she started to undo the packet. 'I should have brought more.'

'Don't worry, I'm not staying. Thanks, anyway. 'Bye, Nicola.' And she dodged through the puddles to her car.

The rain, the darkness and the Sunday returning traffic made the journey wearisome. The shade of a hangover didn't help. Lunch at Amanda's had consisted of two bottles of wine and a bowl of salad with cashew nuts. They had sat there picking out the nuts, leaving the soggy lettuce to be thrown away.

The square was liquorice black and devoid of parking spaces, everyone being prudently home for the start of another week. Sukie parked in a side street and walked diagonally across to her flat, passing close to the central garden. And there, for a moment, she paused. Was that a figure pressed to the railings?

She continued to walk, stepping out into the road, looking over her shoulder. Was that a movement, there, under the tree? A leaf falling? Water running from a branch? Sukie walked on slowly towards the steps.

Once inside the main hall she heard herself let out a sigh. With the relief of tiredness, she climbed the stairs, pressing light switches as she went, hearing them click off behind her.

In her own little hall, a pathway from the moon slanted from the sitting-room, peaceful, ordered as she had left it, the clock ticking. She looked into Jemima's room, empty, and Alex's with school clothes scattering the floor. And there again, in the kitchen, moonlight fingered comfortable objects: the bowl of fruit, the coffee machine, the edge of the table, the shivering plants beyond the pane.

The force of rain had splashed earth from around the herbs. Sukie lifted the sash and began to press them down again. It was then that she heard the sound. It came from the bathroom. A tapping sound. No, much louder. She reached the door. The room rattled. It howled as she entered the eye of a storm. And there was the window, swinging wide, banging against the brick outside, filling the room with wind and rain. Quickly she went across and shut it. There was instant calm.

Her bedroom no longer smelt of mould. It was robust with the scent of wood and leaves. The covers of the bed were pulled back as she had left them, mattress swiped of Henry Whippet's imprint.

Sukie tore the pillowcases from the pillows, the sheets from the blankets and punched them straight into the washing machine. Then she slammed down the sash on the herbs. Only the answerphone requiring attention, then fresh warm bed linen and sleep.

Following the moon-path, stretching out her hands to the darkness Sukie went into the sitting-room. There was Nicola's message, three in fact. Then one from Jemima: 'Where the hell are you? Either of you? It's Sunday, for Christ's sake! And I've just finished my exams, and I'll be home in a couple of days.'

Sukie stopped the machine. She had quite forgotten the exams. Had sent no card. And suppose Jemima had arrived home on Saturday night?

There were a couple of beeps with no message, and then, relaxed and from another world: 'Sukie, Scotland was wet. Luckily I had some very hairy tweeds. Call me. You have a date with a horse.' Bob didn't give his name.

The final message threw her into total panic. '. . . Belinda here, just checking you're on board with the two hundred canapés for tomorrow. I know you're very reliable, but you're never in! Just checking. Hope you don't mind.'

Mind! The fresh warm bed would have to wait. She shut her eyes for a moment to gather strength, concentration, anything. It was when she opened them again that she saw it.

It was where the moon-path was lifted by the angle of the chaise-longue, velvet seat frosted with light. Her address book, open, and placed quite carefully, where she had not left it.

Sukie crossed the carpet and looked down. It had been pressed out wide to show the letter 'W'. And there, typed on a label and stuck on to the page, was the address and phone number of the White Tie Escort Agency.

# Chapter Twenty-One

The canapés were a good thing. All two hundred of them. Leaving the address book to dematerialize upon the sofa, Sukie worked through the night, making what she could from ingredients to hand. At five o'clock sleep came easily.

At eight-thirty next morning, a quick reassurance call to Belinda, a dash to the shops, there to gather up packets of bread, bacon, smoked salmon, watercress, soft cheeses; the sitting-room a no-go area, a thought that might just go away. No mere displacement activities, the spearing of bacon round chicken livers, the cutting into coils of smoked salmon, herb cheese, brown bread. These were the means of living. And then she was off to the City, stepping over the post on the mat, slamming the door on the phone's ring.

When she returned, they were still waiting. She picked up the post from the floor and took it into the sitting-room under the green eye of the answering-machine. While the address book, at its smart casual angle, the pages lifting spontaneously from the spine, remained as though she had left it there herself.

Still in her mac, still holding the post, Sukie looked down at it, as she had done last night. Someone had put it there. Someone had entered her flat while she had been in Suffolk, disturbing nothing, had stuck that label in and left. How? And why? As some sort of warning?

She looked at it a little longer, unable to decide to touch it, to study the label closer, try to remove it with her fingernail, or just shut the book and put it back on her desk as though it would then become of no consequence. She turned away.

There was only one message on the answerphone. 'Hullo. This is Anne Marriot speaking. We have had some difficulty in contacting you, due to a confusion over names and telephone numbers, but I believe at last we have got it right. We also have someone who we think might fit with your requirements and have given him this number. His name is Tony. He is very discreet. Please contact me, personally, if you have any problems whatsoever.'

Sukie sat back on her heels, the post sliding to the floor. She played the message again, and then switched the machine off. She shut her eyes, sore from lack of sleep. Then she opened them, stood up, went to her desk, found a card, returned to the telephone and dialled.

'Hullo. This is Mr Teichgraeber's office, Margot Mainwaring speaking. May I help you?'

'Oh. Yes. Mr Teichgraeber, please. My name is Sukie Buckley.'

'I'm afraid he's in a meeting at the moment. Can I take a message?'

'Oh, yes. Thank you. Nothing complicated. Could you just tell him I'd love to see the horse run at Sandown on Friday evening and that I'll be in the Cavalry Bar five minutes before the first race unless I hear to the contrary.'

'Right. I think I've got that. Sandown, Friday, Cavalry Bar five minutes before first race. Miss? Mrs?'

'Mrs Buckley. Thank you. Oh, thank you too for sending those lovely flowers to my friend.'

'What flowers were those?'

'To Miss Officer? I believe you are clients of hers. A week or so ago. She was mugged.'

'Oh, yes, I remember. Well, those flowers were from Mr Teichgraeber. He is really the one you should thank.'

'But you actually sent them.'

A little laugh, 'Oh, no. They were from Mr Teichgraeber. I'm sorry, you must excuse me, there's a call on the other line.'

Sukie dropped the receiver on to its cradle and began to rip into the post. Intruding between a secretary and her man was like lighting up between the fish and the meat. But Sandown, at least, was on.

More bills. A couple of cheques, long awaited, to the state of her bank account virtually obsolete. A card from Rosamund, dashed off yesterday on hearing of George's death, sympathizing with Sukie for 'always being in the wrong place at the wrong time', as though she were somehow the subject of her discoveries rather than the predicate.

But now, as when she had looked at that other vellum-coloured card, which Rosamund had written to Nicola, something caught her attention. The date. Something odd. And suddenly she knew what it was.

The drawer of her desk was still open. The training bill lay there, turned over so that the number of the White Tie Escort Agency showed uppermost. Sukie took it out, still holding Rosamund's card, looking from one to the other. A game of pelmanism. They matched. The figures for that telephone number and the date had both been formed by the same hand. The person who had written the White Tie contact number for Jerry had, of course, been Rosamund.

'Mosie, now that I've broken up, how about moseying on down to the old Star of India tonight?'

'Can't. I have a date with a horse.'

'You put a horse before your son?'

'And daughter. It was ever thus.' Sukie looked into the glass and ran a hand back through her hair.

'Why are you pouting?'

'I wasn't pouting. Do you think it will rain?'

'You always pout in the mirror. So why do you have a date with him?'

'Her. Because I know the owner.'

'So your date is with the owner. Who is he?'

'Why do you presume the masculine?'

'Because I know that little simper.'

'I never simper! It doesn't look like rain.' She went over to the window and peered up. 'Does it?'

'Who is he?'

'Bob Teichgraeber.'

'The mild-mannered American. So you'd put a date with an American before your son?'

'And daughter. Before a jog down to the old Star of India, yes. And, by the way, it's changed. It's the new Star of India now. You won't like it at all.'

WELCOME TO SANDOWN PARK said the notice above the rhododendron walk, and beneath the two-faced clock. One face inclined towards the Cavalry Bar where Sukie settled herself to wait for Bob. The other inclined to the paddock where Henry Whippet would, at this moment, be waiting to ride in the first race.

Despite the mellow evening air, a paddock full of horses, and stretch of soft turf, the room was convivial with people who preferred fumes, television and loud carpet. Sukie bought herself a vodka tonic and opened her *Sporting Life* to study Atlantic Drift's race. Thankfully, Henry Whippet had been booked to ride something else.

'Mind if I join you?' Sylvia Irvine pulled out a chair opposite and flopped into it. She had the figure of a schoolgirl in old chinos and blue Aertex shirt but her face was mapped out for an old woman's.

'No, of course not.' Sukie closed her *Sporting Life*. 'Good to see you.'

174

'Don't let me interrupt.' Sylvia took a slug of what appeared to be whisky and stared into space.

'It's OK. I'm waiting for someone.'

'I'm just about flat to the boards. We were at Nottingham this afternoon. Three seconds. And Marcus was on them all – win only. I've left him in the owners' and trainers' bar. Ghastly about George, hey? And you found him.'

Sukie smoothed out the skirt of her linen dress. 'Yes.'

'Sorry, I expect everyone says that.'

'Yes.'

They looked at each other, smiled, and began to laugh.

Sylvia swallowed the rest of her drink. 'What a complete toss the whole thing is.'

'Gambling?' Sukie tendered. 'Racing? Life?'

'Life just about covers it. Or, as in George's case, death.' Sylvia yawned and began to scratch her head. 'Who are you meeting, anyway?'

'One of your owners. In the third race. Bob Teichgraeber.'

'Oh, of course, Atlantic Drift. She should run all right. Been working well at home.'

'Worth a bet?'

'Nothing's worth a bet. At school with my brothers, George. Can't remember his face, but very small, he was. Hard to believe. And a total creep even then, always running round after Jerry. I expect I could pick him out in an old photo. I don't think I'll bother. Is it true he was dressed in those extraordinary clothes?'

Sukie nodded. 'Like he'd raided the dressing-up box.'

'Fine feathers never did make George into a fine bird.' Sylvia began to pick at an egg stain on her shirt. 'Funny how some people never learn how to dress, whereas others ... Look at Henry Whippet.' She looked straight at Sukie. 'Look at Bob Teichgraeber.'

'You're most welcome.'

'Oh.' She glanced up. 'We were just saying how well you

175

dress.' She licked her fingers and began dabbing at the puckered place on her front.

'Well, thank you.' He smiled at each of them in turn.

Sukie crossed her legs and shook the *Sporting Life*. 'I've been working out form.'

'Yes, I'm sorry, I'm late. I'll just get myself a chair.' He frowned about the bar, as though the noise made it difficult for him to see.

'Don't bother.' Sylvia gave her chest a final pat. 'I'm off.' She stood up. 'Oh, by the way, thanks to a non-runner we've now got Henry Whippet up. Thought you'd like to know.'

Bob watched her go then took the back of her chair, pulled it a little way further from the table and sat down. 'Hell of a hold-up on the M25. I suppose you're used to it, to allowing the extra time?'

'I have a special route. Through Bushy Park and round the back.'

'I wish you'd told me.' Again he wore grey flannel, with a yellow silk tie. He should have looked relaxed, but seemed irritable. 'Roadworks. They're really bad here.'

'There are always problems on the M25.'

'No, I don't just mean that. I mean all over. Even your little roads.'


. . . but he was an American.


'Well, that's because they *are* little. Less space.'

'No, like the other day. Where was I? I can't remember. Anyway, I was really going to be late. Like now. And everything had to go all round the country. It was ridiculous.'

'They have to do them in the summer.'

'Yeah, but it was inconvenient. Where was I? Yeah, on my way back from Scotland, I'd been to see Atlantic Drift and was trying to call in on Nicola – God, isn't this awful about George? And Sukie, so awful for you. I'm sorry. I don't know if owning a horse is good for me. I'm losing all sense of proportion.'

176

Sukie shook her head. 'It's all right. The police have been questioning me on and off all week. Very cathartic.'

'And Nicola, is she OK? I gave up in the end. Gosh, I'm being edgy.' He put out a hand and touched her knee. 'Sorry.'

'You've caught the English idiom, that's all. The new strain.'

'What?' He spoke sharply but left his hand where it was.

'Weather, as a medium to express unease, is now on the wane. Roads, routes and traffic jams seem to be extra virulent. As we become more urban, perhaps?' She looked up at a television screen, sipping her drink.

He watched her, watching the screen; removed his hand. 'Edgy about my horse, I guess. I say, would you mind awfully if we ducked the first race? I could do with a drink.'

Sukie smiled and sprang to her feet. 'What can I get you?'

'Jim Beam, if they have it.' He relaxed back in his chair. 'Thanks,' he called after her. 'That's very nice.'

Atlantic Drift was a lovely filly, a little weak still, but beautifully proportioned with a fine intelligent head. Marcus, arms folded, watched her from the middle of the paddock.

'She looks OK.' Bob stood beside him.

'Yeah.' Marcus didn't turn. 'Still quite a bit to work on.' The filly was now being led towards them. He put his hand on her neck. 'Still rather have this than a piece of Triumvirate?'

'Sure. I have no regrets.'

'Mr Teichgraeber.' Henry Whippet came up behind them, his hand outstretched.

Bob shook it then looked to include Sukie, who was facing the wrong way.

'Mrs Buckley,' Henry Whippet said, obliging her to turn, to extend her fingers to him.

As he took the tips, Sukie felt for a breath he might raise them to his lips, but he merely nodded and let them fall, before approaching the horse.

177

'Of course,' Bob was still talking to Marcus, 'it might all have been different if I'd known Jerry a bit first.'

'Jerry was all right.' Marcus was tightening the girth. 'Knew him at Eton. Knew him pretty well.'

'How come? You look a good bit younger.' Atlantic Drift was tossing her head up and down at the increased pressure of the girth. 'Were you his fag or something?'

'That's right.' Marcus went round to check the noseband. 'He was always fair to me. There you are.' He took Henry Whippet's boot and gave him a lift into the saddle. 'You know how to ride her. Just let her settle, not too far off the pace, and let her work her way through if she can. Don't give her a hard race.'

'But I'll let her win if she looks like it.'

'Of course.' Marcus backed away. 'Of course. That's what you're bloody there for.'

But Henry Whippet had wheeled the filly about and his only answer was her swaying backside.


'She did run so well. She really did. How many times have I said that?'

'I lost count with the drinks.'

'Fourth. I find that most promising, for some reason.'

'Isn't it because of the jockey?'

'Why?' Bob, his arm along Sukie's shoulders, paused to look down at her.

'Never known to get a place when fourth will do.'

'Really? In that case, even more promising. I get the feeling you don't care for Henry Whippet.'

'I don't know him.'

'Then perhaps his reputation?'

'Either to like or dislike. God, this feels like an ocean liner.'

They were lurching along an upper corridor in a London hotel after a very good dinner. Shaded lamps glowed from cream panelling, carpet pile so deep Sukie's heels kept catching in it.

'The *Titanic*, perhaps?'

She halted. 'Is that a joke in bad taste?'

Bob also stopped. 'I'm not sure.'

Sukie started walking again, slower. 'I've never really known, you see. People always joke about the *Titanic*. But when was that OK? I mean, does something happening a long time ago make it fair game now?'

'That depends.'

'On what? Will we one day joke about the Holocaust?'

'I hope not. But that's different, surely?'

'Why? But then, perhaps you're Jewish? Your name could be Jewish.'

'No. Did you have relatives on the *Titanic*?'

'No.'

'Well then?'

'My son says we ought to be able to joke about everything.'

'Your son is fifteen.'

'That is true. Almost.' She bumped into a table of flowers.

'And you can't walk straight.'

'That is also true. Neither can you.'

'That's because we're on a ship.' He fiddled with some keys and opened a door. 'The stateroom.'

'What a gorgeous bed!' Sukie shook her head as though there were water in her ears. 'I shouldn't have said that. I know I shouldn't have said that.'

'Why not? I'm glad you like it.' He took off his jacket and put it around the back of a chair.

'Neither should I be acting coy.' She also took off her jacket, kicked off her shoes. 'It's spectacularly unbecoming at my age.'

'Or at any.' He came round behind her. 'I like your arms. That flat little piece over bone behind the shoulder, I like that. Put your shoes back on.'

Unhurriedly Sukie slipped on her shoes. 'Better?'

'Better. I like shoes.'

Sukie watched her feet progress across the carpet to the open window, where she leant on a rail and looked out at the bright lights. 'Do you live here?'

'For the time being. Why aren't you wearing those nice high ones with the ankle-straps?'

'At the races?'

'Too much to ask. I am looking for a home.' He was pressed up against her, not touching her with his hands. 'Some place of my own. Where I can be comfortable. Inside. Each night.'

She did not feel him undo the zip of her dress, only felt the gap as it opened. Backdrop of night as she turned. Exposure as he moved away.

He had gone to sit in a chair, long legs stretched forward, head tilted back, his forehead high and weary.

They watched each other.

'Take it off,' he said.

It was a narrow dress, shell-pink linen with a silk lining. Still watching him, Sukie bent to touch its hem, to lift it, just a little, to see him smile. Stealthily watching she drew it upwards, folding it in on itself until it reached her face, a cross-your-heart yashmak. His lips parted. And still they eyed each other, in hope perhaps, as she drew it higher, to halt, lids dropped against the plunge of blindness, arms sheathed in panic, while he observed from his chair.

She heard him sigh, the creak of wood as he got to his feet, but no sound as he crossed the carpet. Only felt hands round her waist defining its structure, moving up the scale of her ribs to release her underwear, the arousal of helplessness. And so he carried her and laid her down, arms bound stiff above her head. And she felt the slithering counterpane under her warm skin, the soft flannel of his trousers, then the smell of fresh cotton, the rasp of a tie, the click of his spectacles as he placed them on a hard surface, a zip. But her eyes, folded in linen, saw nothing of what he did.

180

# Chapter Twenty-Two

No longer would the bedroom smell of mould. Roofers had attended to the leak and decorators were about to move in. Time for Sukie to move out, a cue to talk turkey, to earn money for paint and paper. Having changed into tailored trousers and heraldic silk shirt, brunched on boiled egg and soldiers, she was ready to engage with the phone. In spite of it being Saturday, by a quarter to one she had organized work to take her through the next two weeks and, when she left the flat for the King's Road, Alexis and Jemima still had not stirred.

The paper she chose was not sprigged. It was white lining paper which she planned to have painted a muted orchid mauve. It would probably mean changing curtains as well. The rolls bounced together in their bag on the back seat of the car.

Jemima and Alex sat with their feet up in the sitting-room, arms wide with newspapers, the television on unwatched.

'Have a good night?' Jemima turned a page.

'I've been shopping. It's four o'clock in the afternoon.'

'How was the horse?' Alex had picked up the remote control and was flicking through channels.

'The horse was fine. Very pretty. Pretty fast. How about the Star of India?'

'Brilliant.'

'Well, of course.'

'No, I mean it. Wasn't it, Puddles?'

'What? Oh, yes. Brilliant.'

'But I went there a couple of months ago and it was all pink tablecloths and carnations . . .'

'And beautiful young waiters.' Jemima hugged her knees and looked up at the television. 'Can't be bad. Oh, that reminds me, Henry Whippet phoned.'

'I don't see the connection.' Sukie dropped the bag of wallpaper on to the floor.

'And the food's much better.' Alex put down the remote control and jumped up. 'What have you got there, Mosie?'

'Wallpaper. But what about the family who used to own it? I hate the idea of them just being taken over.'

'Best thing that could have happened for them. They'd been wanting to go back to India for ages, get their daughters married there. Hey, this is plain white. You are branching out.' He picked up a roll and handed it to Jemima.

'But they were so friendly. I thought they were settled here.'

'Apparently not.' He went to stand on the balcony, stretching out his arms so that light through the sleeves of his shirt made them look like wings. 'Why is it no one else is allowed to change, Mosie? You, yes. Everyone else, no.'

'I haven't changed.'

Alexis and Jemima exchanged a look.

'I haven't.' She bent down to pick up the bag. 'Anyone else phone?'

'Amanda.' Jemima handed her the other roll. 'The decorators – they're coming Monday, so they say. Oh, and some strange chap called Tony. Something about a white tie?'

Sukie sat on the bed in her room. She had opened one of the rolls of wallpaper and held it up with the colour chart. The paper still looked white and all the varied rectangles of mauve looked black. It wasn't easy to get an effect. Jemima and Alex had both gone out. Optimism was slipping away.

'You shouldn't have been left alone' – the words of Henry

Whippet – 'a pretty woman like you on a Saturday night.' And then Tony from the White Tie rang again.

'Good evening. I'm Tony.'

'Sukie.'

'What a lovely name.'

'Come in.'

Tony was gorgeous: the sheen on his skin, the gloss on his hair, his dark, dark eyes.

'Can I get you a drink?'

'Will I be driving?'

'No. We won't take a car.'

'Then, thank you, I'll have a gin and tonic.'

He stood in the centre of the room facing towards the balcony. 'This is a wonderful flat you have.' He looked carefully about him. 'Such lovely furniture, the real thing.'

'It was my husband's before we were married.' She handed him his glass.

'Your husband . . . ?'

'I'm a widow. Cheers.'

'Cheers. Of course. I'm sorry.'

'So am I.'

They drank together.

'Yes, it is a lovely flat. Perhaps that's why I don't get out of it as much as I should.'

'Hence . . . ? It's not always easy for a woman alone.'

'Not always for a man either?'

He didn't reply, kept the light smile about his lips, glancing at the room.

'Why do you do this?'

'I . . . I enjoy it. I like to please people.'

'Women?'

'I like to please people.' His tone was firm. 'And I have to support myself. London's not cheap.'

'You don't sound as if you come from London. There's something in your voice – American, is it? Intonation rather than accent.'

'Yes, well, I lived in San Francisco for a couple of years. Clever. Actually I come from Woking.'

Sukie smiled at his beautiful eyes. 'What about the girls?'

The eyes widened. 'Sorry?'

'The girls that work for the agency?'

'Oh. What about them?'

'Do they also like to please *people*? Or men in particular?'

'I don't quite understand the question.' He put his unfinished drink down on a low table. 'You said we weren't taking a car. Where are we going?'

'Just a small place, down the road. Unpretentious.'

'Good.' He looked uncomfortable without his glass, took a step towards the balcony.

'Go on, go out there. Have a look at the square. Everyone does.'

She continued to drink while he stood with his hands on the rail. When she had finished she put her glass down beside his, and picked up her bag. 'When you're ready?'

'Shall I lock these doors?'

She moved towards the hall. 'Yes.' Stood, half in the corridor outside the flat, hearing them come together, the key turn, wondering why the thought had not occurred to her before. Tony, the beautiful young man now moving through her flat, was the same young man she had seen laughing with Rosamund in the mews.

'Why did you engage me?'

They sat in a corner, at an angle to each other, so that they could both watch the other diners. The restaurant was small, only about half a dozen tables inside, three on the pavement. Sun slanted across the wooden floor, catching Sukie's hands where they were folded on the check cloth.

'Curiosity.'

Tony had leant into the light as he spoke, the bone of his short nose translucent. Now he drew back. 'I see.'

'I believe you escort a friend of mine.'

'So?'

'This friend was attacked.'

His expression did not change.

'She was attacked one night after she'd been out with you.'

'Rosamund. You're talking about Rosamund.'

'I mean, what sort of agency is this?'

'It's an escort agency. Long established, respected. Started by Anne Marriot's father. We provide a service for people. We look after them.' One of his hands gripped the stem of his glass, the other fiddled with the tines of his fork.

'Well, why weren't you looking after Rosamund?'

'I'd already left.'

'You didn't go in? For a nightcap, or whatever they call it these days?'

'No. I need a clear head in the morning. I'm a student. A mature student. I do this because I don't get much of a grant.'

'Sounds like you weren't prepared to do what you were hired for.'

'Oh, really? Is that why you hired me?'

This time it was she who drew back. 'No.' Back pressed against the bars of her chair. 'I hired you because two people have been killed.'

He started as though she had spat in his face. 'That can't be true.'

'Why?'

'Well, I . . .'

'Pepper?' A waitress stood between them with Caesar salads. She lowered them to the cloth and picked up the mill.

'Thank you.' Tony watched the pepper fall, wrinkling his nose. He sneezed. When the girl had gone he looked after her. 'I don't understand. What do you mean about people being killed?'

'Two people. Well, one was killed. The other died in strange circumstances. Friends of Rosamund's. Part-owners with her of a horse.'

'Triumvirate. She told me about him. She didn't tell me about the other owners being killed.'

'Odd.'

'No.' He picked up his fork. 'Not really. We only talk about the good things. That's the deal. We have fun. It works.'

'But she told you about the attack?'

He shook his head while he finished chewing a leaf. 'The police came to see me. I was already home when it happened. The guy I share with was out when I got back but he came in soon after. Rosamund went to put out some rubbish, I gather.'

Sukie pressed lettuce against the sides of the bowl, replicating its form, gathered croutons into a little pile at the centre. 'It is certain that she actually was attacked?'

He was eating with energy now. 'I'd left my camera at her place that night. I called in for it the next morning and saw the bruises.'

'Camera?'

'Yes.' He said it patiently. 'I took some pictures of the birds in her garden. She's very keen on them. As a friend, you would know that.' He speared three croutons. 'Although, I must say she's never mentioned you. And, of course, you don't believe me.'

'I'm not sure.'

'Well', he added a wad of leaves and packed the lot into his mouth, 'tough! As for the agency, it's all above board. A perfectly normal agency. I'd hardly work for any shady set-up intending, as I do, to be a solicitor. But, of course, why should you believe that either?'

*

'Amanda's been on again,' Jemima hailed Sukie as soon as she opened the front door.

'Oh, no, I can't call her now.' Sukie kicked off her shoes and went into the sitting-room.

'You weren't long.'

'I never intended to be.' The remains of the sun filtered through the leaves of the tree. Jemima was on the sofa, her face taking on the glow of a shaded lamp. Sukie had seen the light from the street and presumed it would be Alexis. There was a book open face down, quiet Vivaldi in the background. 'I'm sorry if I disturbed you.'

'I was just doing a bit of work. It was pleasant.'

'Not going out?'

'I came back. Want a coffee?' She was already upon her feet.

'That would be lovely.' Sukie turned the music up a little, calling, 'Thank you,' out to the kitchen and 'You're very kind,' when Jemima brought the mugs.

'I'd like to be.'

'I don't think I've always appreciated you enough.'

'I haven't always made it easy.'

'That's not your job. Where's Alex?'

'Out with friends. Pretending they're eighteen. I'll wait up and let him in.'

'You don't have to worry about him.'

'I'm not. The stupid little tosser's lost his keys.'

'When?'

The phone began to ring.

'That'll be Amanda again. She sounded pretty frantic.'

'When did he lose them?'

'I don't know. Neither does he, I shouldn't imagine. Hurry up.'

'I'll take it in the bedroom. That means new locks on the door.'

'You really think . . . ?'

'I do!'

It was Amanda. And she *was* frantic.

'Sukie? Thank God. I don't know what to do. I was out with the dogs this evening, you know, just pottering round the garden, the outside edges where it doesn't matter where they crap, when I noticed that one of the old outhouses wasn't shut properly. I went to take a look, because I don't like them left open, in case of vagrants or whatever. And, you'll never believe what I found?'

'What? What did you find?'

There was a pause, a gasp, before Amanda said, 'George's Mercedes. I found George's car. Inside. Sukie, what am I going to do?'

'You should tell the police.'

'Oh, God, I know what I *should* do. It's what I *do* do, I'm asking about. And *you're* not to tell them. Promise. I mean, the implications. I just can't get a grip.'

'Don't touch it.'

'I haven't. Should I get a padlock?'

'No. Leave it. For the time being. I'll get back to you, but don't tell anyone else. No one at all.'

'I suppose you are including Simon?' The panic had gone from her voice. Her tone was businesslike.

'Of course.'

# Chapter Twenty-Three

Nicola's mules clacked down the spiral staircase from her office. 'Let's go into the juice bar.'

She was still beautifully turned out, honeyed waves of hair, clear brown skin, but she seemed to be carrying a little too much condition. Her haunches in their cyclamen casings dimpled as she moved.

'What'll you have? The peach and lime is favourite.'

Sukie smiled. 'Then I'll follow the money.'

'One PAL and one spa water, Emma.' She pulled out a chair and sat down. 'I haven't got long.'

'Neither have I.' Sukie sat opposite. The place was empty, quiet except for wall to wall MOR music.

'Well?' Nicola did not acknowledge the girl as she put the drinks down. 'You said you had something to tell me. Something I should know.'

'Yes. George's Mercedes has been found.'

She was busy fishing out a slice of lemon. 'Where?' She dropped it back into the water again where it pitched and fizzed.

'Where do you think?'

'I don't know. How should I know? If I knew why should I need you to tell me?'

'Perhaps so you can get your story right this time?'

'What story? I told you too much as it was.'

'And maybe not enough? It won't surprise you, I'm sure, that it was Amanda who came across the car. In an outhouse, at the edge of her garden.'

Nicola said nothing. She was sucking the lemon.

'Because it was either you or Simon that drove it there.'

'It was Simon.' Her eyes were watery above the stripped rind. 'He was protecting me. Then it all just escalated. When you came up with George's body. It made things so much more unpleasant.'

'Especially for George.' Sukie drew in a long squirt of peach and lime.

'You know what I mean.'

'No I don't.' She spat the straw away from where it had stuck to her lip. 'No, I don't, actually. So perhaps you'll tell me before I give Amanda the go-ahead to call the police.'

'All right.' Nicola dropped the lemon rind into the glass and pushed it away from her. 'As I said, Simon thought I should have some time off, so he met me on Friday morning, just after I'd started work, and insisted he drive me home. We took my car and left his in London. There wasn't any sign of George when we arrived, and we weren't expecting him yet anyway.'

'You checked?'

Nicola lowered her eyelids. 'Around the house. So, anyway, Simon stayed. If George did turn up, we could just say I'd not been feeling well or something and that Simon had driven me home.'

'George didn't know about you and Simon?'

'No. Absolutely not. I'm sure he didn't know. Anyway, he never arrived. We waited. One thing led to another . . .'

'You went to bed?'

'Not to *bed*.' She looked shocked. 'On the carpet. And so we never heard the car . . . We heard something a bit later, but that can't have been it.'

'What did you hear?'

'Well . . . afterwards, you know . . . we did feel a bit uncomfortable.'

'Well, you would. I hear carpet burn can be horrid.'

190

'That's *not* what I meant.'

'What did you mean?' Sukie also pushed her glass away.

'I *meant* that we did actually wonder if George could have arrived *during*, so to speak. So Simon suggested he take a look around. He didn't come back for ages.' She turned her head away as fear changed the shape of her eyes. 'When he did come back, he said that George's Merc was in the garage but there was no sign of George.' A tear dropped on to her hand. 'You can imagine what I thought?'

'No.'

'I thought he'd been there, watching us. All the time. I thought he might have killed himself.'

'A bit drastic.' Sukie reached for her straw and whipped it round the empty glass.

'I don't see why. Anyway, I told Simon to go and have another look.'

'Was that when you phoned me?' Sukie sucked at the base of the straw, making a crackling noise.

'Yes. I was in such a state. I really did feel I was being watched.'

'But you thought George had killed himself?'

'I told you. It was a *feeling*. So, when Simon came back, I told him *you'd* called me, that you were dropping in on your way to see Amanda. I really wasn't thinking very clearly.'

'Or even at all.'

'If George had done something stupid I didn't want it linked to my relationship with Simon. If he was just playing some horrible trick, then serve him right. I suggested to Simon that he took George's car.'

'Why?'

'It was raining. He always left the keys in it, so I suggested Simon drive it back to Tancred House and hide it there until George turned up. It was raining really hard. Simon didn't want to go and look for a bus; he made a dash for the car before it could get worse. It never occurred to either of us George'd been murdered.' Her last word was a whisper.

. . . Simon is in his place.

Sukie said, 'But he came back? Why did Simon come back? I saw him in the wood.'

Nicola looked up. 'He was worried about me, I expect.'

'So, what is Amanda to do about the car?'

'You won't tell the police?'

'Of course not. I'm leaving that to you.' Sukie put down three pound coins beside her empty glass and left the juice bar.

Continuing north, through South Kensington, and into the Cromwell Road, Sukie knew where she was going, and yet it wasn't a decision that was driving her. After completing her itinerary of viewing luxury flats through the eyes of luxury clients, the prospect of derelict carpet over the bath rim was too much of a shock to the culture. She needed a gradual letting down. So, parking in the same spot as before, she walked down the slope to the mews.

In the intervening weeks, the window-boxes had burgeoned. Twigs of helechrysum splayed over the ledges, and geraniums lifted shell petals to their reflections in the panes.

The rest of the scene then slipped into *déjà vu*. There was a sound within the cottage that caused Sukie to dart behind the conifer in a tub. The front door opened and Rosamund emerged laughing into a large white handkerchief with which she was mopping up her nose. She wore a silk kimono and velvet slippers, and behind her again came the ravishing young man, also laughing.

But this time Tony did not hand her into her car. It was she who leant over to see him into a small black Fiat, then backed on to her doorstep and, still laughing, waved him out of the mews. The front door shut. Sukie waited. She heard the car drive two parts about the square, turn off, then mingle with distant traffic. And this time she stepped from her hiding place, approached the cottage and rang the bell.

There were sounds of water and heavy feet coming downstairs. The door was opened. 'Well hullo.' Rosamund's voice indicated extravagant pleasure. Her eyes did not.

'May I come in?'

Rosamund was wiping her hairline with a towel.

'But, of course.' She pressed herself back against the wall. 'If you don't mind catching my cold.'

She led the way through a narrow door into a room that ran the depth of the house, the rear wall with wide sliding glass doors that were open on to a leafy paved garden. There were scents of jasmine, honeysuckle and damp earth.

'Plenty of fresh air, that's what I need. What can I do for you?' Rosamund continued to rub at her face.

'It's about this.' Sukie took the training bill from her bag and held it out with the telephone number uppermost.

Rosamund dropped the towel on the floor and took the bill. She turned it over. 'Oh, that.' She handed it back, dismissing both it and Sukie. 'I knew it was only a matter of time before that came up.'

'You were expecting it?' Sukie continued to hold out the bill for Rosamund to acknowledge the number.

But Rosamund was looking behind her for the sofa. 'Well, as I dumped it on Jerry just before he died . . .' She flopped down. 'Obviously nothing's been done about it.'

'Why did you give it to Jerry?'

'Because it hadn't been paid, of course.' Rosamund put her feet up. 'George hadn't paid it. Surely you knew that?'

'Yes, yes, of course.' Sukie looked away at the garden. There was a wire bird-feeder hanging from an apple branch. A great tit swung on it, his feathers glistening in a ray of sun. 'So you handed it on to Jerry?'

'Well, I thought he should deal with it. George was his friend. Sylvia just made out a duplicate and shoved it at *me*. Probably too frightened of Jerry.'

'Most people were. Sad, really.' Sukie went to look out through the open doors. There was a swish of bamboo and a cluster of birds flew away. 'There's something written on the back of the bill. A telephone number. It's in your writing.'

'Oh? I'm always scribbling things on the backs of things.' Rosamund heaved to her feet and blew her nose loudly. 'Do excuse me, I'm a little fragile.'

'I tried phoning it. It's the number of an escort agency: the White Tie.'

'Good God, of course!' Rosamund took hold of the piece of paper. 'I gave that number to Jerry with the bill.'

'He'd asked you for it?'

'Jerry? No. What is the matter with you? No, no, no. They got an extra number, and this happened to be beside the phone. It was strictly for personal use.'

'I see.' Sukie gave a little cough.

'Do you?' There was a white metal table in the garden with two chairs, one of them pushed askew. 'Of course, you saw him just now.'

'You're a lucky woman. He's very handsome.'

'You like that, do you? You think that's important?' A cynical smile lifted a corner of Rosamund's mouth. 'Yes, Tony is very handsome. And very young.'

'I hope you don't think I'm making assumptions about your life?' Sukie held out her hand for the bill. 'Perhaps I should give this to Amanda.'

'Yes, I think perhaps you should. We all make assumptions, my dear. Sometimes they're even right.'

. . . Rosamund seemed the most comfortable.

'There is something.' Sukie fiddled with the fastening of her bag. 'I'm sure that I'm being followed and, however unconnected, while I was in Suffolk the Sunday before last, someone entered my flat and stuck the details of the White Tie Escort Agency in my address book.'

'Well, well, well,' Rosamund was steering her out of the room, 'what a jolly jape. Why didn't I think of it first?'

# Chapter Twenty-Four

'Quick, quick, quick.' Amanda stood on her doorstep cheering on Sukie's sprint across the glistening gravel.

There was sunlight but no sun. Tancred House appeared the light source, golden, wistaria painted, detached from an indigo sky.

'God, what a moment to choose.' Sukie landed on the step, shaking herself like a dog.

'Careful.' Amanda backed away, frowning at the transparent spots appearing on her silk shirt.

They retreated to the hall to stare out together at the crashing rain as it slicked off bushes and drilled holes in the drive.

'It's been so hot.' Amanda shivered and shut the door. 'This should clear it.'

The drawing-room was part extension, so that a third formed a conservatory, opening on to reconstructed terrace with steps down to the lawn. Water streamed down the roof, the wall of glass. Sukie, pressing her face to it, saw the serpentine beech hedge, the veiled horizon.

'We can't go skulking round outhouses in this.' Amanda watched her over the cigarette she was lighting. 'Want one?' She tossed the packet across. 'Go on.'

'All right.' She just managed to catch the lighter that followed.

'We're supposed to be off to Newmarket this evening. Unlikely, as it seems.'

'We?'

'Oh,' Amanda waved her cigarette, 'Reggie . . .'

'Simon?'

'Simon wants to get back to London. He left his car there, I gather. Been angling for a lift to the station. Ha, picked his element.'

'Have you told him about finding George's car?'

'No.' Amanda pressed her lips together.

'Because I've heard a version of how it came to be there. I'd like to talk to him about it.'

'What do you mean?' Sukie could feel the skin on her skull tighten as Amanda came up behind her. 'What do you mean?' As if she were about to receive a sharp tug on her hair. 'You're not implying' – Amanda, so close she could smell the smoke on her breath, see the pale concealer beneath her eyes – 'that Simon had anything to do with George's death?'

'No.' By maintaining eye contact Sukie managed to give the word its opposite meaning.

'Because, of course, that would mark a complete betrayal of our friendship.'

'I'm sorry. I wasn't aware that friendship depended upon untruths.'

Amanda's eyes were almost closed, her lips again pressed together. Then the eyes snapped open, the mouth laughed. 'Ridiculous nonsense, all this. As if you'd really think anything like that. As if, anyway, I wouldn't know.'

Sukie wandered away across the room, picked up the ashtray from the arm of a chair, put it down again.

'Oh, come on. Why don't you come to Newmarket with us? Bob's coming too.'

'So?'

'So. It should be fun. Where's your sense of humour? Ever since you did the business with Henry Whippet.' Amanda folded her arms and picked at a rain spot on her blouse as if it were likely to become permanent. 'Simon's almost certainly gone by now.'

'Mother, you do talk nonsense.' He stood in the doorway not apparently about to come in. 'You know I can't go without a lift.'

'I thought you might have called a cab.'

'For goodness' sake, I'd have said goodbye.'

'Oh, well,' she flapped her hand, throwing up smoke signals, 'I don't know anything about your arrangements. Sukie wants to speak to you, by the way. She thinks you had something to do with George's death.'

'Oh?' He looked from one to the other, his boy's face puzzled but equable.

'That's not what I said.'

'Anyway, George's Mercedes is still in my outhouse. And how did it get there, I wonder?' She looked straight back at him. 'How? How?'

'I really think I ought to be going.' Simon looked at his watch. 'Is that lift still on?'

'I wasn't aware it ever was.' Amanda lifted her head at the sound of the doorbell, and hurried past him.

'I'll give you a lift.' Sukie stubbed out her cigarette and picked up her bag. 'I'm driving back to London now.'

'Terrific. Thanks, I'll get my things.' He eased out to the hall to let Bob and his mother into the room.

'Where are you going?' Amanda called after him. 'Excuse me.' She turned and they could hear her running up the stairs.

'Well,' Bob took a step towards Sukie, 'how are you?'

'I'm fine. A surprise.'

'No.' He put out a finger and ran it up her bare arm. 'Goosepimples. Are you cold?'

'Not really.' She smoothed the arm, the little bright hairs standing up where he had touched. 'It's just the change in the atmosphere.'

'Oh, it *is* changeable. Gentle, then violent. I hadn't realized

198

that. I've not experienced an English summer before. I tried to call you.'

'Really?'

'You were never in.'

'Never?'

'Well . . .'

'You never left any message.'

'I didn't know what to say.'

'How about your name?'

'Must have slipped my mind. Anyway, here we are.'

The doorbell rang again.

'Oh, God, I shall have to dig out some boots.' Amanda returned, equipped with Reggie.

'Sure thing, my darling. Absolute must in the bar, wellies.'

Behind them, dusty in the hall half-light, Simon's face sought out Sukie.

'OK.' She took the car keys from her bag.

'Have I missed something?' Amanda looked between them.

Simon stood beyond the door-frame, prevented from entering by the bulk of his wax-jacket and baggage.

'I'm giving Simon a lift back to London.'

'But you wanted to see round the garden.' Amanda rallied from Reggie's surprise. 'Sukie, you're coming to Newmarket.'

'No.'

'But you are. We arranged it.'

'No. I was never planning to come. As you see – espadrilles.' And she led Simon out into the shining air.


'She's been acting pretty oddly lately.'

As soon as they were on the motorway Simon had undone his seat-belt and begun to manoeuvre himself out of his Barbour, eyes fixed on the road.

'Who?'

'Mother, of course.' He freed his left arm, jogging the steering wheel with his right, so that the car jerked towards the barrier.

'Careful!'

'Sorry. Frankly, I can't stand being around her at the moment. She suffocates me.' He leant at an angle away from the wheel to extricate the other arm which stuck out as though encased in plaster. 'At the moment.'

'So, where do you want me to drop you?' Sukie pushed the arm out of her vision.

'Froggy's.'

'I thought he lived in Wantage.'

'His stables are at Wantage, but he's got a little bolt in Fulham. Froggy just uses it when he's on the booze, then hits the M4 in the morning.' He shifted his buttocks, pulled the jacket from under him and threw it over the back. 'Lets me use it too. Good old Froggy.'

'Would you mind putting your seat-belt on again now?'

'Got to go into hiding from the women.' He pulled the belt over his shoulder and clipped it shut. 'Women get so complicated. Take Mother. She's always said I should cut my own way, but whenever I do and give her a preview, she starts tweaking at me, like one of her suits.'

'We mothers are all the same. And other women?'

'You know.' He began watching cars through the side window. 'Nicola. Complicated. For me it was just a bit of fun. You know. I thought it was the same for her. Frankly. She was married, for Christ's sake. Shall I tell you the latest?'

'What?' Sukie put on the brakes, resigned to the approaching jam.

'She wants me to "support" her at the funeral. George's funeral. Can you imagine? Her *husband's* funeral. I mean, can you imagine? I shall go with Mother, of course.'

'When is the funeral?'

'Next week. They've just released the body. Will you go?'

'Of course.'

'That's a relief. I gather it might be a bit thin.'

They had stopped and the rain had started again. They sat listening to the rhythm of the wipers. Counting them like moments, before Sukie licked her lips and asked: 'Simon, did either you or Nicola drive over to Tancred House in George's car and put it in the outhouse there?'

He waited for the wipers to complete six further beats. 'What did Nicola say?'

'She said that *you* did.'

'Right. Well.' He folded his arms. 'It was a damned stupid thing to do. But she was in one hell of a panic. And it *was* absolutely slashing. Nicola gets pretty odd. She's like Mother.'

'Amanda misses Jerry.'

'You think? I don't know. I was actually relieved when he died.' He glanced at her before continuing, 'I was shocked, of course. Upset. But relieved nonetheless. Now I really miss him. I'd really like him back. I'm not sure that she would. Odd.'

'She's angry with him. Hard to want someone alive when you want to kill them.'

'I suppose it must have been pretty humiliating for her.'

'Pretty.'

'I haven't really thought about that. More about him. Jerry. What he was like. Not just as a father. We actually had things in common.'

'Like?'

'Well, take women.' Simon tried to heave himself into a relaxed position against the restraint of the belt. 'Jerry wasn't really a one for the women; he was much happier with the boys. I don't mean gay or anything, just more fun, less *complicated*. And I'm like that. All this with Nicola showed me. I can't see Jerry inviting some hooker back to the flat. What d'you think?'

'I think – ' Sukie put the car into third, speeding towards a clearer stretch – 'I think – ' judging the speed of the traffic –

'that he was there with someone he knew.' She released it into fourth. 'Quite well.'

'Who?'

'Oh, someone . . . someone who persuaded him to join in the game.'

'What game?'

'I don't know.' She said it with surprise.

'Well . . .' he shrugged, drawing away from her. 'Well, George had certainly been playing fancy dress. You know something, don't you?'

'I know nothing at all.' The car was doing ninety now, the road hissing away behind them. 'Except that I saw you in the wood at Meadow View shortly before I found his body. And that you saw me.'

Simon folded his arms. 'Did you tell the police?'

'Not yet.'

'So, what was your game, then?'

'Mine?' Sukie's head turned.

'Careful! Nicola had said you were dropping in on your way "to see Amanda", but when I arrived home, Mother knew nothing about it.'

'Ah.' Sukie had relaxed her right foot and they were now doing a steady seventy. 'That does make a sort of sense. I had no plans to see Amanda. I had no plans to see Nicola either. It was she who phoned me. While you were outside, looking around for George.'

He nodded. 'But you can see why I came back. I wanted to know what the hell was going on. I left the car a couple of lanes away and walked. I didn't expect to bump into you. I thought you'd be safely in the house by that time. I'd even thought that if you really were planning to see Mother, you could give me a lift and I could put George's car back in the damn garage.'

'So, you hung around for a while. Until you saw me coming from the barn?'

'The look on your face. I just knew I'd got to get the hell out.'

Sukie sniffed. 'Nicola thinks your return was proof of your concern for her.'

'Are you sure?' Far from appearing uncomfortable, there was the cynicism of youth in his glance.

'So, you're going into business with Froggy?'

'That's the plan. Assistant trainer. If he can get a certain owner to give him some horses. He's working on Henry Whippet to put in a good word.'

'I should hardly have thought that were possible.' Sukie wound down her window and a huge draught of damp air buffeted the inside of the car. 'Let's find out what's happening in the world.' She pressed the switch on the radio.

'Fine.' He settled back and shut his eyes.

'I shall ask you to direct me to Froggy's place when we get near Fulham.'

When they reached Parson's Green he guided her down a narrow street made even narrower by cars parked end to end on either side. There, halfway along, she stopped in the middle of the road to let him out.

'By the way,' he was leaning into the back to pick up his jacket and bag, 'I think I owe you an apology.'

'Oh?'

'The night of the fash bash. I didn't want you to see I was waiting for Nicola, so I hid outside. I think you must have heard me or something, but you went haring off down the road as if I was going to attack you.'

'Oh,' she laughed. 'That. You did make me jump. Was that the only time?'

'How do you mean?'

A car, coming up behind them, hooted.

'Forget it.' She laughed again. 'Just teasing. 'Bye.' And hardly waiting for him to slam the door she set off fast for the end of the road.

Neither Jemima nor Alexis was in when Sukie let herself into the flat with her new set of keys.

It was an unsatisfactory time, no longer day but not yet appropriate to settle down to night. A bluebottle drilled into the window pane. And then the phone rang.

'At last.' Nicola sounded cross. 'Where were you?'

'Out.'

'Listen, something else has happened.' It wasn't crossness; it was fear. 'When I got back here this evening, I found I'd been burgled.'

'What was taken?'

'A whole load of stuff. Mainly from George's study. The police have only just gone. I'm beginning to feel really jittery.'

'There may be no connection at all between this and George's death.'

'Oh, thanks for reminding me. Is Simon with you?'

'No. Should he be?'

'Of course not. I just don't know where he is, that's all. He's been pretty funny with me lately. So have the police.'

'What do you mean, "funny"?' Sukie leant over to the window-catch.

'They asked me for a sample of my hair the other day. Why would they do that?'

'DNA. There could be any number of reasons.'

'That means you don't know. What are you doing?'

'Liberating a bluebottle.'

'You what?'

'So you're not yet sure what was taken?'

'Well, the lap-top, his camera, stuff from the drawers. A few valuables from the rest of the house. There wasn't much, for goodness' sake. Do you really think there is a connection?'

The bluebottle drifted through the window, butting the heavy air, then slowly spiralled skyward until it became too small to see.

'It's hard to make out what.'

'Brilliant. Well, just let me know when you can.' She slammed the receiver down.

As Sukie also replaced the receiver, it was wet under her hand. Dense grey sky encased the square. She had to get out. Walk somewhere. Time to give the Star of India another chance? Takeaway was now standard in the repertoire, she had heard.

Down in the street, leaves shuffled the air about them. Her skirt stirred it about her legs. Walking amongst other people shifted the matrix of images in her mind. She could believe herself free, not composed of memories which informed her there was only one true pattern.

The Star of India indeed revealed itself in a new light. Crowded with diners: the waiters dodged amongst tables with no time to impress. Sukie's brown carrier-bag was quickly filled and she was on her way home. The music still, she recalled, quite beautiful.

When she reached the square there was some light left in the sky but at pavement level all was dark, except for soft patches directly under the lamps. She crossed diagonally as usual, passing close to the railings of the central garden. And then she heard a step behind her. There was no mistake this time. Turning sharply, Sukie swung the bag, but already it was too late. The brown paper hit its target with a tearing sound and immediately became weightless. At the same time she felt an arm across her throat, fingers digging into her biceps, and she was being dragged backwards between broken railings into the wilderness of bushes at the centre of the square.

# Chapter Twenty-Five

Everywhere there was the smell of curry. It spread like a stain through the newly washed air. It was in the moisture rising from the earth, in the fading sap of the leaves into which Sukie's face was pressed. It was in the sweat of the man who held her down with strength rather than weight. The blood in her mouth tasted of it. There was no other smell, no other taste. The only sound was the sound of their struggle, and then, above in the lime, the last night call of a blackbird, the call of danger. Sukie could see nothing at all.

He was sitting astride her, holding her left wrist by which he had pulled her arm behind her back. He was not heavy and yet whenever she moved he would raise himself just a little to bounce down again with such force that all the air was crushed out of her.

Now she was still. No more strength. No more breath. He gave her arm one more jerk up her back but she did not cry out, let the arm go limp in his grip. No more will.

'This'll teach you, you bitch! Messing up people's lives.' It was a whisper close to her ear.

As he leant over she could feel the shift in his weight, no longer bearing down upon her lower ribs, no longer preventing her filling her lungs. In one violent movement she took a deep breath, arched her back and threw him from his seat. And then she was scrambling to get up, clutching at earth, at tree roots, at the bulging bushes that bent and swayed and withdrew their support, running before she was even upright, running head down before she could see, charging at shrubs, not knowing if she was making for the road or just going deeper into the garden.

And, of course, he was behind her.

'Bitch! Bitch!'

The words in her ear again. So close.

The glint of metal, caught by the moon.

Sukie lunged forward, buoyed by a laurel, then crashed through it, scratching her face, her hands.

And he is on top of her once more, hand over her mouth, forcing her head back so far she believes her windpipe will split. But he doesn't speak again. He is very still. Sukie also has become still, and she can feel that he is listening. His attention not fully with her any more, his body twisted away to the sound.

It is the sound of a car. It comes so slowly round the square that it can't be a normal progress, so close to the central garden that it can't be looking for a house number. It draws level with them. She can feel him trembling, sense his eyes widen to the darkness. The car has stopped.

Panic, so violent that it could be mistaken for relief, waves through her. Sweat breaks out in pinpricks all over her body, hot or cold?

Very gently the handbrake is applied, a door opens and is pressed shut. Footsteps. Hands trying the gate, that will not open. Silence. And then words. Hissed, agitated. 'Are you there? For Christ's sake! It's me. I've got the car. Quick.'

For a breath, her assailant looked down at her. Shaking his head. Seeming to study her face. 'You asked for it.' Then he was off. Between the bushes, through the railings and out on to the road. There were the sounds of running feet, doors slamming, the firing of an engine, the squeak of tyres. The car had skidded round the corner of the square and was gone.

Sukie rolled on to her back, looking up through the jigsaw of leaves to a cloud that billowed across the moon. The earth was a bed, down into which she could sink unresistant, while the trees waved their branches, lulling her to sleep with clusters of roosting birds.

And then she was awake. Shocked and sick, and trembling, she heard herself say, 'This is a pretty pointless way to behave.' She didn't know where she was or why she was there, only that she had to escape the terrible smell of curry.

Sukie staggered to her feet, shaking out her skirt, stamping where her espadrilles were full of earth. But nothing could get rid of the smell. Hands extended, clutching at anything she could touch, she made her way to the gap in the railings. And the smell followed. She stood on the narrow paving that edged the garden, contemplating the road that had to be crossed. High on the other side, her flat twinkled its distance.

'Steady on. You look like you've overdone it a bit.'

'What?' She was immediately angry. 'I am not drunk!'

'I didn't say what you'd overdone.' Henry Whippet put a hand under her elbow.

She jerked the arm away, pressing it across her chest. 'What the hell are you doing here?'

'I got fed up with phoning. Don't you ever return your calls?'

'It depends who they're from.' Her fingers felt the bones of her shoulder. Even that hurt.

'So, I came to see you.'

'At this time of night?'

'I was riding at Newmarket this evening. Gave up my early night on the chance of catching you in.'

'Well, now you have.'

'Yeah, and you don't look good. What you been up to?'

'Nothing that concerns you. I'm perfectly fine. Goodnight.' She turned away, missed the kerb and almost fell.

'I'm not going till I've seen you home. You're filthy. You've got blood on your chin, and you pong something awful.'

'I know.'

'And you're right, it's not drink, it's curry. You stink of it. What the hell have you been doing?'

She continued to walk towards the opposite pavement. 'I bought a takeaway.'

'Couldn't you wait till you got it on a plate?'

'I didn't *eat* it. I *hit* someone with it.'

'Why?' He stopped in the middle of the road.

'Because he attacked me, that's why.'

'Who attacked you? When?'

He was following her quickly now.

'Some man. This evening. Some man. Then he got in a car with another man and they drove off. I need to have a bath and wash my hair.'

''Course you do. Curry gets everywhere. I think I smell of it and all. Did you see his face?'

'No.' At the top of the steps she leant against the front door. 'I'm very tired. Goodnight.' Without looking back she went inside.

'And where have you been?' Alex, hands on hips, was instantly out of the sitting-room when she opened the door to the flat.

'Stop looming at me.'

'That's nothing to do with it. Where have you been?'

'Then don't loom. What's the time?'

Without looking at his watch, he said, 'Five past eleven.'

'Gosh. Is it, now?' She tried to slip into the bathroom.

'What have you been doing? You said you'd be in this evening.'

'Did I? Well, I'm here now.'

'You promised you'd watch the football with me, and have a curry. Jesus, you've already had it!'

'No! Darling, I'm so sorry. God, I'm sorry. How could I forget? But you're wrong about the curry. I have not had it. It had me. Let me just have a bath and then I'll explain. Please, please, please, let me have a bath.'

'All right.' He went into the bathroom and turned on the taps.

'I was worried about you.' The smell of bath oil and the sounds of splashing.

'There was no need. Why don't you order some takeaway now? Anything you like – not curry.'

'It's OK.' He came out of the bathroom. 'I was starving so I had something from the freezer.'

'I'm sorry. How was the football?' She sidled past him.

'All right. Except I kept being interrupted by the telephone. Mostly for Jemima.'

'Any for me?' She shut the door, kicked off her espadrilles and began to drop the rest of her clothes over them.

'A couple. Henry Whippet and some woman. An officer, she said she was. What rank I couldn't gather. Said she had something to tell you. Said to call her tomorrow. Where were you, Mosie?' His voice was close to the locked door.

'Oh,' she flapped her hand in the water, 'all so silly. I thought I'd try the Star of India again, after what you'd said. Surprise you. And I was in such a hurry to get back that I had a confrontation with a moped. Curry everywhere.'

There was silence on the other side of the door.

'Alex?'

There was still no reply.

She turned off the taps and listened. From across the hall was the sound of the sitting-room door being shut. She climbed into the bath and slipped down into unresisting water.


Sukie was sure she had flu. It was the only thing, on waking, that could account for the soreness in her mouth, the pain in her throat and the difficulty she had in taking even the shallowest breath. Then she felt the grazes that stiffened her knees and elbows, saw the inky bruises stamped down her arm, smelt the curry – and remembered. Stumbling to the bathroom she found Mrs Tribe contemplating her discarded clothes, looking very tired indeed.

'I'm sorry. I'll deal with those.' She scooped the pile and carried it off to the kitchen, stuffing it into the washing machine with a generous dollop of liquid, all except the espadrilles. Those she put in a plastic carrier-bag, tied the top tightly and dropped into the bin. Now to get to grips with the day.

It looked untrustworthy. Shafts of mist were ranged around the backs of buildings. It loitered on fire escapes, lurked in doorways, kicked its heels over drains.

Sukie felt sticky inside her cotton robe and longed for another bath, but instead opened the window and watered the herbs, pinching off any dead leaves, wishing she could do the same for herself. Then she made two cups of coffee and carried one through for Mrs Tribe.

'And what happened to you?' Mrs Tribe held the cup and saucer high, facing the bookshelves.

'I wasn't looking where I was going last night and came face to face with a moped. I was carrying a bag of curry at the time.'

'Bill said he thought you'd been behaving a bit peculiar lately.' She took tiny sips of coffee. 'I've had to open all the windows.'

There was indeed a movement of air throughout the flat while all outside was still, the lime tree a deserted hulk behind the mist.

'You chose a good day to come. I'm very grateful.'

'Depends how you look at it.' Mrs Tribe's eyes met hers and withdrew.

'I'm going to have a bath now and then I shall go out.'

'Work?'

'Yes.'

'I won't keep you, then.' She handed over her cup.

In the bathroom, lowering herself with difficulty into the water, to feel it pounce on every abrasion, Sukie thought, aggrieved, Nobody believes me. And then, relaxing into the pain, But, of course, I'm not telling the truth.

*

The mist still had not lifted. Outside, in Rosamund's garden, birds darted through it as in a winter scene. From one corner of the frame, leaves dripped from a branch.

Both the doors were slid back and Rosamund wore a sleeveless dress in an unfortunate green. Her arms looked doughy and unhealthy, as did her face on which there was a dappling of sweat.

Sukie sat with a mug of coffee, in apparent relaxation.

Rosamund lit a cigarette then took a china ashtray from the mantelpiece and wandered the room holding it like a plate. 'It's all come as rather a shock, to be frank.' She waited, looking out at the birds. Then she turned back into the room and began to pace it, head down. 'I thought the incident was just random. Some hooligan on the prowl, seeing his chance. I preferred to think it was random.'

'But it wasn't?'

'No.' Rosamund stopped, cigarette halfway to mouth, recollecting something. 'No, it wasn't.' She resumed pacing. 'Aren't you hot in that long-sleeved blouse?'

'No.' Sukie plucked at the blue chambray. 'So the person who attacked you was someone you knew?'

'No. But I did know *of* him.' She was at the window again. The bird-bath was full of fledglings, jump-jets scrapping for space. 'I knew of him, yet had no idea he felt as he did. That's disturbing.'

'Who was it?'

'It makes one wonder. People wandering about with grudges, feelings of powerlessness, hatred. How are we to know?'

'Unless we know the injuries we've done. Their extent.'

'Oh, I know those I've injured. Usually looked them in the eye when I've done it. That's business. But this person felt injured in a way that I couldn't have known.'

'Who?'

'Tony's boyfriend.'

'Ah.' Sukie tried to meet her eyes but Rosamund had turned away.

'Yes, Tony's gay. I never told you that, did I? Didn't seem any of your business. Didn't seem relevant. Only James, apparently, was jealous. Of me. Can you imagine, poor boy? He hated Tony escorting women out in the evenings. He got lonely. So started to follow him.'

'Why did he pick on you – or perhaps you weren't the only one?'

'Oh, I was. Tony was most insistent about that. It was just that Tony saw me so often.'

'When did Tony tell you about this?'

'Last evening. We'd been going to go out and he cancelled. I knew there was something up. He called again this morning to explain that all our little jaunts would have to come to an end.' She looked down into her mug, swilling it round as though it contained whisky. 'I shall miss him.'

'He'd only just found out?'

'Apparently.'

'And you're sure no one else was attacked?'

'Tony would have told me.'

'You think?' A sparrow landed on the carpet just inside the windows. It stared, startled at its surroundings, then flew out again. 'Aren't you surprised he decided to tell you at all?'

'We were friends. He was very . . .' Rosamund passed a hand over her hair, 'careful of me. Very worried, I think, that I would go to the police. But we were friends.' She crossed to the mantelpiece to replace the ashtray, giving it a little shove. 'He said it was important you knew it had nothing to do with Jerry's death.'

'God, will I never be able to extricate myself?' Sukie began to stand up and, caught by the pain in her ribs, halted on a gasp.

'I say, are you all right?'

'I lay in an awkward position last night. Things happen. Someone phones . . .'

'Like me?'

'And I feel I'm getting nearer. I feel I'm getting to know the person, only I can't see their face. One day I'll just recognize them.'

Rosamund laid a hand on her arm. 'Why don't you leave it, my dear?'

'Because I don't think that I can.'

'It's all in the hands of the police, after all. Shall you be going to the funeral on Thursday?'

'Yes. I gather it might be a bit thin.'

'Yes, I'd heard that. I shall certainly be there. Important to make the effort.' With squared shoulders Rosamund escorted her to the door.

When Sukie arrived home, Mrs Tribe had moved on, leaving all serene and smelling of beeswax. The pains in her ribs were getting worse, the place where she had bitten the inside of her cheek, her throat that she had felt would split open. It was as if she really did have flu. She was even shivering. So she took off all her clothes, putting them neatly away, and wrapped herself up in Peter's bathrobe.

Coming out into the sitting-room again she saw that the mist was being rolled up into the sky like a bale of muslin. She made herself a whisky mac and settled down on the sofa with the telephone. Sandwiched amongst the calls to catering friends was one to the White Tie Escort Agency:

'Tony?' Anne Marriot's voice was full of regret. 'Oh, I'm so sorry but he is no longer with us. He asked to be removed from our books this morning. You see, he's a student. Pressure of work, unfortunately.'

It appeared that Rosamund had been telling the truth – or a part of it . . .

# Chapter Twenty-Six

The chapel looked like a supermarket lowered into the middle of farmland, at a place where four paths met. Halfway along two of the paths were circular areas for parking, one fanned with cars, the other with only two vehicles. The rest of the place was deserted to the boundary walls.

As she stepped from the Renault on to asphalt, Sukie felt ill at ease, in spite of a nearly-new Calvin Klein dress. It was a bright day and a lark sang in an innocent sky, but her bare arms attracted a breeze that raised goosepimples. The word made her shiver.

One of the two cars was an elderly green Volvo with a mess of rope, bits of carpet, and Wellington boots in the back. The other was a Jaguar, new, silver grey. Now, against the brick building, she could just see two figures, a woman and a man. They were not together but slowly approached each other as though it could not be avoided.

Sukie had already surmised the probable owner of the Volvo, but Sylvia and Bob were now talking, and she did not care to interrupt. Besides, another car had come in at the gate. Amanda's dark blue BMW with Simon at the wheel.

'Is this it?' Amanda put a hand to her brow as though sighting land. She wore the same veiled hat that had taken her to Jerry's funeral with a distinctively designed suit. Simon was two paces behind her.

Sukie, who was not wearing a hat, took a brush from her bag and gave her hair a few strokes. 'Not the easiest of gatherings.'

'Who's gathering?' Amanda extended an arm and picked a loose hair from Sukie's shoulder. 'Come on, Simon will look after us.'

'Sylvia's here. In the mackintosh.'

'And Bob. Didn't you recognize him?'

'I didn't recognize the car.'

'It's new. Swish, eh? He took us off to Newmarket in it the other evening. Hullo,' she approached them, holding out her hand, 'I hadn't thought to be early.'

'Who's early?' Bob looked at his watch on the way to taking her hand. 'Everyone else must be late. Just as well.' He glanced towards the red roof, not uplifted by the monotonous strums of a guitar. 'Sukie . . .'

'Hullo. Good of you to come.'

'I had heard it might be a bit thin.'

'Sylvia . . .'

At Amanda's arrival, Sylvia had stuffed her hands into her pockets. Now she nodded towards Sukie, clumsily extricating one of them. 'Marcus couldn't make it. There's a stable to run.'

'Here it comes.' Amanda was watching the entrance where the hearse, followed by three cars, had just turned in.

The guitar sounds had stopped. The hearse slid past with one of the cars from which Nicola, her sister Lisa, and a stout older woman with fine ankles got out, pulling at their skirts. Nicola wore a silk top hat: she looked like something from pantomime.

From the direction of the parking circle, Sukie could see Rosamund stumping up, accompanied by, of all people, Tony. She also recognized Zana from Atalanta's, and DS Crowther and DC Isaacs who had taken their statements at Nicola's house. A seventh car turned in at the gate. It was time to go into the chapel.

Nicola, proceeding with her mother and sister towards the front, looked round for Simon but Amanda had him hemmed in at the back. The others, including Sukie, all squashed up together. Just as the service had begun the door behind them banged to and Henry Whippet walked up the aisle. He chose an unoccupied pew in the second row and settled himself down.

The service was short, impersonal and bleak. As she watched the coffin totter away between the curtains Sukie felt inconsolable. Was this all there was for any of them? And when they emerged it was to find bleakness there too. Cloud had rolled in to cover the sun, to muffle the sound of the lark. Looking into Amanda's eyes she was surprised to see tears.

'Well,' Rosamund surveyed the line of cellophane brightness propped against the wall, 'what a lot of trouble people have taken.'

'Not much of a turn-out, is it?' Henry Whippet was also studying the flowers. 'Shame.'

'I didn't expect to see you here.' Sukie gave him a savage glance.

'Didn't you? Oh, well. I believe in observing forms.'

'Quite right,' Rosamund nodded. 'Are you coming back to the house?'

'Got to get off to Newbury. I'm at Wolverhampton tonight. Floodlit. You should come along.' He was looking at Sukie.

'I think not.' She turned to follow Amanda who was already on her way to her car. 'Excuse me.'

'What's eating you, then?' Henry Whippet was at her shoulder.

'Nothing's "eating" me. I just can't fancy the idea of a floodlit Wolverhampton.'

'It's very nice. You can get good curries round there. How are you, anyway? That's a lovely bruise under those pearls.'

Sukie put her hand to her throat. 'I'm fine.'

''Course you are. I wouldn't be so sure about Mrs Graham-Jones.' He had turned to watch her stepping from foot to foot as she spoke with the detectives. 'Things don't look too healthy there. Right. Got to get going. Wouldn't do to get caught breaking the speed limit. 'Bye.' He ducked into his beautiful car and swung slowly towards the exit.

On a table before the sofa in Nicola's cold drawing-room were three white plates. One was piled with sausage rolls, another with mini frankfurters, and on the third were triangular white sandwiches with a line of something pink running through them. Nicola's mother and sister stood about the table, each holding a glass of brown sherry. The curtains were drawn halfway across and no light had been put on.

Sukie received her drink and went to join Amanda and Simon who had remained near the door. She rubbed one of her upper arms, remembering that long night when she and Nicola had sat together here for a comfort neither of them could give.

Lisa picked up a plate and brought it towards them. Amanda backed away. Sukie said, 'No, thank you.' Simon took a frankfurter and the whole string swung off the plate. 'Oh, help!' He quickly returned them.

Lisa giggled and put a hand to her mouth. 'Mum, you forgot to cut them. Mum and I did the food. Save Nicci the trouble. I'll take them out to the kitchen and do it.'

'Actually, we have to be going very soon.' Amanda was arching towards the hall where the sound of voices and the closing of the front door hailed relief.

Sylvia came in followed by Bob. Bob's head was bent as though he were avoiding a low ceiling. Sylvia frowned at the offer of a drink. 'Got a long drive ahead. Got to get up to Uttoxeter. Bring the horses back. Marcus doesn't trust the lad.' She said the last words to Nicola who had just appeared in the hall, hatless now, her white face hovering in the gloom.

'Yes, well we really *do* have to be going.' Amanda took Simon's arm. 'So sorry. About *everything*.' She shrugged. 'I know how you feel.'

'Do you?'

218

Amanda smiled. 'Thank you for entertaining us. I'll be in touch.' And, keeping Simon ahead of her, she was gone.

'Yes, well,' Sylvia fidgeted her feet.

There was a loud ring on the doorbell and Rosamund steamed in. 'So sorry. So sorry to be late. Dropped Tony at the pub. So good of him to drive me, but he didn't think he'd come up. Ah, thanks,' she took the glass from Nicola's mother and tipped back the contents. 'That's better.' Ruffles sprouting from the reveres of her suit fluttered and subsided.

Lisa was quick to offer the plate of sausage rolls. Rosamund took two and went to relax heavily on the sofa, shifting with her the focus of the room. Light slanted from the front window on to her puffy legs. She brightened. 'I suppose you'll be selling the house?'

'What?' It was Nicola's mother.

'Well,' Rosamund made increasing circular gestures with a sausage roll, 'and the horse, are you going to continue to run the horse?'

'Of course she will.' Lisa was on her way to the kitchen with two of the plates. 'Nobody wants anything else, do they?'

'No.' Nicola picked up the other plate. 'No, I shan't. I shan't be running him.'

'Why on earth not?' Her mother put the stopper into the sherry bottle. 'Don't you think you should consider what George would have wanted?'

'No. I don't know what he'd have wanted. I only know that I shall be selling my share because I don't want to be next.'

'What nonsense.' Rosamund swiped crumbs from her skirt.

'I don't see why? First Jerry, then George—'

Rosamund beamed. 'Because if anybody's next it's bound to be me.'

'Oh, come on.' Bob turned away with a twitch of irritation. 'This isn't some game.'

'No.' The word was like a sigh and Sukie found herself looking at him.

'And yes, I shall also be selling the house, because it gives me the willies and frankly, I need the money.' Nicola opened the door with her hip and left it to bang behind her.

Without a word her mother followed and Sylvia made her escape.

Sukie touched Bob's elbow. 'I think I'll be getting back.'

'Do you have any particular plans?'

'No.'

'Ah.'

'Why?'

'Oh, I thought of going over to Newmarket to look at another horse I might buy, a quick lunch in a pub, a long leisurely dinner, then staying over. Does that appeal?'

'Well . . . yes. Yes, it rather does.'

'Right then, better make our excuses. Are they all in the kitchen, do you think?'

'Did you mention lunch?' Rosamund heaved herself to her feet. 'Good idea. I'm game. The pub down the road's charming. I left Tony in the garden.'

'I'll go and find Nicola.' Sukie slipped into the hall. Somewhere a tap dripped. She went down the passageway that led to the kitchen and paused before the closed door. She coughed, gave a little knock and twisted the handle. As she entered Lisa and her mother turned to face her, their expressions blank yet aggressive. 'Sorry to barge in,' Sukie included Nicola at the sink, 'but we thought we ought to be going. I came to say goodbye, and to thank you.'

'That's OK.'

'Yes, well we're off now. Speak to you tomorrow, Nicci.' It was her mother. 'You'll be all right, won't you?' She picked up a large patent handbag.

'You know me, Mum. 'Bye.' She did not move to see them

220

out, but when they had gone her hands began to move in the washing-up water.

'Are you sure you'll be all right?' Sukie took a step towards her.

'Of course.' There was a choking sound. 'Oh, God.'

Sukie put a hand on her shoulder, at which she slumped over the sink, with heavy sobs.

'Nicola, Nicola.' She was uncomfortable with the hand there but didn't think she could take it away. 'Oh, funerals are such horrid things. So public. You feel you have to hold yourself together.'

But Nicola was shaking her head. Her hair hung forward, almost touching the water. 'No, no,' she sounded angry. 'No, it's not that.'

'So?' Sukie felt able to move the hand. 'What is it, then?'

'They don't understand either.' Nicola jerked her head towards the back door. 'And why the hell should they? But the police'll find out. Of course they will.' She turned round suddenly. 'Didn't you see them there? At the cemetery? They were there!'

'I believe that's quite usual.'

'Oh, quite usual. Quite usual, is it?' Nicola put on a nasty little smile, shaking her head as if to a stupid child. 'Yes, and d'you know when it's usual, and why? Because of the blackmail, of course. They're investigating the blackmail.'

'Why do you think George was being blackmailed?'

'How should I know?'

'You were married to him?'

'So why should that mean I know? These things are not up front. Not in your face. They hint. That's all part of it. Get into the person's mind so that they're never sure what's going to come out. Makes it much worse. All their little secrets. It's the fear that makes them bigger. Why should you think that I know?'

'I didn't realize you knew so much.'

A silence stretched between them. Nicola's eyes darkened in her unlined face. Sukie was aware of the window's view of her own, aware of the age difference. But it was Nicola who turned away, back to the sink where she continued sluicing crockery with a brush.

'Why do you think I'm so upset?'

'It's not unusual. When one's husband has died.'

'No. But you know about me and Simon.' Nicola gave a little sigh that ended in a hiccup. 'I'm upset for several reasons.' She sounded sullen. 'I am sorry he's dead. And for the way it happened. But that doesn't mean I want him back living with me. Once I met Simon I knew I couldn't put up with it much longer.'

'Nicola, you wrote those letters, didn't you?'

Nicola's mouth opened, her eyes widened; the angle of her face, caught in the half-light, was like a newspaper photo just after the shot has been fired.

'I hope I'm not intruding.' Rosamund leant into the doorway.

'Ha, on private grief?' Nicola began to laugh.

'Well,' Rosamund actually looked uneasy, 'I hadn't thought to say that. I was thinking, more prosaically, of lunch.'

'Oh, yes, well,' Nicola continued to laugh, whisking a tea-towel from the rail and beginning to dry a plate. 'Lunch. Now that is important.'

Rosamund looked at Sukie. 'I believe that Bob is hungry. A man needs lunch.'

'Just give us a moment.'

'No, no, I wouldn't hear of it.' Nicola came up behind them with the tea-towel. 'Off you go.' She drove them down the corridor. 'I understand you're desperate for food,' she called to Bob loitering in the hall and flung open the curtained door. 'So good of you to come. George would really have appreciated it.'

Sukie turned on the step, an apology out of reach of words. But Nicola took her hesitation for a question; she looked down at her, wringing the tea-towel with whitened fingers.

'Yes,' she hissed. 'Yes, yes, yes.'

As Sukie walked across the yard to her car, she looked back. Nicola was still in the doorway, the tea-towel loose in one hand like the stretched neck of a fowl.

## Chapter Twenty-Seven

'While you were in the kitchen, Sukie,' Rosamund shifted her buttocks on the thin cushioning, 'I was suggesting to Bob that he take over Nicola's share in Triumvirate.'

Sukie eyed Bob over a forkful of shepherd's pie.

'I said, no.'

They were squashed together in high-backed seats either side of an oak table in the pub where, half an hour earlier, they had found Tony huddled beside a brass firescreen with a large Scotch.

'You'll have to drive back, I'm afraid.' He was on to the red wine. 'I'd forgotten how depressing funerals could be.'

'And now this.' Rosamund cocked her head at the window.

It had come on to rain. Burly clouds jostled outside, slinging water with such force that the car park seethed, and the hanging baskets had spattered their faces as they ducked inside.

'Well, eat up, everyone.' She bent her head to the task.

'School food, most comforting.' Bob put down the knife with which he had been cutting up his carrots. 'It wouldn't suit me, a part share in a horse. Nothing personal, Rosamund. I just don't think it's my thing.'

'Well, Amanda and I have discussed it, and we don't want to go halves.'

'What about the people Jerry rejected before he thought of you?' Sukie took a gulp of wine.

'Ah, the "unsuitable" people. Any reason why they should suddenly be suitable now?'

'And there must always be those who want to own a horse but can't run to buying a whole one.'

'How about it, then?'

'Rosamund, I couldn't even afford a hair of his tail.'

'Perhaps I should try and trace the "unsuitable" people. I might give Marcus a call.'

'You think he'd remember?' Bob had sorted out his food and was about to eat. 'He doesn't seem the most organized of people.'

Tony had finished his fish pie. He stood up and stretched. 'How about I get some Perrier? Could you help me with the glasses?' He was looking to Sukie.

'Of course.' She shrugged and followed him to the bar.

'Thanks.' He stood at the counter but made no effort to attract the barmaid's attention. 'I wanted to speak to you. That's partly why I offered to drive Rosamund today.'

'I was surprised.'

'Yes, well, we keep in touch. Look, she told me you thought you were being followed.'

'I was attacked.'

'I'm sorry.'

'In the square, outside where I live.'

'Look, don't tell Rosamund this, but James has been following all the women I escorted.' He sighed. 'Phoning and following. I've only just found out, and I can't tell you how bad I feel about it. For everybody. And for him . . .'

The barmaid was coming over. Tony leant with his back to the bar so that she couldn't catch his eye.

'The point is, I'm really looking after him now. I know I neglected him. He'll be OK.'

'You're asking me not to go to the police.'

He looked down and, with reluctance, nodded. 'If you can square it.'

'Oh, I can square it, and draw a line through it, and scribble a face on it, but that doesn't cancel my image of his entering my flat and putting the address of the White Tie in my address book. That still makes me feel invaded.'

'Sorry again. I'll speak to him.'

'Do that. And the return of my son's keys would be appreciated.'

'I promise.' He turned to the barmaid with his beautiful smile.

'James is a very lucky boy.' Sukie leant on the bar like a man.

'Yes. I really am grateful. Thank you.'

'That's not quite what I meant.'


'So, this is another whole horse we're going to take a look at?'

'A whole horse. Too right. What do you take me for?'

'The baby of the family who always got sibling-soiled toys?'

'Wrong. I was an only child. Perhaps you were that baby?'

'Perhaps I was. I had an older sister and brother. My sister married a rich farmer and lives in Yorkshire, and my brother is unmarried and lives in Oxford. He's a don. I think he might be gay. No – he is gay. We've just never talked about it. My mother lives near Maidenhead. Do you have parents?'

'The usual number.'

'My father died just after my husband.'

'A bad year.'

Ahead, sunlight split the road, scattering its verges with white water.

'Here we are.' Bob slowed down at high gates and they proceeded up a drive between ordered meadows grazed by mares and yearlings.

'They look so contented.' Sukie leant her arm along the warm metal of the car where the window was open. The rain had been whisked away and the sun bore down with determined heat lifting steam and sweet smells from the earth. 'You're having a preview before the sales?'

'I intend to buy a couple of two-year-olds for next season, as well as an older one to go along with Atlantic Drift.'

'All with Marcus?'

'Why do you ask?'

'Just a feeling. That you're not entirely happy with the set-up.'

'Yes, well. I've said nothing.'

'It was just a feeling.' She continued to look out of the window.

'The fact is, Marcus may have served his purpose.'

'That sounds ruthless.'

'I'm a businessman.'

'So you are.'

They saw some lovely animals, heads raising wary eyes and tender whiskers that caught the light. Bob moved independently of Sukie, relaxed without his jacket, his dark trousers and beautiful shirt not looking out of place. In her black dress and high shoes, Sukie wished she had a bright cardigan to slip over her shoulders.

'Now for the hotel.' Bob held the door for her to get back into the car. 'I believe it's about six miles from here.'

'I haven't anything with me.'

'What do you need?' He was smiling, fastening his seat-belt.

'I don't know. I just feel a bit sparse.'

'Good. I like that.' And he set off down the drive a little too fast.

The hotel was approached down a narrow lane. There was the sound of running water, and clucking blackbirds swooped before the car. The lane entered iron gates and curved round the creepered building, past a green reflecting pond, to a car park at the back. Trees drooped over them as they made their way round to the entrance, leaves turning black against the evening sky. Between the twisted stems of wistaria the walls were faded pink, the front door guarded by sturdy columns.

Bob made his way to the desk while Sukie lingered to study a picture on the wall. It was a seascape in too heavy a frame, the frail greys and yellows distant as though viewed through a long tunnel.

'Let's go.' His heel squeaked on the polished floor. 'I have the key. Just up these stairs. We don't need a porter.'

The room was large with a balcony and an antique double bed. Sukie walked past the bed on to the balcony, and looked down at the drive, then over hedges to fields of vegetable crops and corn. Bob was behind her; she could feel rather than hear him breathe, then he was drawing her inside.

'So, this is all you have?' He ran his hands down the sides of her dress. 'Just what you stand up in?' He was sitting on the bed, hands on her bottom now, pressing her between his knees.

'Yes. Do you like that?'

'Oh, yes.'

'While you are so well equipped. Shirts, ties, brushes, unguents. Everything a gentleman could need. French hand-luggage. Always packed. Always ready.'

He sighed, moving his hands up under her skirt, pressing her in closer, shutting his eyes.

'Such fine trappings.' Sukie smoothed back a piece of damp hair from his forehead.

'You think so?' His hand was inside her pants and tights, stretching them to cobweb, drawing them down. 'That's right.' Her hand was on his shoulder, balancing, stepping out of them. She waited while he put them in his pocket. He waited for her step back into her shoes. 'Now.'

'Now?'

Again, the sigh. He looked so tired, palms losing hold down the front of her dress. 'You're not wearing a bra?'

'I took it off in the pub.'

'Why?'

'I don't know. I expect you do.'

It was the first time she had heard him laugh. 'Oh, Sukie.'

228

Fingers at the nape of her zip. The dress dropped to the floor. Bob looked down at her shoes: 'That's how I like it.' Black suede with slender heels, wisps of strap performing no function. 'Perfect.'

'I must make a phone call.'

'Go ahead.'

'To my son and daughter. They'll wonder where I am.'

'That's OK.' He got up from the bed. 'I have to go to the bathroom.'

'Don't you ever take your clothes off?'

'I shall tonight.'

Sukie dialled the flat. There was no one in so she left a message that, being over the limit, she would stay the night in Suffolk. It was perfectly true: she had drunk three glasses of wine and left her car at the pub until morning. But Jemima and Alex would assume she was with Amanda.

'Are you hungry?' Bob came out of the bathroom, hair slicked back, shiny with water, his face fresher than usual, a little pink on the cheekbones. He was putting cuff-links into a striped shirt still holding the creases from the packet.

'I'm not sure.' She bent to pick up her dress. 'Either very or not at all.' The dress was crumpled beyond decency. 'Hell.'

'Silk.'

'Yes. Do you have something I could borrow?'

'Like what?'

'Like anything. A sweater?'

'I do have one with me.'

It was a V-necked cashmere, a gorgeous clear scarlet. 'I could wear it over the top so that only the skirt would show. I don't usually wear red.'

'It suits you.' He stood behind her at the glass.

She held out her hand to his reflection. 'In your pocket?'

229

'What? Oh, no. You don't want those. You're better as you are. Believe me.'

Deep in the night a phone was ringing. Deep in the bed Sukie heard it. Deep from darkness and warmth she surfaced, seeing only darkness at the window beyond the room, feeling Bob breathe, smelling the scent stretched between them. She reached out of the down and put her hand to the cold receiver. 'Hullo?'

A voice she recognized, slurred with drink. 'Sukie?'

'Tony. It's the middle of the night.'

'Twelve o'clock.'

'I thought it was later.'

'You've been in bed a long time.'

'How did you know where I was?'

'Rosamund knew. Bob mentioned where he was staying.'

'What do you want?'

'Something I've got to tell you. I talked to James. He's never been in your flat. Never, ever. He swore to me. It wasn't him, absolutely, who put the White Tie address in your book. I'm sorry. Be careful. I'm so sorry. It must have been someone else. 'Bye.'

Sukie replaced the receiver. The shapes of the room had come into relief, the bulk of the wardrobe, the glint of the glass. Beside her Bob slept, gleam of collarbone, the exposed throat, lips parted. He had the most perfect mouth. She hugged her knees, watching him, with a furtive sense of power.

## Chapter Twenty-Eight

The flat presented chill and abandoned when Sukie arrived back the following morning. It was also tidy, in the way it was after a party when everything has been washed and put away. But it was not welcoming. Wondering what Jemima and Alex had been up to, she sat on the floor and took down phone messages: three offers of directors' lunches, the minding of the boutique again for a week while Poppy was in Umbria, one from Nicola, and two from Henry Whippet. She put the pad aside and went to the french windows, folding her arms and staring out across the square as she often did when unable to act: it was better than eating.

Bob had made it clear he needed to leave early; businesslike and polite he had strode about the room, collecting, folding, arranging his immaculate possessions.

'Can I extend the loan of the jumper?' she had said, looking out over fields obscured by mist. 'I'll take it into Jeeves when I get back?'

'OK,' he had said, 'whenever.'

They had hardly spoken on the way to the pub where she recognized the Renault with surprise, unflanked now by yesterday's lunchtime throng, a little on the skew, desolation dripping from its windows.

'Thank you.' She leapt out before he might or might not kiss her. 'Thank you,' she waved from across the damp asphalt, and by the time she had backed and turned he was gone.

The jobs, all next week, would require some juggling. Sukie

231

liked working at the boutique and arranged to call in that afternoon for an update. She was just about to lift the receiver to confirm the lunches when the bell pre-empted her.

'I tried you last night, but your son said you were at Amanda's. I tried Amanda and she had no idea where you were.' It was Nicola. 'I want to talk to you.'

'Yes?' She surprised herself with her sharpness.

'I wanted to explain – about the letters. I did write them, yes I did. Well, I wrote one, just to get some money for Atalanta's. I thought that was all it would take. But he wouldn't cough up so it sort of got out of hand. I had to keep writing them, hinting at more and more things that I knew.'

'You knew things?'

'I knew about some shady deals when he was in Hong Kong, but that didn't bother him. It was when I wrote about his family that he began to get twitchy. I noticed it the morning he opened the letter. It wasn't anything much. The double-barrelled bit. Stupid. His real name was just Jones. I saw it on his birth certificate. Graham was his middle name and he'd just shunted them together.'

'Did you ever speak to him about it?'

'Oh, yes. He said I was never to tell anyone. Said he'd lose all his friends if they knew. He was ever so peculiar. Pretended to be what he wasn't all his life.'

'What was he, then?'

'His father was a petty crook in Brighton. Pick-pocketing. Fraud. Always round the racetracks. Somehow he managed to send George to a posh prep school where he met Jerry and Sylvia's brothers and the like and decided that was the life for him. Only, it all went wrong. His dad got put in gaol and George into the comprehensive.'

'While Jerry et al. went on to Eton?'

'You what? He never told them, of course. Made up some

232

story about the family going to Australia on business. He even had a cousin there who he got to post letters for him.'

'So, they never knew?'

'They'd have dropped him like a brick if they had. Not that Jerry bothered much anyway. But George *was* clever. Good at telling people what they wanted to hear. Good at believing his own lies. He believed them, so other people did too. Like his dad really – only higher stakes. I think he actually forgot what the truth was.'

'So, when he got your letters . . . ?'

'I didn't know they'd have such a bad effect on him, I really didn't. But he changed. Seemed to lose all his confidence . . . I don't know . . .' Her voice faded and Sukie heard a sniff.

'Did George tell you all this?'

'Oh, no. I found a letter.'

'Another blackmail letter?'

'No, just a letter. It was what gave me the idea. It wasn't signed and it wasn't dated. And it didn't ask for anything. It just sort of gloated.'

'Have you got it?'

'No. The police had everything like that. I suppose George thought all the letters came from the same person. They were all computer printed.'

'I expect he did.'

'There's another thing. When I was frightened, when I felt I was being watched and phoned you to come over, well, you probably realized it was Simon I meant.'

'No. No, I hadn't realized at all.'

'Of course, because it was all so silly. Anyway, I just wanted you to take no notice of that. It was just the way he looked at me, probably just the light before the storm, as if he really didn't like me.'

Sukie caught the glint of her wedding ring on the hand

holding the receiver, the cuff of scarlet cashmere. 'Look, I have to go. I have things to do.'

'What shall *I* do?'

'Nicola, I don't *know*. Did Simon walk on the grass?'

'You what?'

'On the way to take George's car, the grass beside the house?'

'Hang about. I think he did, actually. Didn't want to get his shoes muddy. Why?'

'No prints. That's all. Thanks, Nicola. Goodbye.'

Sukie took hold of the ribbing of the jumper and drew it up over her head, trapping herself for a moment within his smell; then she tore it inside out and threw it on the floor. Afterwards, when she had bathed and washed her hair she set off with the jumper in a carrier-bag for Jeeves and the boutique.

A little over the limit and with a new carrier-bag containing a red cardigan that had cost as much as she could earn in a week, Sukie scurried up the darkening stairs to the flat. From the street below she had seen a light deep in the drawing-room with a leap of joy at the thought of an evening with Jemima or Alexis. 'Hullo,' she called, pushing open the door with the rustling bag, 'I'm back.'

'Hullo,' came Alex's voice.

'I've been trying to get away since four o'clock, but you know what Poppy's like.'

'Do I?' He was sitting in an armchair, one leg bent with the foot resting on the opposite knee. In his hands was a large album and all about him on the floor were spread piles of photographs. On the sofa, sifting through more photographs, was Henry Whippet.

Sukie dropped the bag on to the floor. 'Alex, what are you doing?'

'What? Oh,' he looked up smiling, but not at her. 'These. It's been years since I've looked at them. I had blond hair, didn't I, when I was small? I'd forgotten that. God, I remember that plant pot with dragons on it. Whatever happened to that?'

'It got broken.'

'I used to sit on it, look – ' he showed the album to Henry Whippet. 'Turned upside down.'

'That's how it got broken.' Sukie picked up the bag and was about to leave the room.

'Mosie, I've got my new school photo. That's how we got looking at these. I left it at Paton's when I was there for the weekend. I saw him today and got it back.' He brought it over to her, holding it under the standard lamp.

'Where are you?'

He pointed.

'Oh, yes. It's good. It looks like you.'

'You should see some of the prep school ones. Some of the people are quite unrecognizable. Though *he's* quite good at it.' He looked over his shoulder at Henry Whippet. 'He managed to match up practically everyone from prep school who moved up with me and are in this photo.'

'I wonder if I could?' Sukie took the wide frame from him, scanning the ranks of boys, even in uniform all so different.

'Oh, yes, you could. But you knew them all.'

'That's true.' She put the photograph carefully on the table, still looking at it, finding it sad. But not as sad as after a war. Not as sad as Peter's. 'So, what do you want?' She turned on Henry Whippet and caught Alex's frown.

'I tried phoning you, but you was never in, so as I was on my way back from Goodwood today . . . I like looking at photos. Tell you a lot about people. Yours look very happy.'

'Snapshots are always happy. They're taken on happy occasions.'

'But you should look after them better. Some of them was all crushed up by the drawer. Those albums you did were very nice.'

'Yes, well, I don't have time for albums now.' She began to

235

gather up the pile from the floor. 'Let's just put them all away, shall we?'

'But, Mosie, I thought you'd look at them with us.'

'For goodness' sake, I'm tired. I've been out all day. I'm looking after Poppy's boutique next week and I've got three lunches to do as well.'

'Goodnight, then.' Alex put away the remaining albums and shut the drawer with his foot.

'But it's only nine o'clock.'

'You said you were tired.' And he left the room.

'You do look tired.' Henry Whippet had stood up.

'Good. I really needed to know that. I would also like to know what you are doing here.'

'I came to see you. Wondered what you was up to.'

'Well. Now you know.'

'I suppose I do. I'll be getting along, then.'

Sukie stood with her arms folded, watching him to the door. In the silence the phone began to ring. She lifted the receiver, eyeing him. 'Yes?'

It was Amanda. 'Where have you been? I've been trying you all afternoon. And yesterday people kept trying me.'

'What do you want?'

'Don't sound like that. When did I ever want anything? Well actually, I want sympathy.'

'What for?' Henry Whippet had not moved. Sukie lifted the instrument off the table and swivelled away from his gaze.

'Well, firstly for having to field enquiries about you last night. Secondly because I got a call from one of Simon's friends to say he'd had an accident on his way to Froggy's this morning and could I go and collect him, but when I got there, Froggy knew nothing about it. And thirdly because when I got back here it was to find that I'd been burgled.'

'What was taken?'

'The usual: stereo, camera, a clock, a few pictures, some plate,

236

none of it valuable. But that's not the point. I was very fond of some of it. You know, things I'd known as a child, comforting things, pictures of rabbits having tea, you know ... and photographs. Simon as a baby, Jerry at school and Christ Church ... my Christening spoon – that was silver ... All so pointless ... I feel absolutely gutted ...' She began to cry.

'Amanda, I'm so sorry. I'll come over, shall I? Would you like that?'

'Yes, I would. I would like that. But there's one good thing. Would you believe it? They took George's car from the outhouse.'

'I'll come over now.'

'So, was that another burglary?' Henry Whippet had moved a little further into the room.

Sukie replaced the phone on the table. 'What do you mean – another?'

'Well, like Mrs Graham-Jones. She had one, didn't she?'

'How did you know about that?'

'News gets about.'

'You always say that. You said that about something else.'

'Did I? Well, it's true. Small world, racing. What was stolen? With Mrs Graham-Jones it was stuff from the study, camera, pictures.'

'Yes.'

'Are you answering my question or just agreeing with me?' He had taken another step nearer.

'You'll have to work that out. Now, I must speak to Alex and get going.' She began to move past him.

'OK, doll, I'm still on my way.' His voice was close to her ear. The faint waft of meadows, his apple breath. 'Be careful.'

'I'm an excellent driver.'

Henry Whippet shrugged. ''Course you are. 'Bye.' He lifted his head to call to Alex through the door and was gone.

*

Amanda was swaddled in a cashmere dressing-gown and an outsize pair of ski-socks. 'They were Jerry's,' she said, tripping over the toes.

The curtains were closed the full width of the room, yellow silk, a colour Sukie's mother would have called 'old gold', edges pressed together against the darkness. Sound was muffled, their voices hushed between discs of light. A bottle of Glenmorangie was on a table. Amanda fetched a glass, filled it and handed it to Sukie.

'I'm upset.' She sipped from her own glass. 'I've been thinking about that phone call. It was obviously made to get me out of the house.'

'Have you spoken to Simon?'

'He's away, now I learn. Taken off for a day or two, according to Froggy, God knows where.'

'And Froggy's no idea who the caller could have been?'

Amanda shook her head. 'Neither have I. It could have been anybody. Nothing distinctive, young, English . . .'

'Male?'

'Yes, of course, *male*.'

'What exactly did he say? Can you remember the words?'

'I'm not sure. Well, he said, "May I speak with Mrs Wearing?" and then, "I'm sorry to trouble you, etc." and "I'm a friend of Simon's and please don't worry," and so, of course I instantly did.'

'Of course.'

'Then he says Simon's had a bit of a bump in his car, nothing serious, he's not hurt, only a bit shaken but the fender's badly twisted and he thinks it's illegal so he doesn't want to risk driving. And could I pick him up? That was more or less it.'

'You didn't think to ask his name, or why Simon hadn't made the call himself?'

'No. Well, would you? I was worried. I presumed it was worse than they were letting on.'

'Yes, of course.' Sukie began to pace the room. She needed to disturb the space about her. Enclosed as they were, they could have been anywhere; underground with curtaining to lend pretence of windows, or high in a scraper with nothing but white sky and whining wind on the other side of the glass. Something stopped her thoughts for a pace before she said, 'Nicola was burgled too.'

'I'd heard.'

'The same sort of thing.'

'The police say they'll keep a lookout. Galleries, auctions, car boots.'

'I'd be surprised if anything turns up.'

'So would I. By the way, that reminds me. George's car has been found in a lay-by. Police slithering all over it, now. Thank God I never touched it. You'll stay the night?'

'I'll stay the night.' Sukie lifted her glass to meet the whisky bottle. 'There's someone I want to visit near here tomorrow morning.'

# Chapter Twenty-Nine

After breakfast, eggs and bacon, Amanda drooping over the Aga, 'I have to have protein, it's the only cure,' Sukie set off in her car, undeflected by pressure to persuade her to stay.

Still comforted by the cashmere dressing-gown but less harmonious, Amanda had clutched at her sleeve. 'I still miss him, you know. You don't have to go. People don't think that I do, but I do. Just because I keep myself in good nick.' The dressing-gown flapped open as she ran across the drive, her satin nightdress dingy in the morning light.

. . . Amanda Wearing, eyes like gentians.

'I know you do.'

'Yes.' Amanda's head drooped, hair springing from nacreous parting.

She dyes it, of course, only horses have manes that colour. Sukie opened the driver's door then turned with one foot inside. 'Why don't you ring me this evening and we'll arrange to go to the theatre.'

'I haven't been to the theatre for ages.'

'Exactly. See you soon, then.'

'Hey,' Amanda stepped forward, 'didn't you say you were visiting somewhere round here?' She was leaning down to the open window. 'Give me five minutes and I'll come with you.'

'No.' Sukie started the engine, pulling away so suddenly that

Amanda was thrown back and almost fell. 'Sorry,' she called, waving. 'It's all very boring and I'm already late.'

Hands high on the wheel, driving slowly to give time for thought, Sukie took the road to Newmarket. The idea had come into her mind while she had been looking at Alex's school photographs. The plan had emerged on her way to Suffolk last night. She wondered if she could remember the way. And she wondered if she wanted to get there at all.

She found the way disconcertingly well and was there before she felt ready to arrive. The gravel was not as neat as it had been in the spring; a season of cars had worn it bare in places and sprayed it into the circle of tired grass. Hers was the only vehicle this morning; shiny from the recent rains, Sukie observed after she had pressed the front doorbell. No one came. The windows of the house had an empty look, reflecting the scene outside. She tried the bell once more, studying her feet in their glossy loafers amongst the scatter of small stones on the tiles.

'Yes?' The voice was behind her. 'Oh, it's you.' Sylvia never had to strive at being inhospitable. She stood, arms a little away from her body, a red and white kerchief drawing back her hair from tight freckled cheeks.

'Oh. You are in, then?' Sukie looked down on her from the step, feeling a tad vulgar.

'No.' Sylvia seemed to expect a reply but then continued, 'I'm out. I was in the yard. Creosoting.'

'Of course.' Sukie could see now that they weren't freckles at all but a fine brown spray.

'First chance I've had. We've just lost three to Froggy. It's an ill wind.'

'Very ill. Whose?'

'Millfield's.'

'Reggie Millfield, I know. Friend of Amanda Wearing's.'

'Not top class, but they helped pay the bills.'

'Simon Wearing is supposed to be going to work with Froggy Frencham.'

'No *supposed* about it. He *is* working with him. We shall lose all Mummy's next, no doubt. Except for Triumvirate. Marcus'll put up a fight for Triumvirate.'

'How will he do that?'

Sylvia blinked then said, 'I'm off back to the yard. If you feel like telling me what you're doing here you can follow on. If not, I'd be glad if you'd shift. I don't have time for chit-chat.'

She moved across the gravel, so light there was hardly a sound, and yet Sukie had to scurry to catch up with her. Sylvia was working on a loose-box at the end. It had been swept clean and a large pot stood in the middle of the floor with a brush.

'I should stand back if I were you.' She eyed Sukie's loafers. 'OK, then, spill.' She picked up the brush.

Sukie stood her ground. 'I want you to lend me something.'

'Oh? What?'

'If it's the one I want, that is. I need to have a look.'

'Oh, really?' Sylvia was not being sarcastic. She held the brush, bristle upwards, like a fan in front of her face. 'Someone else said that to me this morning.'

Half an hour later Sukie climbed into her car carrying a long package wrapped in Waitrose bags, then drove down the lane towards the town. What she was to do with it she hadn't considered. And as she entered the High Street she realized that she had no idea. The object itself had so obsessed her with the hard light of truth that the implications of it coming into her hands had not dawned. With truth went responsibility. Sukie was not sure she was up to it.

Her mouth tasted of dust. On an impulse she stopped at a pub. A very ordinary pub, noisy, smelling of chips. Sitting in a corner, while extricating flakes of brain food from within its batter overcoat, she arranged the fragile scraps of truth she had

242

absorbed since Jerry's death around the backbone now locked in the boot of the car. There were gaps, but no morsel that hadn't a place. A depression waved over her so that she could no longer hold her knife and fork and as she put her hand round her tankard of cider she was unable to lift it from the table.

She hadn't asked Sylvia who it was who had been there before her, because she knew. And while she knew, and now had proof of that knowledge, she had not wanted to hear the name. Always, she now realized, she had hoped, so naively, that the guilt would lie with a stranger.

And yet, something *was* odd. Something didn't quite lie flat. Why had both Nicola and Amanda been burgled, yet Sylvia receive a visit with nothing removed? The fish was a mess in her plate, everything taken apart, black skin revealed, sharp bones and soft flesh all mixed together, wasted.

It had been an effort to contact Amanda, an even greater one actually to meet at the theatre. Sukie was experiencing a reluctance to leave the flat. It was fear, of course. And a hollowing sense of loss. Her children had gone. There had been a note, on the kitchen table, decorated with cartoons: Jemima dancing, Alexis underwater face to face with a huge fish. 'To Greece.' 'Only for the summer.' They had hoped to cheer her up. The whole summer. It explained the tidiness of the flat. Both of them. Flown.

They were aware that she was busy, had found a list marked 'Suspicions' in a drawer. An invitation had come their way. All very respectable, from Paton's parents. A villa. With a private beach. They would send lots of cards. She *needed* a life of her own. Sukie had lain on the bed and wept, while under it skulked the package in its Waitrose bags. The truth. Not always the true picture.

'You seem somewhat morose?' Amanda had made an effort: a Ronit Zilkha suit, sky-blue silk. She looked startling. The more so at this serious North London Fringe. Was it spite, Sukie pondered, that had restrained her from mentioning that dress was also seriously casual?

'I'm not sleeping well.'

'Not enough sex.' Amanda squinted at the programme. 'This is *Greek*.' She fumbled for her spectacles. 'Ancient!'

'It's *in* English.'

'What dementia made you choose it?'

'The usual sort.'

'Ah. Tremens.'

'That's delirium.'

'What's the odd DT between friends? You're much too sharp, Sukie.'

'Have you heard from Simon yet?'

'That's what I mean. No.' Amanda frowned as though she did not understand the question. 'No. So?'

'Well, he was missing the last I knew.'

'He wasn't missing. He was never *missing*. Whatever you and the police like to think. You do get stirred up sometimes. He's just off. With some girl, I imagine, before settling down with Froggy.'

'The odd couple.'

Amanda sighed, 'You've never taken him seriously, have you? Just because yours always do all the right things. Simon and Froggy are really going to make a go of it together. Why are you laughing?'

'If you don't know, I'm not going to tell you.'

'Reggie's sent them his three already.'

'I know.'

'You're still laughing.'

'I can't help it. It's hysteria. Don't take any notice.'

'It's difficult. Everyone's looking at you.'

'No, only you are looking at me, Amanda. All right. I'm better now. See. No hands.'

'You're talking nonsense.'

'It's the only thing that makes any sense at the moment. Are you going to send your horses to Froggy?'

'When I can organize it.'

'What about Triumvirate?'

'Ah. I'd like to. Rosamund isn't so sure. And then there's Nicola's share.'

'Rosamund was trying to persuade Bob to put up for a third but he's not interested in part ownership.'

'I should think that runs to everything with him, wouldn't you?'

Sukie did not choose to reply.

'Not like Henry Whippet.' Amanda gave the hem of her jacket a little tug and walked down the black stairs to the acting space.

So there was to be no more racing. Time was reeling away. Kneeling on the sitting-room floor, with a large pad and dark pen, Sukie drew a picture of the tree. She put all her original suspects like unopened presents at its base. And then she began to hang it with baubles: bright scraps of information, one or two sweetmeats, a lollipop, the odd red herring, looping some of them together into strings of lights until she reached the top where there was no angel, just a name.

Afterwards she felt too calm. She had missed out her usual half-bottle of wine, so went to the decanter and poured herself a brandy. Then she put on a CD of Mozart's Concerto for flute and harp and sat with the curtains open although it was getting cold. She thought of what she knew and set it aside, then she thought of Jemima and Alex and was thankful after all that they were far away and happy. And she thought of Peter, which she did often though not deeply because that was too difficult. And she accepted the tears and wondered if she would ever grow up. Then, when the music had finished, she switched off the player, washed her glass and dried it and put it away and, leaving the curtains open to the fluttering leaves, made her way to bed.

In the night there were sounds, the rattle of windows, the creak of a branch, a step on the landing outside her front door. The door heaved with sustained pressure but the lock had been fixed and the wind, or whatever it was, withdrew.

# Chapter Thirty

Unlike Poppy, her boutique in St John's Wood was not inclined to extremes. It purveyed reliable elegance to the reliably rich: an outfit designed to interface their sprees with comfort and gravitas. Women with preoccupied husbands and dress allowances to match the preoccupation. The clothes were gorgeous. The weight of them, or the lightness, the butter-curl curve of wool suits, the scrunch of silk blouses, the cashmere ... Sukie sat at a gilded desk in a chair upholstered with ivory dupion. She wrote in an Italian ledger with a slender pen, rising at the sound of the street bell, smiling across the approach of carpet.

The women liked Sukie. They liked women of their own age whose bodies had also had children; who understood that they knew their own style; who did not flatter to secure a sale, and who would never enter a fitting-room without being invited.

And Sukie liked them too. They made her feel safe. She understood that although rich their lives were not always easy. There was a courageousness about them, that somehow they would always come through if they made up their faces each morning and sallied forth, hair moulded into shells, buttons shining. The boutique made her feel safe as well, its rose-pink walls, indirect lighting, its ponderous curtains and cords. Was this, then, real life?

She had spent Sunday making canapés while it rained outside. Nothing else had happened. At night she had gone to bed exhausted and a little drunk, having swallowed her half-bottle all in the short time it took her to clear up. She saw no one. And no one phoned. That hadn't felt real.

Teresa did. The woman who came into Poppy's to do alterations part time. The woman who every day handled such beautiful clothes, and every day herself wore a navy pleated skirt, a cream nylon blouse and down-at-heel shoes. Middle-aged, her dark schoolgirl hair, held aside with a kirby-grip, was quite without shine.

'What terrible weather we're having.' She stood at the window, arms folded, eyes slumped within their nests of lines. 'Terrible. So depressing, isn't it?'

It was Tuesday and still raining.

'Sorry?' Sukie whisked into the back room to make lusty sounds with the coffee maker.

'And there's me having to be at the dentist's this afternoon on top.'

'Sorry?' Sukie was holding out Teresa's mug.

But Teresa was not to be lured through the flap. She was at the desk now, drawer open. 'All right if I put this in here, for security?' She held up a flower-papered package.

'Yes, yes, of course.'

'Birthday present for my sister. Going round there tonight after work. No peace for the wicked, eh?' She smiled, mouth turning down at the corners.

'What have you bought her?'

'Oh, just some notelets. Well, I thought, you can never have too many of them, can you? And it's the thought that counts.'

'Coffee?' Sukie lifted it to Teresa's attention. 'There's a yellow jacket and a green skirt on the rail here, both needing shortening. I've put the pins in.'

'Oh, right.' Teresa approached the mug. 'Did you hear that medical phone-in on the radio last night?'

'No, no, I didn't.'

'It's very good.' Teresa shook her head. 'They're so good, the

248

experts. So interesting. Makes you wish you had a disease yourself.' She closed her eyes to sip the hot liquid. 'You know, so they could make it better.'

In the afternoon still it rained. Lights in the opposite shops made it seem like night, while water ran from the corner of the blind. Sukie could hear the relentless flow, the brisk flurry of drops as the wind caught the canvas, and was glad that she was not responsible for getting it fixed. She was also glad to be cut loose from Teresa.

The reason she enjoyed herself in the boutique was the autonomy and because next week she wouldn't be there. She shied away from routine as most people did from danger. Dipping into people's lives was what she enjoyed, dipping out of them, perhaps so she could feel her own had not yet started.

A Lady Lyons had bought a Valentino suit. It looked quite beautiful on her; she was a beautiful woman with natural style. The suit was navy, very plain with dull gold buttons and fitted perfectly, except for the skirt which she wanted shortened to just above the knee. With Teresa absent, Sukie suggested that she pin it to length as she had always done before. Lady Lyons agreed, lifting a hand to smooth hair from her immaculate forehead, as she stepped into the fitting-room. Sukie followed with the pins, unlooping the cord from around the padded curtain to let it fall.

It was peaceful kneeling on the rose pile of the carpet, handling the fabric, easy smiles passing between them. They both heard the sound of the bell out in the shop as the door opened, then closed.

'I'll be with you in just a moment,' Sukie called round the edge of the curtain.

The task was almost finished. When they emerged, both expecting to see someone seated in one of the gilt chairs, Lady Lyons raised her eyebrows at Sukie. The shop was empty. Picking up a carrier-bag that she had left by the desk, with a light wave she was gone. The bell rang as she opened the door and again as

249

it swung behind her and Sukie was left, in a glass case, lit for view.

She began to tidy up, uneasy now, glancing about her as she put things into drawers and shut them. Outside it was quite dark, the street draped in rain, shop lights revealing only bent figures hurrying by. Suddenly, with extra-loud ringing, the door was flung open and a man butted his way in, shaking his head so that water spun across the room.

'Careful.' Sukie was eyeing the silk hangings while he stamped on the mat.

'That's better.' He tossed back his head and looked at her between strands of hair.

'Marcus! What on earth are you doing here?'

He tossed his head again, so that the hair resumed something of its usual poise. 'God knows! It's hell out there. I came on Westway, though one would hardly have known; saw two shunts before the Paddington turn-off. There were probably more but one was too busy minding one's own back – or rather front.'

'But why are you here? Can I get you some tea or coffee?'

'Is that all you've got?'

'It's all I'm offering.'

'I'll have a coffee, then. Black.' He flopped into one of the chairs.

'Please – ' she darted forward. 'Your mac.' She was pulling at the shoulders. 'These seats mark very easily.'

'Oh, sorry.' He went to hang the mac up then followed her through the curtain at the back to where the coffee machine was kept on a small draining board in a room mainly taken up by free-standing rails supporting plastic-shrouded garments, while stairs led to Teresa's workroom above.

'It's ready.' She poured the coffee into a cup, leading him back into the main shop. 'I hope you don't take sugar. Virtually none of our customers does, so we just slip them a sweetener if necessary.'

Marcus took the cup and saucer, standing up to drink it, looking larger than she had thought him, and less spruce. It wasn't just the effect of the rain which was, after all, his natural element for much of the year. There were veins on his cheekbones she now saw, not like Sylvia's, not simply reaction to weather; some of them replicated on his nose. In his fingers, the delicate Coalport cup shook.

'So, why are you here?' She stood behind the desk, hands resting either side of the Italian ledger.

'Ah,' he took in a deep breath, letting it out again as he placed the empty cup and saucer before her. 'That's better. A bit. Sudden impulse.'

'Aren't they always?'

'What?' He turned an ear towards her.

'Sorry. Amanda says I'm getting sharp.'

'You're very friendly with Amanda. Go back a long way?'

'We were at school together.'

'Exactly. So, you confide in each other.'

'Not necessarily.' Sukie gripped the edge of the desk.

'Well, it was she who mentioned you were working here. And, on the spur of the moment I took the chance. On my way home from Kempton, took the opposite direction to the M25 and came on over.'

'Why?'

'It's common knowledge that Simon Wearing took Nicola Graham-Jones off to the Cotswolds for a few days recently.'

'Is it?'

'Oh, yes.' He folded his arms. 'And it's also common knowledge that any interest he had there was well curbed before George's funeral. OK? So, why go away with her, you might ask.'

'I might?'

'Oh, yes.' Marcus cleared his throat. 'Now, I think, and Sylvia does too, that Simon took Nicola away to soften her up and

251

persuade her to let Triumvirate go to Froggy's before she sells her share.'

'Was that a question?'

'What? Yes. I mean, in talking to Amanda, you know...' Marcus made a circular movement with his hand. When Sukie did not respond he lifted the hand to beside his mouth. 'Could we be right?'

Sukie was considering an answer, when an involuntary shiver roused her. 'Did you come in here about a quarter of an hour ago, when I was in a fitting-room, and go straight out again?'

'No. 'Course I didn't. Do you think I'd rat all the way here from Kempton to wait out in the rain?'

'No.' Sukie contemplated him. 'It's possible, I should think, that Simon would do what you suggest. Hardly the conduct of a gent, but who's a gent these days?'

'Exactly. Right.'

'You're worried you're about to lose your best horse.'

'Got to keep ahead of the game. Forewarned is forearmed, and all that. Better go.' He was already at the door. 'Had a bloody break-in the other day. Sylvia's a bit jittery.'

'How horrible. Was much taken?'

'Nothing of value. Haven't *got* anything of value. Only a few cups and stuff and that's all down at the bank. Heigh-ho. Christ, I think I'd better go A1, what with the North Circular from here it'll be bloody murder on the M11.'

'Not to mention semi-permanent roadworks.'

'Roadworks. Fuck! I'd forgotten them.' He was hunching himself into his mac, pulling up the collar.

'So had I.' Sukie stood watching him to the door. 'Then I suddenly remembered.'

The bell gave a ping and then another one, and he was gone. Sukie took the cup and saucer through to the sink and continued to tidy up. She arranged the curtains and re-hooked the cords. She smoothed the seats of the chairs, the silk making a light sigh.

Then she put the ledger, pen and papers in the desk drawers, the pins and tape measure in their basket, all the time aware of how she must appear from the street within the frame.

Keeping her head down she slid the cheques, credit card slips and cash from their box and took them through to the safe and had just locked the door when the phone began to ring out in the shop.

It was Teresa: she was sorry she was so late but the dentist had kept her waiting. She knew it was past closing, but she'd got to collect her sister's birthday present. She'd be there in fifteen minutes at the most. Would Sukie wait?

Sukie did not care to wait for Teresa.

Teresa did have a complete set of keys, but if the alarm was set she wouldn't be able to use them. Sukie agreed to leave the alarm for Teresa, who could set it when she left. Poppy would have done the same. She picked up her bag, turned off a section of lights and left the shop, Chubb-locking the door, before thrusting up her umbrella for a dash to the car.

The rain continued and Sukie made more canapés and Coronation Chicken and lemon tarts while the night pressed itself against the windows of her kitchen, rattling like plastic sheeting. As she focused on the task, spectacles on the end of her nose to read the nice fractions of quantity, events of the previous months receded to a story, a play half heard over the radio from the corner. This was her concern: bread and butter. She had driven her children away . . .

# Chapter Thirty-One

The food had to be delivered early so that Sukie could get to the boutique by five to ten: a journey out of the City at that time could take ages, stuck the wrong side of King's Cross. She had to leave before the post could arrive, fresh-faced and clear-eyed in spite of only three hours' sleep. At least the rain had gone and the pale streaked sky offered hope of a sparkling day. Even now, ahead, the tall blocks of the City gleamed like bullion as she drove through the swishing streets. Carefully she carried her trays and baskets into the entrance hall of the company accountants', past weary commissionaires, down marble steps into the basement where the kitchens and some of the hospitality suites were situated. There was no one there. The place was in total darkness. Luckily she knew the layout, so laboriously unloaded herself to switch on the lights. The walls like the floors were marbled, with the odd scandepsis and etiolated palm standing against them in functional white pots.

Sukie took everything through to the preparation area and waited. She waited half an hour and was just scribbling a note when Belinda arrived, blue chiffon scarf flying: 'I'm *so* sorry. I really am. *Do* forgive me. But Paul was going to Bristol today and at the last minute decided to take the train so I had to drive him to Paddington.'

'Right, well I'll be off now, then. Here's all the stuff – what you asked for. I didn't really feel I could just leave it.'

'You're cross.'

'No, I'm not cross, but I have to go.'

'Oh, God, you *are* cross!'

'All right, I'm cross, but I still have to go. I'm late.' And she was up the marble stairs, through the iron gates, and driving north to the Euston Road.

It was ten-fifteen when she arrived at the shop and was irritated to find that Teresa had forgotten both to set the alarm, and to double-lock the door. Everything was in order, but they would have to have words when she came in at eleven.

Luckily no one was waiting, and it might well be a quiet day. The rain had made people begin to think of autumn clothes; today that would be an aberration. It was hot. Sukie slipped off the black jacket that she wore over her white crêpe dress and went through to the back to make coffee, smoothing her bare arms while she waited.

She took her coffee back to the desk and began to check through a stock list as she had to decide whether to take delivery of certain outfits that day. Part of the list appeared to be missing. She looked through the drawers to try to find it. In the bottom of one was a small package wrapped in pink flowered paper. Had Teresa then decided not to come back to the shop after all? They would certainly have to have words. No sign of the rest of the list.

The thing to do was to check the rail and see what was there apart from the things on display. Taking a quick gulp of coffee Sukie went through with the list in her hand. The light was so bad that without her spectacles it was hard to read the labels through the plastic coverings so she put the paper between her teeth and attempted to pull the rail to directly under the central fitting. It was heavy work. Her mouth came open with the effort and the list floated across the floor. She stopped to retrieve it and to get her strength back. It shouldn't be so difficult, a rail of clothes. She tried again. Perhaps something was jamming the bar, underneath?

Sukie crouched down and began to lift the skirts of the

garments to see what might be there. Wool pleats, silk linings, cashmere panels fluttered through her fingers until she felt something that did not flutter. It was something one might expect to find amongst the folds of a skirt. She withdrew her hand with a giggle of apology. Knowing that none was needed. Knowing that it was an unsuitable response. It was a leg. A woman's leg, astride the bar, in flesh-coloured tights, scale-textured to catch the skin like the body of a fish, and colder.

Sukie remained crouched on the floor, hugging herself, rocking, shivering, cold sweat trickling down the inside of her dress. She stood up and wiped a palm hard down over her hip bone. Then, leaning forward, she parted the clothes.

For a moment there was relief. Because Teresa was smiling. Behind one of the plastic coverings, like a child's picture protected with polythene, was a great upward-curving mouth. It had not been well painted. The yellow face was smudged downwards so that where the mouth should have been was just more dappled yellow and pencil lines. Only the eyes, anthracite bright Sukie had not remembered, lit memory to a likeness. Death, the moment, had brought life brimming to them, rising from what rush of blood? For the upward curve, vermilion, rose madder, crimson lake, was painted on the neck so that Teresa smiled from ear to ear. She had finally seen the joke.

Sukie continued to wipe her hand down her dress. She wanted to cover up the smile, the glare through milky plastic, but felt unable to choose something to do it with. And knew anyway that there was no point. A pair of tights had been tied under Teresa's arms and with these she had been hung upon a hook at the end of the rail, the plastic cover placed over her to keep the blood in.

Sukie turned her back, and pushed aside the curtain to stare out at broad daylight in the shop. It stretched the room to horizontal blindness, only the edges of the picture defined. The open wardrobes of clothes down one side, the two fitting-rooms at the other, one with its curtain drawn back and secured with the cord as Sukie had left it, the other released to cover the cubicle as she had not. She stepped across and drew the quilted fabric to its fastening point, wanting to correct an error, wanting to achieve some order. It was then that she saw it. The dress, laid out on the chair. Red chiffon over panels of thigh-revealing silk, a clasping bodice: the most expensive dress in the shop. Still on its hanger it had been given the touch of a fine black scarf which partly obscured a small card pinned to the breast. Leaning forward to lift the scarf Sukie found between her fingers the toe of a stocking that had been tightly wound around the throat of the hook. The name printed on the neat card was her own.

In seconds she was on the telephone.

'Your third body, then?'

'I'm not claiming possession.'

The police had seemed impressed. Or perhaps they were trying to make her see the positive side? Perhaps they were covering up their suspicions of her? It did look suspicious. *She* would have been suspicious. She *was* suspicious. But they didn't believe her.

Robbery was the most likely motive. There had been several in the area lately. The thief had seen Teresa return to a dimly lit shop; had followed her in. Teresa had a key to the safe on her ring. The safe had been opened, the keys left hanging, and was empty. No fingerprints.

But what about the red dress? The strangled dress with Sukie's name on it? Ah. Is she sure she had no designs on it herself? She shakes her head. They shake theirs back.

Why should they believe a woman on her third body that the murderer had been lying in wait for her? Why should they believe a woman on her third body about anything?

Another signature to another statement. But when a name had been between her lips about to be spat in their faces, they had asked her if she had a good doctor, so Sukie had only said, 'Yes,

257

but I never go to see him.' And they had suggested that today might be a good time to renew the acquaintance.

She had insisted on driving herself home. 'Auto-no-me!' she had kept repeating through the traffic; and, 'I think actually I am a little crazy,' as she kicked off her shoes and flopped on the bed; then, 'What am I doing here? I'm not an invalid. There's cooking to be done.'

More canapés, pâtés, mousses, terrines, two whole salmon with mayonnaise, chicken breasts, baby potatoes, lemon tarts and gooseberry fools. In the light summer evening, birds perched on fire escapes and sang from chimney-pots, against a golden sky. And Sukie watched them as she worked until they faded into the trees. Then the trees faded into the sky, and she put the light on and she shut the window to see the black plastic pressed instantly to it again. Only now there was no rattle. There was total silence. She could hear herself breathing and did not like what she heard.

It had been like that in the shop today, with the fear ... The fear, that had not been of attack. She had known she was alone. That was the fear. The fear that only she had to take action. There was no one else. And it was still the same.

The phone was ringing. It had been ringing for some time. Sukie ran into her bedroom.

'I was about to hang up, but I couldn't believe you were out. No answerphone?' Bob's voice was energetic.

'No, I'm in. Cooking.'

'I'm glad. That you're in. Didn't you get my card?'

'No.'

'Things have cropped up. Exciting things. I want your expert advice.'

'I've learnt never to give advice.'

'Quite right. Opinion will do?'

'Sorry.' Sukie wiped her hand down her apron. 'Cooking brings out the prig in me.'

'Oh. All that washing of hands, I can imagine. Look, do you have time? I can call back tomorrow.'

'No. I need a break.' She sat down on the bed. 'Now, I'm listening. I've even put my feet up.'

'What shoes are you wearing?'

She contemplated her legs from knee to ankle, gleaming with summer, the extension of bare feet. She smiled. 'You'd like them.'

'Tell me.'

She laughed, 'No. Come on, what's this advice you want?'

'Opinion. Have I . . . disturbed you?'

'No.' She felt a lurch inside. 'They're black patent, with ankle-straps.'

'Thank you.' There was the sound of him shifting the receiver to his other ear. 'Right, Marcus wants me to buy Triumvirate.'

'I thought he might. And?'

'The whole horse. I'm seriously tempted.'

'Well, you would be. So why do you want my opinion? You've already decided you want him.'

'Yeah. I think I just wanted to tell you. It'll cost me.'

Sukie moved her toes like the notes on a piano, watched the bones moving with them.

'There's something else.' He shifted the receiver again. 'And I really do want your opinion. I think I've found a house, one that I seriously feel I could live in. I wanted you to come take a look at it.'

'Oh.' That lurch again. 'Where is it?'

'Hampstead. Right near the heath.'

'I'd love to see it, but you're usually so decisive. Aren't you?'

'We all have our areas. You don't really know me.'

'I wouldn't presume . . .'

'That's not what I meant.' His tone was gentle, or was it sad? 'You have the impression I'm a lot tougher than I am.'

'Do I?'

259

'Oh, yes. So, will you come see the house? Hold my hand?'

She was still looking at her feet. 'I'll come. When were you thinking of?'

'Tomorrow. Tomorrow evening? I'll pick you up?'

'OK, about seven, I should be back by then – oh, but I probably won't be working.'

'Why's that?'

'Oh. Something ... I'd better tell you. The boutique I'm looking after – ha – this week. Well, the seamstress, she was killed. Last night. The police think it was robbery.'

'That's dreadful.'

'Yes. She wasn't exactly an appealing woman – I don't know if that makes it worse or not. It could hardly *be* worse. She was middle-aged, but it was like her life had never started. It never will now.'

'It probably never would have.'

'No. I must go. More cooking to be done. Look forward to seeing your house. 'Bye.'

But she lingered, lying on the bed, watching her toes as they stretched and curled. Then she sighed and sprang up to go to the kitchen, on her way pausing to check the locks in the hall, catching the edge of the morning's post where it had been pushed under the mat by the door. A couple of bills which she opened and put on the table, a letter from her mother that she would read later, and two cards: Jemima and Alex, identical scenes of brash blueness with few words and lots of exclamation marks. She slid them into the pocket of her apron and continued through to the kitchen.

It seemed essential that everything should be absolutely clean, not a smear, not a speck, shining. Even after they had been taken from the dishwasher, all the items had to be dried, polished. She polished individually each bowl of a spoon, frowning under the hard central light. And while she did it she knew something of what it was to have been Teresa who, with her finicky ways, had held life at arm's length. She had an image of Teresa that kept recurring, her lips pressed together bristling with pins, and yet she wasn't aware she had ever seen her except with her pins in a little painted box. And we were not so unlike, Sukie thought, for I am only a spectator, reluctant always, as I am now, to take any action that will make this real. Studying form has always been an end in itself for me. I have never staked much. It has always seemed my role just to stay watching, while others take the risks.

She untied her apron and hung it on the door hook, then wiped her hand down her white dress as she had done earlier that day. Repulsed, she snatched it away, looking at the place. Very faint, but quite distinct, like dots that make up a picture, was a clay-brown smear.

Sukie raised her arms so that the dress lifted at the hem, then twisting them round to the back of her neck, she began to slide the zip down. She eased the fabric from her shoulders, dropped it to the floor and stepped out of it, leaving the kitchen, glancing back to where it lay empty, the stain hidden. She went into her bedroom then and put on some shoes, high black patent with ankle-straps.

In the sitting-room, moving with stealth, drawing the curtains across her lace-stripped form, she crossed to the desk, switched on the Chinese lamp and opened a drawer.

She was shivering, not from fear, and not because she was cold. She was shivering from rage. She had known, and she had done nothing, kidding herself she was a participant, taking a risk, thinking she was brave. How easy to risk one's own safety, to watch while the killer got on with the plan, as though there had been a choice. For a long time now there had been no choice. If she had acknowledged that, had acted as she should, Teresa would still be alive. That disease from which she had suffered, life, could yet have been held up to the attention of the experts, could yet have been cured.

From the desk Sukie withdrew some headed paper and wrote a letter. Then she meandered towards the bedroom, unfastening her bra to let it fall to the floor, fingers exploring this body veiled in darkness, feeling what it was to be someone else.

# Chapter Thirty-Two

The house in Hampstead was in a broad avenue rising northwards for Golders Green, shaded by ancient trees excluding the world of the High Street, of boutiques and pizza bars. Opposite, the undersoil of the heath rose sharply from the road, topped by yellow tufts that brushed the sky.

Bob had stopped his car and they were looking up at the façade. Birdsong was all around and in the distance the faded sounds of traffic. 'So, what do you think?'

'It looks very expensive.'

'Tell me something I don't know.'

'It looks very big for one person.'

'I know that too. I need space. Look, if you can't say anything positive, at least say why you don't like it. Come on, enjoy yourself. Feel free.'

'I'm sorry. That's really not how I was thinking.'

'OK.' He began to get out of the car. 'Let's take a look.'

He was standing on the pavement with his back to her, a hand shielding his eyes, head tilted back. There were wrought-iron gates and a stone-paved drive overhung by a lop-eared magnolia. Someone was obviously being employed to keep down the weeds, but shrubs flopped forward revealing woody stems at the backs of the beds, and clematis disappeared into the heights of trees. The petals of rock roses had fallen as though a wounded animal had passed that way until a hydrangea blocked its path.

'It's rather beautiful.' Sukie was looking about her.

'If you like chaos. It'll need a lot of work. There are cracks in most of the ceilings and the wiring's all to pot.' He went up to the front door and took a bunch of keys from his pocket. 'But I gather the basic structure's sound. Victorian, yes?'

'Yes. Gothic.'

'Does that appeal?'

'I always used to like it in story books.'

'Oh, the princess in the tower, all that stuff. Is that how you saw yourself?'

'Didn't most young girls, then?'

'I wouldn't know. If so, you haven't changed. Amanda's become the Wicked Queen, though I guess she started out Snow White.' He walked down the length of the hall to meet his reflection in the glass at the far end.

Sukie stayed where she was. There was a comfortable smell in the house of wood and books. '"Hair as black as ebony and skin as white as milk", you're right.' But he had disappeared.

'I'm in the kitchen,' he was calling. 'It's big. A real cook's kitchen. Come and take a look.'

She followed him through to a soup-green room, with shelves, a built-in dresser and a great space at its centre where a table would have been.

'I remember . . .' he began, then shook his head.

'What?'

'Nothing.'

She went to the window and looked out on a freshly mowed lawn, the evening sun laying great shadows of trees across it. 'You remember a kitchen like this?'

He was very still, then gave a sharp intake of breath, a sigh. 'Like this. Much like. In New England, of course. Childhood memories,' he smiled, 'like you being a princess.'

Sukie smiled back. 'Except mine was imagination.'

'Do you want to see the rest of the place?' He took her arm. 'I like the shoes. They're the ones you were wearing on the phone.'

'I wore them for you.'

'I know that.'

The downstairs rooms were panelled like the hall and the smell of books was explained, for some still remained in the shelves, while there were others in piles about the floor. A sofa was there too, at an angle in a corner, as though it had just been let loose across the polished boards. People seemed to have been packing to leave in a hurry and had then just given up the struggle.

Bob paced about, shaking his head. 'This is all so strange, don't you find it strange?'

'I find it sad.' She picked up a 'Just William' book.

'Do you?' He looked at her intensely. 'Do you really?'

'Oh, yes. It must be awful, as a child, leaving everything one knows behind, and in such a hurry. Children often prefer to stay with something bad than go into the unknown.'

'Why do you presume that?'

'I was a child.'

'Oh, sure, a princess in a tower with golden curls.'

'Not really. I wasn't particularly pretty. I had to work at it.'

He gave a cynical laugh. 'You don't know what you're talking about. You know nothing.'

'I do too. Curls were an *essential* for the pretty child. My hair was always straight.'

'Why did you use that, "I do too"? That's an American expression.'

'A joke. You use English ones.'

'I don't.'

'You do too.'

'Like what?'

'Like, "goosepimples" instead of "goosebumps". And others. You also said that you'd forgotten how chilly summer evenings could be, then another time said you'd only been in England in the winter.'

'What are you trying to say to me?' He had come very close,

265

his beautiful mouth shaping the words, the lenses of his spectacles catching the sunset.

'That you're inconsistent.' She could see his eyes now, smell his smell, healthy and faintly scented from within his clothes. She felt she might open his shirt and kiss him.

'OK.' He took her arm again, the one that held the book tightly in front of her, leading her out of the room. 'I need to be sometimes. I'm in business. Obliqueness becomes second nature.'

The stairs were shallow and they climbed them slowly. He was watching her feet and she heard him sigh. As they reached the top he looked up as though preparing himself for whatever he might find. 'Bedrooms . . .' he flung one arm out and then the other. 'Take a look. There's a billiard-room at the top, I believe.'

Sukie nodded and wandered into the room on her left. He didn't follow, just remained leaning against a window frame, looking down into the garden. She glanced into all the rooms, where unrelated possessions lay abandoned in unrelated places: a dressing-gown hanging from a curtain rail, a man's shoe in a hatbox, an extension lead in a corridor, a Bunnykins mug on a chair. They continued up to the next landing, and on again up a narrower staircase to the top.

'A billiard-room, you said?'

'Yes.' He opened the door with his foot, hands in his pockets. Then he switched the light on.

It was a billiard-room, with a billiard table still in it, a massive full-sized table with a bright green baize under the bare bulb.

'Too difficult to get out, I suppose.' She touched the baize. 'However did they get it up here in the first place?'

'Had it built up here.' He surveyed it from near the door. 'I imagine.'

'So it's a part of the house?'

'Oh, yes.'

'So, we could play, if they'd left the balls?'

266

'There are other things we could do. Byron wrote feelingly of billiard tables. I've always been an admirer of Byron.'

They were in what had once been a loft, the slopes from its apex bestriding the whole house. High up, front and rear in the upright walls were windows with wooden bars across them, through which one could only see the sky: a deepening twilight at the front, streaks of plums and custard at the rear.

'There was someone out there.'

'Where?' She looked sharply from front to back between the two windows.

'Down by the kitchen under the walnut tree.' He had shut the door and come towards her, backing her into the table, pressing her hard against it.

She put the book down. 'Who? Who was it? What were they doing?'

'I don't know.' He lifted her up, sat her on the edge and began to undo her buttons.

'Is this why you brought me here?' She was watching his knuckles.

'In part. I thought it would be pleasant. What do you think?'

'It feels pleasant. I'm not sure.'

'What about?' He was slipping off the red cardigan.

'I've learnt not to trust my feelings. What are your other reasons?'

'One at a time.' There was the sound of the zip of her skirt.

'Suppose we were to reverse the order?'

'I think not.' He had lifted her a little so that he could pull the skirt away.

'Do you always like to have fun before . . . ?'

'Before what?'

'Oh, undressing, dressing up, undressing. It's all quite import-ant to you. Even the champagne.' He had begun to kiss her, her arms were around his neck. 'I just don't understand about the roadworks, you see. Just explain that. Please. Who you are wouldn't matter then.'

'Who I am?' He had drawn back. 'I am precisely who I say I am. My name is on my passport.'

'Oh, I know that. I know you are exactly who you say you are. So what's in a name?' She took a breath of the scent of him through the cotton of his shirt. 'Actually, I wanted to talk to you about someone else, a boy who was at prep school with Jerry and George Graham-Jones, one of several whom they bullied.'

He had taken a piece of her hair and was twisting it round his finger.

'Who was that? I did hear Jerry and George talking once.'

'He was a very fat boy, unable to join in, or take things in the right spirit. "Sad people" my son calls them, and they are. But this boy had a second chance. To reinvent himself. His mother went abroad and took him with her where he learnt new ways, and a new language. A land of opportunity. For him as well as for her. The flight over the sea lifts him high above all the misery that has weighed him down so he grows tall and slender and very handsome. He also becomes very rich so that he can have anything he wants – he believes.'

'Is this the prince in the tower?'

'More like the ugly duckling, don't you think?'

He was looking over her head, his fingers lightly on her shoulders but she could feel a hair on her forehead lift from his breathing.

'Many, many years later, he returns to England believing that things must now have changed. He has turned his life around, so why shouldn't things also change around him? He traces Jerry Wearing whom, in spite of the bullying, he has never ceased to admire; even modelled himself upon Jerry, perhaps. He learns that Jerry has just bought a horse which he has called Triumvirate in honour of a group of three at school, himself and his two blue-chip friends, Rupert Fabian and Richard Manningtree. But

Rupert, now a diplomat, is posted to the Far East so, under pressure, Jerry lets in George. Then Richard is killed in a hunting accident and Jerry is left looking around for yet another owner for the third share – another "suitable" owner.'

Bob had begun to kiss the side of her face, moving his lips down to her neck, her shoulders. Sukie's voice was dreamy.

'The former victim hears all this so writes to Jerry, reminding him of school. saying that he would be happy to make up the Triumvirate; he has the money. His offer is rejected. He then hears not only that a woman has been chosen to fill the position, but Jerry joking about the ghastly people he has turned down. He has by now, of course, met Jerry, using his bright new name, sure that he will never be recognized.' She looked down at Bob, head on one side, hair stroking his face. 'Until one day at Newmarket. The day of Triumvirate's first run. When you so honourably intervened to stop Jerry attacking Henry Whippet with a knife. I saw that look on his face. I didn't understand it. But you did, didn't you? It was recognition.'

'Of course.' He had straightened up and moved in closer to her again, his hands under her shoulder-blades.

'Bob is short for Robert, isn't it?' She put out a hand and touched the fine lawn of his shirt, finger worming in between the buttons. 'But there are other abbreviations: Bobby, Rob, Robbie, Bert even, Bertie . . . ? And if a woman remarries, a child might take her second husband's name if he is adopted, as you were by Mr Teichgraeber. A strange name, but I'd guess you were happy to take it in exchange for Fowler.' She was resting back now against his hands while he still pressed between her legs against the table. 'I've seen your photograph.'

'What photograph?'

'You know. At prep school with Jerry and George. I have it under my bed.'

He removed his hands from her and went to look out of the high rear window. 'I wonder what they were doing out there?'

'I wonder if they were out there at all?'

'You don't believe me? Ah, well.'

'I'm not sure. You almost have Triumvirate.' Sukie propped herself back on her hands.

'I do.'

'So, with Jerry and George dead . . .'

'Jerry died of natural causes, George . . .'

'And Teresa?'

'Who?'

'A woman in a boutique in St John's Wood. She went back to the shop after closing time and disturbed someone. Someone who had laid out a dress for me. Just the one I would have chosen.' Sukie lay back on the table, watching the naked bulb hanging from its flex.

He had turned away from the window so that there was only his outline against the lurid sky. 'What do you think of my house?'

'I don't think you'll be happy here.'

'Oh, that's too bad,' he stood contemplating her, 'because I've already bought it. So, you see . . .' He came nearer, as though with the idea of rearranging her in some way. 'You're right, of course, I don't expect to be happy.' He was between her legs again now, leaning over to stroke her forehead, frowning at her face as though it were something distant that he could not properly discern. 'Do you expect to be happy?'

'I always hope. Sometimes I succeed.'

'I suppose you do. So English. Smiling through.'

'Is that what I'm supposed to do now?' His hands had moved under her head down to her neck to grasp it like the scruff of a dog. She recognized panic in a flash of white across her vision, in a sensation of weightlessness. The laws of nature given way. She was floating. She would fall. This was fear. And this was reality. She had never before felt so alive.

Her eyes must have been shut for then she felt his tongue in her mouth, and lazily turned her face away. 'Don't,' he said. He

270

had put his hand up inside her panties and hoisted her to the edge of the table. She made an attempt to wriggle away from him, but it was only a token, for he was so heavy and filled her so with warmth and sufficiency and everything she'd always wanted, and 'That's better,' a whisper in her ear.

Touching his mouth with hers, she spoke the words she knew she should not speak. And all the while she spoke them, tasting his lips, shaking her head, cheeks touching the baize from side to side, denying the words that were coming from her mouth, what it was that she was allowing him to do to her on the table.

'School photographs. You've been collecting them, haven't you? You phoned Amanda saying Simon had had an accident with his car. He'd bent the "fender" you said. Not the "bumper" as an Englishman would say. You'd overheard our conversation at Sandown but thought of Sylvia too late. I got there first.'

There was no interruption in his breathing. In what he was doing. Perhaps he was too preoccupied to hear . . . ? Perhaps she also . . . being under occupation . . . harbouring a fifth column, as it were . . . was too implicated to know . . . what she was saying? Oh God, what was she saying? Oh, God? Oh, God!

He was looking down at her as he tidied his clothes. 'You and someone else.'

'What do you mean?' She tried to sit up, graceless and cold.

'Someone else saw those pictures. Sylvia mentioned it. She thought it was pretty strange, I guess.'

'Who else?' She was hunched on the ridge of wood now, damp, shivering. 'And why?'

'Someone whose name can't be in his passport. As to why, I can't imagine.' He ran his hands back through his hair; he looked as fresh and well-pressed as when they'd arrived, but drained, thin, absented. 'OK, I took a couple. You can surely understand that? I didn't want it known who I used to be; not after the way they'd all behaved.'

'They were all dead.'

271

'They'll never all be dead.'

'Who?' she whispered.

'Henry Whippet, of course.'

And then there was the sound.

They both turned. A sound within the house. Footsteps, slow, inevitable, coming up the stairs. They looked at each other. 'I didn't believe you,' she said.

'I knew that you wouldn't.' He was over at the door. 'Get behind me.' He pressed himself against the wall.

Both silent, listening, they waited, as the steps came nearer, rising to the surface of the landing. Sukie could not control her breathing and thought she would faint. Then, with a crash, the door flew open and there stood Henry Whippet with a gun.

'I got here in time, then. You all right?' He frowned at Sukie in her panties.

'What are you doing here?' She crossed her hands over her chest, rubbing her shoulders.

'Don't you know?' He had moved further into the room, covering them both with his gun.

'Surely you're not going to tell us?' Bob leant against the wall with his forearm, hand level with his face. He looked relaxed, almost cheerful.

'Hardly necessary, wouldn't you say? Get dressed.' He jerked his head in the direction of her clothes.

'You didn't believe me, did you?' Bob was watching Henry Whippet.

'I don't know.' She had collected up her skirt, bra and cardigan. 'I don't know!' She pulled up the skirt roughly, twisting to fasten the zip, dropping the cardigan. Getting dressed with the two of them there, not watching, was humiliating in a way that undressing had never been. She retrieved the cardigan – and flung it.

'Christ!'

There was a shot. The light went out. Then there were the sounds of feet.

272

'Oh, God.' Sukie stood alone in the darkened room. 'What have I done?' She hugged herself again, listening to the sounds: a car in the distance driving up a hill, the sharp insistent notes of a blackbird. In the house: nothing. Only darkness.

She felt around for her cardigan but could not find it, only the book, lying on the table. She picked it up, pressed it tightly against her chest, then with her back very straight emerged from the room to the top of the stairs and began slowly to descend. She was still wearing the shoes, strapped round her ankles so that every step was a clatter signalling where she was, and yet she hadn't the care to remove them. All around the sky had now faded to an inky transparency, holding a little of the sun's light but letting none of it through into the house. The blackbird had ceased its call. Around her and her shoes was silence.

Down on the second floor Sukie paused, looking still into darkness: not a movement, not a breath, she knew there was no one there. On, down the next staircase to the floor where Bob had first seen someone in the garden. The window against which he had leant stretched broad and black with the shapes of trees, the sky almost gone. And then the lights went on. Sukie stood at the window, hands spread apart on the sill, looking into her own eyes, knowing, absolutely knowing, that she had got it wrong. And in a way, now, after all, she didn't care. She really didn't care any more.

There was an arm round her neck, and a mouth close to her ear. 'That was so stupid,' it said. 'What on earth did you do that for?'

She didn't reply, feeling the arm tighten, the stroke of cashmere.

'Because now I've got to look after you. I was hoping to manage without that.'

Still she didn't answer.

'Where do you think he is?'

'He'll find somewhere,' she said.

There was the sound of water. They both heard it. Somewhere in the house. Fast running water, pouring, splashing, gurgling, with great force. The arm around her neck loosened.

'The bathroom, the bathroom.' She was off down the passage. There was a bang. Darkness again. Feet sounding behind her. And a smell.

She knew the room before she reached it, mildew damp, and that other smell which she recognized and understood. He was lying in the bath, his fine suit under water bulky as cardboard, both taps still gushing. And a little old electric fire was in there with him. It trailed from the red extension flex she had seen in the corridor and had given all the warmth it had to give, all Bob would ever receive. Flare from a street light caught his hands clasped around it, his head thrown back, his perfect mouth open, framing for Sukie what she would always believe was relief.

Henry Whippet had pulled out the plug. Now he stepped forward and turned off the taps.

Silence rushed in to fill the room. The first drip, when it came, took all her attention, then the next, and the next . . .

Sukie felt something soft on her shoulders.

'Here's your cardi,' Henry Whippet said. 'Put it on.'

Obediently she pushed her arms into the sleeves, recalling how as a child she had done much the same before an electric fire.

'Sorry it couldn't be me, doll, but I told you I like things natural. If I killed anyone it would be just the same, natural. You should've known that.'

'I did.' She continued to stare into the bath. 'I think I knew for a long time, perhaps even before the roadworks he saw that weren't there. Tonight I knew for certain but, just for a moment . . .'

'You didn't want to.'

'This may sound very rum in the circumstances, Henry Whippet, but I'm desperate for a bath.'

# Chapter Thirty-Three

Newmarket is like no other racecourse. It has not the graciousness of Ascot, the historic worldliness of Epsom, the charm of Chester, nor even the solid comfort of Sandown. Despite its recent red-roofed buildings, it has a grandeur that amounts to the classical. It is not to be contained. It spreads itself across the arched landscape confident that everything it touches is its own: the gallops, the training establishments, the studs, the salesrooms, the administrative offices, even the jockeys' substantial but practical homes. It is 'headquarters'.

Triumvirate swaggered round the paddock, his head arched low, the muscles in his great hindquarters turning patterns like oil on water.

'He does have to be the most beautiful beast one has ever seen, don't you agree?' Amanda's smile was ecstatic.

'He is truly splendid.' Sukie contemplated the horse wistfully.

'You've brought him on brilliantly, Marcus.'

'Glad you feel loyalty's paid off.'

'Loyalty, stuff it. I just asked myself what Jerry would have wanted. It was all quite simple then. A very proper use of his life insurance to boot. Decent of Rosamund to let me buy her out as well. Even Simon seemed to understand. Everything to continue as before – even Henry Whippet up.' She glanced at Sukie: 'Not such a little runt after all?'

Sukie was looking to the far end of the paddock where the jockeys were coming in. 'Oh, I don't know?'

*

She hadn't seen Henry Whippet since the evening in Bob's house three weeks ago. He had taken care of everything then, called the police, driven her home, even waited while she made a phone call, had her bath, and brought her a big mug of coffee and brandy afterwards.

Henry Whippet had been alerted to the same idea about Bob when they had been looking at Alex's school photographs. He had also remembered the names of the 'unsuitables' from Marcus mentioning them. Riding in France over the weekend, he had telephoned Sylvia from the airport to ask if she had any pictures of her brothers at prep school, but before he arrived back they had all been taken in the robbery. Sylvia had then found one in the attic, put away because the glass was cracked, and he had immediately recognized Bob as Bertie Fowler. He had tried to leave Sukie a message, but she had forgotten to set her answering machine. So, straight after racing that day, he had driven down to her flat to find her out but Bob's postcard jammed under the door.

Sukie had asked him, holding her coffee and brandy in both hands, how he had known where she would be, and he had produced the 'Just William' book from the abandoned sitting-room that she had been clutching.

'I had another idea, a long time ago. When I heard him volunteer the word "fag", meaning like a little boy looking after a prefect at school. No American uses it like that. To them it just means pansy. That's what made me perk up, when we were looking at your son's photo. I also sent a fax to the embassy in the Far East, to Rupert Fabian. He came up, amongst other things, with an address. The house where Bertie Fowler lived as a child. The house where I found you. He'd been determined to buy it back, especially bearing in mind who it had been sold to.'

'Who?' Sukie had asked, dreaming into her warm mug.

Henry Whippet had handed her the book, its cover open. Inside, on the flyleaf, was the name Richard Manningtree.

'They bought it off of the Fowlers when Bertie's father shot hisself. He'd suffered from manic depression for years, poor sod. Not much fun for Bertie.'

'Richard Manningtree was killed out hunting . . . ?'

'Yeah, well I guess we'll never know about that, but Bob did go hunting, didn't he?'

'Yes. I thought it strange at the time. It didn't fit with other things he seemed to believe in.'

Henry Whippet had got up to go then. 'Get some rest, doll. Tomorrow won't feel good.'

She watched him to the door, where he stopped.

'Why did you do that? Go there with him? When you knew? You got a death wish or something?'

'No.' She had looked up, gloom filling the space between them. 'Perhaps I felt I owed it for not doing anything sooner? To be the bait. It was what I felt like by then. Or perhaps it was something more complicated?'

'Yeah, well . . . I said once I thought you was weird.'

'At least I'd written a letter.'

'Oh?'

'To Barnie. An old friend and his wife, suggesting some dinner dates, and telling them where I was that evening and what to do if I didn't phone him by a certain time.'

'Bit late then.'

'I had planned to tell Bob about it . . . if necessary.'

'You went on hoping that it wouldn't be.'

'Yes.'

'You hoped it was me.'

'Yes.'

He nodded once, looking at her from the dark edge of the hall, eyes shining as if lit by a candle, then, shaking his head once, he turned away.

277

'Although I knew that it wasn't,' Sukie lifted her chin and called after him.

But the front door had already shut.

He was coming towards them now, stepping lightly over the grass, his whip in his right hand. And when he reached them, instead of raising it on the move with his usual insouciance, he stopped, feet smartly together, and touched the brim of his cap, nodding as he did so to each of the women.

Amanda held out her hand and said how pleased she was that he was to partner her horse. Sukie checked the zip of her shoulder-bag to see that it was properly shut.

The mounting bell sounded and Triumvirate swung in towards them; Marcus checked the girth and stirrups, then Henry Whippet was up in the saddle and doing a circuit of the paddock, the lad backing himself into the horse's chest to keep him steady.

And this was how it always should have been. Triumvirate skimming to post over the good to soft ground looking tremendous value at eleven to two, third favourite in a big field; and two hundred and fifty pounds on the nose. Sukie had never risked such a bet before. Two hundred and fifty pounds. The price of a cashmere cardigan.

Through her binoculars she could see him being led into the stalls. He was one of the last but still hadn't got too fussed. Then the stalls were open and Henry Whippet had him handily covered up on the rails just behind the leaders, going sweetly, not pulling too hard. At the two-furlong marker he pulled him out to make his move, and Triumvirate instantly slipped into another gear, while those in front were already being scrubbed along. All except the favourite. And he, still with two lengths in hand, was going for home. Then Henry Whippet let out another notch and Triumvirate really began to shift. He simply thrust the ground away behind him, pellets of mud flying from his heels, and while the favourite put in a great effort to make a duel of it, the result was never in doubt and Triumvirate passed the post a comfortable two-lengths winner.

It was a party in the unsaddling enclosure: Amanda greeting the sympathetic reception with moist eyes, fluttering handkerchief and a smile. Sukie watched her turn to congratulate her jockey, but he had slipped from the saddle; beneath the noise of the crowd, between the back-slapping and shaking of hands, even past the friendly questions of the press, the photographers' shutters. There were other races to ride. This had only been one of them.

The journey home was euphoric; the little Renault disposing of the ground like Triumvirate's heels. Buoyed still, Sukie leapt out on to the pavement, up the stairs, racing to fling open the door of the flat. And then came to rest, leaning against it, hearing it close behind her.

There was a card from Greece on the mat: 'Still having a marvellous time. Wish you were here. (Sic). (To both). Will inform of imminent return. Love. (Sic. Sic. Sic.) J. and A.' Sukie propped it against the Kenwood and poured herself some wine from the fridge, taking it through to help with the checking of the answerphone. Only one communication there as well: a rather sheepish invitation to drinks the following evening from Sylvia. She didn't seem to require or even want any sort of response, as though she might prefer that Sukie did not take her at her word.

The Chanel bag was on the floor in the hall where she had dropped it when she picked up the postcard. Still with her glass of wine, she went and collected it by its long chain, carrying it through to her bedroom where she swung it on to the bed. Pausing for another swallow, she put her glass down and unzipped the bag, turning it upside down.

The money was resistant at first: stuffed so tight, it preferred its own company. But she thrust her hand in amongst it and gouged it out, layer by layer, so that some of the notes were nicked by the teeth of the zip. When the bag was empty, she knelt, leaning on the bed, drinking the rest of her wine, staring at the litter.

'I probably am a great embarrassment to everyone nowadays,' Sukie told it. 'Myself included. Tough. I shall certainly go to the party. Nothing else to do.'

The following evening, flogging up the M11 through thrashing rain yet again, she did consider that rereading a Thomas Hardy interspersed with some Mozart and a bottle of Pouilly Fumé was certainly not 'nothing'. And yet she continued to flee, made anxious by yet another card on the mat this morning: 'Have just heard the *most disturbing* things about you and your goings on. Returning at once! J. and A.'

The gravel circle was well and truly churned up when she arrived. Eight cars and the rain had scored furrows so deep that, as she parked, her wheels spun. She tried to make out Amanda's BMW and any other familiar vehicle, a green Porsche, but all cars are black in the dark, especially with one's eyes screwed up and a newspaper over one's head.

He was there, of course, Sukie saw as she came in, still shaking herself from the dash to the porch. He was standing by the fireplace talking to Simon, a glass in his hand, not drinking. In the dark low-ceilinged room, he appeared sombre, insubstantial. And then the fire flared up and caught his eyes before he looked down again.

Sylvia thrust a glass of wine at her, frowning as if not quite sure what it was. 'Marcus's idea, all this,' she glanced about her, still frowning as if not quite sure who the people were either.

Sukie shivered violently. 'Sorry.'

'What? Do you think I should draw the curtains?' Sylvia nodded and went to yank them across. They were thin and the night still guttered through the weave. In spite of the fire, the place was chill. Sukie took a large swig of wine.

'I was sure you wouldn't come all this way.' Amanda's heels clattered across the bare floor. 'I'm really touched.'

'You should know I'll go anywhere for a drink.' Sukie received her kiss and took another swig. 'It's in honour of the horse, I imagine.'

'Of course. And Sylvia has done her best. There's bread and cheese in the kitchen.' She raised an eyebrow. 'Luckily I've some smoked salmon at home.'

'I wonder what Marcus actually lives on?'

'Looks like he goes to the pub. Their friends know what she's like, so they'll have made arrangements. What about you?'

'I don't know.' Sukie waved her glass. Henry Whippet and Simon were joined by Marcus and another trainer at the fireplace.

'You can come back with Simon and me if you like.'

Sukie didn't reply, just smiled and sipped her wine.

'We've never really talked, have we?' Amanda touched her hand. 'Since it all came out.'

'Not much to say.'

'No. But I was so glad. Relieved that Jerry was cleared of all that nonsense. I feel I owe that to you. It makes such a difference, people knowing that he wasn't unfaithful. And *weird*.'

She said it fiercely, looking to Sukie for confirmation.

Sukie shook her head. 'I'll just get myself another drink.'

'Then you'll have to stay,' Amanda called after her.

She was holding the neck of a bottle in the harsh kitchen light, splashing wine over the rim of the glass, when she felt a light touch on her back.

'I like that cardi. Cashmere. Very nice.' Henry Whippet put his untouched drink on the draining-board.

She looked down at the red cardigan, spilling more wine. 'You probably think I'm weird still wearing it. Anyone normal would have thrown it out. But I couldn't afford to. It cost too much.

So, I just decided I'd wear it all the time, so that I'd get used to it, so that it could acquire new associations.'

'Very sensible. Shame to throw it out. It suits you.'

'Does it?'

''Course it does. That's why you bought it.'

'Maybe?'

'Want to talk about it?'

'Maybe?'

'I'll get your coat.'

'I haven't got one.'

'Nothing to keep us then, is there? Just say our goodbyes. They know I'm a stickler for my early nights.'

Sukie drifted through the firelit room, Marcus gave her a vague wave, Amanda a meaningful stare. Sylvia followed close behind to prevent her changing her mind. She looked determined, hopeful that this move would inspire others to peel off.

Out in the rain again Henry Whippet bundled her into his car. 'We'll pick up yours in the morning.'

'Oh, God.'

'I'm not going to attack you.'

'I know. I think I'm just sad, actually. Everything reminds me. Sorry.'

The Porsche floated backwards; Henry Whippet's wheels didn't spin as he steered it round. 'It was his name, wasn't it, that made him do it the way he did?'

'Yes. Fowler. They'd used it, of course. They pick on anything when they want to bully. If it hadn't been that it would have been something else. But that was perfect – with him being fat – lots of scope. I heard Jerry once refer to him as "Paxo". They used to stick their compasses into him to see if he was done.'

'Little sods, kids.'

'Yes. One trusts that most of them grow out of it.'

'But Jerry didn't.'

'Bob didn't feel so. The triumvirate rejected him. Then he

heard Jerry joking about the way they'd baited him at school. Bob had changed. He'd come back to England to prove it. To heal poor Bertie, I suppose.'

'But they wouldn't let him do that.'

'I think it came as a terrible shock. He began to feel like Bertie again. He felt so threatened, he felt himself disintegrating . . .'

'So?' Henry Whippet had turned off Newmarket High Street towards Bury St Edmunds, trees like seaweed overhead.

'He knew he couldn't exist alongside Jerry unless he could, in some way, reverse the past between them. I don't think he ever intended to kill him.'

The car swung into a narrow lane. 'Almost home. Nice and warm there.'

'But he had to dominate him – ' she was watching the movement of the wipers – 'humiliate him, get him under control. Otherwise Bob wouldn't exist at all.'

Raindrops appeared and were wiped away, the glass clear as if they had never been, except for a trail of water at the edge of the screen. A trail that, however clean the car, always contains flecks of dirt.

'So champagne. Nothing but the best. Cigarettes that Jerry had always smoked at school. *Marrons glacés*. Giorgio. What *is* in a name?' Sukie gave a giggle that turned into a shiver. 'I think he smelt it on Nicola one Sunday lunch at Jerry and Amanda's. It amused him, the name of it, so he sprayed it around the flat to lay a "false scent". For Amanda to pick up, probably. Jerry was trying to fight back when he died. He'd managed to reach his paper knife.'

She could sense Henry Whippet turning his head to look at her, but he didn't speak.

'It was a game. He liked games. Dressing up. Undressing . . . Being dressed.'

He had stopped the car in the drive and was listening to her.

283

'I think he must have used a knife, with both of them.' She nodded to herself.

'He'd have to have used something. People don't willingly take to being made oven-ready. Poor old birds neither.'

'Went to Jerry's flat after racing that evening. It was him in the lift. Met George at the house on his way to Scotland. That was when he saw the roadworks. But, of course, he intended to kill George. Nothing else would do any more. Dressed in his finest feathers.'

'Yeah. Well, let's go inside. Nice and cosy inside. Here's the key. You let yourself in while I put the car away.'

It was a Georgian house, with the scent of flowers and leather as she opened the door. There was a Persian carpet on the floor of the hall and a long-case clock by the stairs.

'Come on, then. I left a fire in.' He guided her to the sitting-room, where there were more carpets and dignified comfortable furniture. He leant over the fire and removed the guard. 'Now, you sit down and I'll get you a drink.'

She sank on to the velvet sofa. 'Do you have any Calvados?'

''Course. Nothing I haven't got.'

'I knew he'd killed George.' She laid her head back and shut her eyes. 'I knew he'd been there that day because he'd seen the roadworks. But I got so sidetracked, what with the White Tie Escort Agency and Nicola and all her lies. She thought Simon had done it, perhaps. Explains some of her behaviour. Why she insisted they hid George's car. The roadworks had been there earlier in the day that George was killed. Nicola had warned me about them. However, by chance, they'd been taken away by the time I arrived. Bob didn't know that. Mentioned to me that he'd come across them two days later. I didn't realize for a while. I didn't realize what he'd said that was so odd. And when I did, I just hid it away. I didn't believe he'd kill again. There was no one else to threaten him.'

He picked up her hand and put her fingers round a glass. 'Except that you was getting too close.'

'Was I?' She lifted the glass to her lips and took a sip. 'I don't know. I wasn't really close. But . . .'

He sat down beside her and lit a cigar. 'You don't mind?'

She shook her head. 'Not really close. Not really. It was he who stuck that White Tie label into my address book. To frighten me. Put me off. Easy just to pick up Alex's keys. I've lived a very regular life, Henry Whippet. Married at twenty. Widowed at thirty. I've had boyfriends – lovers – of course. But nothing significant. After a few weeks we'd part with puzzled smiles. I didn't feel ready, not with the children around. But now . . .'

'They're growing up.'

'I suppose so.'

'And you thought that Bob might have been significant?'

'Oh, I don't know that I did think that.' She sat up, knees together, looking into her glass. 'I think I just trailed the idea. It excited me. He . . .' She tossed back the contents of the glass. 'Bob was . . . Now I just feel disturbed.'

'Would you like to sleep with me?'

'No.'

'I'd put my cigar out first. You liked it last time.'

'Did I?'

'Oh, yes.' He was holding the cigar upright, watching the thin smoke twirl upwards, then he tossed it into the fire. 'I've got a lovely bed upstairs, very clean.'

She turned to face him on the sofa, fingers braced either side in the seat.

He had put out a hand to the top button of her cardigan. 'Can't resist cashmere.'

She watched his hand. 'Neither can I.' It was such a beautiful hand, smooth and brown with shining nails. 'It's age, I think. Texture becomes more important than style.' She recalled seeing that hand weave tenderly in and out of a wriggling ferret. She gave a little sigh.

'It doesn't have to mean anything. Or it can mean whatever you want. I don't mind. I just want it to be nice. Make you happy. I like that.'

She watched the last button of the cardigan come undone then slowly shrugged and began to ease it down from her shoulders. 'New associations?'

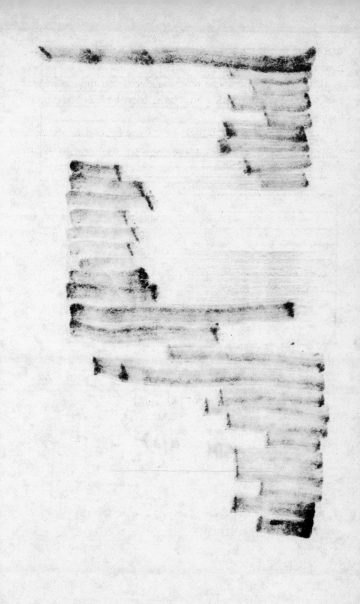

W/Q JAN '06
40  5.9.03
STH  8/07  w/Q 6/03

21-5-98